Love in a Carry-On Bag

Kelli,
Never stop Believing
in Love!

Love in a Carry-On Bag

Love,
Light
& Laughter!

Sadeqa Johnson

Sadeqa 8.3.13

12th Street Press

12th Street Press • Hillside, NJ

This is a work of fiction. Names, characters, places, and incidents either are the product of the author's imagination or are used fictitiously, and any resemblance to actual persons, living or dead, business establishments, events, or locales is entirely coincidental.

12th Street Press
1215 Liberty Avenue
3rd Floor
Hillside, NJ 07205
www.12thstreetpress.com
info@12thstreetpress.com

Book design by Mary Brown
Production Assistance by *Marra*thon Editorial Production Services, www.marrathon.net

ISBN 978-0-9847289-0-9
Library of Congress Control Number 2011962619

Printed in the United States of America
1 3 5 7 9 10 8 6 4 2

To Glenn,

I married well

In loving memory of:

William T. Murray,
who said that one day I would be the monkey
that stopped the show.

And

Tommy Getter,
I still have your back.

Acknowledgments

Thank you, Heavenly Father, for using me to touch the lives of others. To my father, Tyrone Murray, for raising me to be strong, brilliant and true to my creative self, and to my mother, Nancy Murray, for your overwhelming love and support. My second mother, Francine Cross Murray, you complement our family so well, lots of love. I'm grateful to my mother-in-law, Paula Johnson, for mothering me and my children, and for her thoughtful edits of this book. To Tauja, Nadiyah and Talib Murray for being the greatest siblings a girl could have. To Geraldine Murray and Yvonne Clair for your nourishment. To my in-laws, Marise, David, Michelle, Pacita, Nneka and Kris for letting me in. Ilov Grate and Zurn Porter, HOOTY-HOO. Shaunte Durham, Maudjah Henriquez Francis, Tonya Smith, Ranesha Hunt and the Right Away Bail Bonds crew, thanks for believing. Thanks to my writing group, The Furious Flowers, for being true. My sister circle—Althea Aikens, Dana Cobbs, Monique Moody and Valerie Hopkins—for waving your pom poms. My Tuesday night meditation circle and Sensei Haress Goodson for giving me a stage. Maisha Johnson for getting me out of the house, and the Scholastic crew, hugs.

To my teachers: Marilyn Ducksworth, angel Bebe Moore Campbell, Benilde Little and Jackson Taylor—who taught me how to make it sound good. To Dara Stewart and Gilda Squire for the sound advice, Dawn Hardy for creating magic, and Mary Brown for your wonderful graphic designs and patience. To my Queen Bee editor, Cherise Fisher, for giving me confidence, courage and the connections that I needed, and pushing me to go deeper—period. You have restored my faith, thank you.

To my beloved children: Miles, for telling everyone that his mother is about to be a famous author; Zora, for demanding that I work harder and keeping me cute; and Lena for those infectious hugs and smiles—all that I am is because of you. Thanks to Swara, Janelle, Britni, Alexis and Rodganya for looking after my precious gems. To all of the supporters of my blog who cheered me up and on.

It is with extreme gratitude that I thank my husband, Glenn Johnson, for drying my tears and sitting me back at my computer when I had enough. It was you who called me an author when I insisted that I was just a writer. Your unwavering belief has gotten us here. Yin and yang, baby. Thank you.

PART I

To love is to make of one's heart a swinging door.
Howard Thurman

Chapter One

Chocolate-Covered Sundays

Erica knew she shouldn't have answered the telephone. She was already running late for her train from New York to D.C. Her carry-on was propped next to her office door, her desk had been tidied and the computer was shut down for the day. But in her haste to get out of the office, she dropped a manuscript all over the floor. She was on her knees reordering the pages when the call came. Her initial thought was to let her assistant, Prudence, pick up, but by the fourth ring it was apparent that she had stepped away from her cubicle. Letting it roll to voicemail was another option, but something told her to answer it. Daughter's intuition maybe. The moment she heard her mother's breathy voice, she regretted her decision.

"Slim, the heater's out again," her mother belched. "Mr. Handy down the street said he'd fix it, but I won't have money 'til Tues-dee and it's cold as the dickens in here."

Erica felt her shoulders tense. "I'm rushing to catch a train."

"You goin' see Warren?"

"Yeah, and I'm late. He's performing tonight."

"That's nice, glad to see you guys making it work. What ya'll been dating, a year?"

"About that."

"Well can you just stop at the bank real quick? My back's aching from the cold and I ain't goin' make it through the night with just blankets."

Erica should have been immune to her mother's needs by now. The last time she cried for money it was because her electricity was shut off and Erica had to shell out for the six months that was past due. Before that, there was a leak in the roof. The decayed tooth back in February had Erica on a monthly payment plan, and last week there was the ingrown toenail that needed to be removed before it caused gangrene. Her mother had more problems than a prostitute on her way to jail. But once again Erica gave in. It was just easier than arguing with her.

"How much you need?"

"Said he'd do it for sixty bucks."

"Ma, I want it back. My rent is due and you still owe me from the last time."

"I'm selling my percocets after I go to the doctor's on Tuesdee. I'll give it all to you then."

Erica stuffed the manuscript in her shoulder bag and flipped off the light in her office. Even though the bank was a half block from her job, it was Friday and the teller's line snaked without mercy. A grayed woman with a walker and too many plastic bags slow-footed it in front of her and the room felt like the thermostat was stuck at ninety degrees. After transferring the sixty dollars from her account to her mother's, Erica speed walked the two blocks to the 1/9 subway station only to watch three jammed packed trains pass her by.

By now, she knew she had missed her Amtrak. The thought of disappointing Warren pained her so much, she shelled out an additional seventy-five bucks for the Northeast Corridor Accela express leaving in an hour. She was going to be two hours late, but with any luck, the venue would be operating on colored people's time, so maybe she'd catch some of his performance.

By the time she hopped out of the taxicab in the Adams Morgan section of D.C., anxiety had taken over her belly. She hurried down the steep steps of the basement jazz club, making careful not to catch her four-inch heels in the metal grooves, and stepped through the heavy velvet curtains that separated the entranceway from the ground floor into the darkened room.

Warren had left her ticket at the door. While the coat check girl stashed away her carry-on, Erica touched up her lip gloss, raked her reddish brown hair around her shoulders, and adjusted the belt to her pencil skirt. After dropping a few bucks in the girl's tip jar, she headed up the inside flight of stairs to the main lounge. The music grew stronger as she reached the top landing, and her ears recognized Warren's horn wailing before she entered the room.

Maybe he wouldn't notice that she was late. The club was jam-packed with Friday-night patrons, old school jazz enthusiasts, college students and a handful of after work sophisticates. Erica tried to blend in unnoticed, but when she glanced over at the stage, Warren pointed his trumpet at her, firing three sharp notes in her direction. Their eyes met and her breathing slowed to a sway.

It was always beautiful watching Warren play. His almond-brown skin glistened with sweat under the spotlight, and his shoulders hunched around his ears, keeping time with the rhythm. She loved his lips—thick like braids of licorice—and when he pursed them against the mouthpiece of his trumpet and mashed the brass valves, the notes flowed like he was singing high-pitched vocals.

The bassist was strumming with his eyes closed, rocking with his upright instrument and plucking the strings, while the drummer answered with soft, sexy brushing. The pianist joined in, playing staccato, but Warren topped them all with a whine that was so long and clear, it got under your skin but felt good at the same time. The quintet went on like that for a while, and then Warren raised his trumpet in the air, shooting off notes back to back like firecrackers, with the others behind him, snapping, pounding and popping.

Erica clapped along with the crowd until her palms stung and he tipped his trumpet at her before taking his bow. A couple rushed Warren as he left the stage, but he barely took his eyes off Erica while he spoke to them. After the admirers drifted on, Warren strolled towards her, smiling that crooked grin that she liked to think was reserved just for her. She finger waved him over, knowing she was blushing like it was a first date.

"Took you so long," he dipped his lips and Erica fell against him like syrup. He smelled like a mix of salt and cedar.

"My mother."

Warren looked concerned, but the worry eased from his brows as Erica recounted her latest tale.

"You need some cash?"

"Thanks, but I'm good." She always declined money from Warren, but somehow he still managed to slip bills in her purse before their time together ended.

The narrow bar was packed, but they didn't have to wait for service. Warren exchanged pleasantries with the bartender and a young trumpet player who said, "You dig, baby," after every breath. Erica sipped on her martini carefully in an effort to balance the triangular-shaped glass in the jostling crowd. Once the young cat moved on, Warren set all of his attention on her.

"I got you something." His voice sounded husky.

"Me, first." She swiveled in her seat and handed him an envelope from her purse.

Warren flipped two tickets out and turned them over in his hand. Stifling a laugh, he snickered, "The bitch-ass Nets?"

"Watch your mouth, trumpet boy. They're a gift from my author, Lacy Pope. Her book landed at number one on the *New York Times* bestsellers list."

"Nice." He clicked her glass. "But you must not have been too good on the job, since she got Nets tickets instead of the Knicks."

Erica slapped his wrist, "I'm a proud Nets fan this year."

"So then my gift is appropriate." Warren put his drink on the bar, reached into his back pocket, but stopped abruptly.

"See, you messing with me," she tugged, urging her gift forward, but dropped her chin when she saw it.

"A damn bumper sticker." And worse, it read "Washington Wizard's biggest fan." They shared a healthy love for basketball, but Warren knew she would never root for his team, the Wizards. "Talk about stinkin' up the place? Have they even won a game yet this season?"

"Careful girl."

"Or what?" Her mouth took on a pout. Warren used it as an invitation to kiss her, lightly at first but with each second the intensity wavered between hunger and greed. Goosebumps sprouted across her arms and she looked around to see if anyone was watching them.

"Let's go," he wiped her gloss from his lips, and then helped her to her feet.

His Yukon Denali was parked a half block down from the club, and the two hurried against the night's cold before it had a chance to sneeze. Once inside the car, Warren's hands seemed to be everywhere. Erica loosened her coat and leaned her head back so that his lips could find her tender spots. His fingers pressed against her thighs and the rush of heat made Erica's breath quicken.

"Those are twenty dollar nylons."

"Bill me," he whispered, breaking the seam.

Chapter Two

Dream Crusher

They had barely made it through Warren's front door before they began sipping, tasting, and gorging on each other's body like starved animals. Clothes were strewn throughout the living room and Erica was splayed on the sofa, basking in the afterglow. Warren sat opposite her in his boxers, pushing the muter into his trumpet. A plushy sound emerged, clear and full, and with each note Warren slipped further between the rhythm and cords, filling the air with a thick sweetness. The music soaked into Erica's pores, as she stored him up like she did every weekend; his scent, sound and touch. It was the only way she made it through the week without him. He lowered his horn.

"Nice," she leaned up on her elbows.

Warren placed his trumpet in the hard case, then propped it in the corner next to his vinyl collection. Everything in his apartment had a place. "Did you eat?"

"I nibbled on the train," she reached for the chenille throw. Warren strolled into the kitchen and then returned with two beers and a bowl of salt and vinegar potato chips, Erica's favorite. After her fourth scoop, Warren offered, "I could order you something. I think Chinese is still open?"

She shook her head. It was late, and she hated going to bed on a full stomach. They found a West coast basketball game and settled into their usual trash talk about the other's team.

"Come on, take the Spurs with me? The Mavericks can't buy a bucket," Erica teased.

"They'll be back."

"I doubt it. You have a knack for picking the worst teams," she made an L with her thumb and pointer finger.

"Yeah, it's called loyalty. I don't bounce around based on who's winning like you do."

"Well, you should. Maybe you'd win an office pool or two." She popped another handful of mix into her mouth. Warren leaned in closer to the television, and she reached for his chin.

"When was the last time you washed your hair?"

"This morning, why?"

"Here, sit," she dropped a pillow on the floor in front of her, grabbing her purse wedged in the corner of the sofa. Warren eased onto the floor and rested his shoulders against her thighs. She carefully parted his curls, then dipped her fingers in jojoba oil and slid them through his scalp. Warren's hair moved like short balls of cotton, and as she worked she found an easy rhythm.

"I have this first time author who is making the most ridiculous demands."

"Really?" Warren's head was pressed against her inner thigh, and she could tell by his voice that he was being lulled.

"She's crazy, telling me that she needs to stay at the Ritz-Carlton. With the budget that marketing gave me she'll be lucky if I can afford the Marriott."

"Hmm."

"I hope Claire pulls me in on Reverend Black's campaign. It's high profile and will really give me the experience I need."

"How's Edie?"

"Tacky and pregnant. I can't wait for her to go out on maternity leave. She called me at home last night complaining about a typo on the Chang schedule."

Warren shifted his head so that she could grease the other side.

"Meanwhile I'm thinking isn't that what you have an assistant for." Her fingers moved as if she was buttering a piece of bread. When all of his hair was oiled she moved into a head massage.

"What's up for tomorrow?" Warren muttered. He usually left the weekend plans to her, and Erica hesitated before telling him she had to stop in on a book signing.

"That's two weekends in a row." He turned to face her.

"I'll be ten minutes." She tilted his head back towards the television and started raking the comb over the tiny hairs above his neck. "I just need to show my face."

"I'm not going." He stretched out his legs and slipped from between her knees.

"Please, honey, we'll be in and out."

He reached for his T-shirt and pulled it over his head. "Why can't someone else handle it? You do too much."

"Because I'm here, and I'm trying to line things up so that when Edie leaves I slide right into her director's position." She stood next to him smoothing down the back of his shirt. "I did a good job on your hair. Doesn't that feel better?"

He nodded without distraction. "It just seems like it's always something."

"I know, Muffin." She wrapped her arms around his waist. "Soon you'll be moving back to New York and this won't even be an issue."

Warren pulled away from her and slipped on a pair of sweats. "You want anything from the kitchen?"

"Nope, I'm good."

Erica took his question as a truce, picked up her beer and then patted the seat next to her on the sofa.

Late the next morning, Erica slipped out to the corner shop for food and was placing their continental brunch on the living room coffee table when Warren walked in yawning. "What's this?" His shawl-collared robe was open at the waist.

"Bagels, morning glory muffins and a few slices of melon to get the day started," she handed him his coffee. "Your blackberry kept ringing this morning but I didn't answer it."

"Probably one of the geeks from the job. We have our monthly metrics meeting on Monday." Warren worked under contract as a software engineer for mobile telephones.

"How much longer on your contract?"

Warren shrugged. "What time do you need to be at the bookstore?"

"Two."

"I'll go with you. But ten minutes, tops."

Erica hugged his neck.

When they arrived at the Books a Million in DuPont Circle, Warren held the door for her and reminded her once again not to take all day.

"Promise," she said and was off.

Brandon Sykes was a midlist mystery author that Erica's company was trying to build, and like many of her authors, he was demanding and filled with self importance.

"I asked for navy Sharpies, not black," he chided. "I never write in black, it's too easy for people to forge my signature,"

Brandon tapped his wire-rimmed glasses. His eyes were the same storm gray as his receding hairline, and matched his wool vest.

"I'll take care of it," was her signature line, but when she returned with the correct pens, he continued to complain.

"I can't go to the podium and pour my heart out to a handful of people. It kills my creative flow. How was this advertised?" he demanded. Erica turned up her publicist smile and told him to give it five more minutes. She asked the events manager to make another in-store announcement.

Warren had strolled to where Erica could see him and mouthed, do you need any help? She winked at him and shook her head no. Turning her attention back to the stack of books, she lifted the dust jacket and flapped the books to the title page to make them faster for Brandon to sign. A few stragglers arrived, and once the folding chairs were half-filled, she pushed Brandon to begin.

He cleared his throat, took a sip of water, adjusted his glasses and read. Erica had not intended to stay, but after the first few minutes, she could tell that Brandon needed help with his presentation. She took out her turquoise note pad and jotted a few notes.

1. *He's speaking too slowly; the audience is falling asleep.*
2. *Start the reading with chapter 1, instead of 13. I've read the story and I was lost.*
3. *Don't wear so much gray.*

Brandon took a few questions, autographed books, and posed for a picture with the staff, which was clearly the highlight of his day. It was the first time Erica witnessed a hint of a smile. Gathering Brandon's things, she walked him out to his hired town car and pressed a business card into his hand.

"Call me if you need anything," she said, deciding to wait until she got back to her office in New York to give him her notes.

"Oh, I intend to," Brandon called from the window as the car pulled away from the curb.

Warren walked out of the store with a bag biting his bottom lip.

"What did you buy?"

"Nothing. You ready?"

"Sorry, the guy was terrible, I just couldn't leave him stranded." She reached for his hand.

"It's cool." Pulling his skull cap down on his head, he started towards the car.

The problem with long distance relationships was that there was no time to fight. With only seventy-two hours together and a good portion of that reserved for sleeping, things needed to be resolved and fast.

Warren put the key in the ignition. Erica reached over to the dashboard and pressed the buttons to warm their seats. After driving a few streets south, he parked on Wisconsin Avenue down the block from one of their local hangouts.

The Big Hunt was an unpretentious dive bar that offered twenty-seven varieties of beer on tap, flat screen televisions, a pool table, lots of seating, and a jukebox with good soulful music.

Warren held the door open and then led her over to empty seats at the bar. "What're you having?"

"The Raging Bitch I.P.A," she said, and watched him hold back a smile. It was what she drank the last time they were there, when Erica dedicated a karaoke song to him. Even though she sucked at singing, her theatrics had the audience cheering her on and Warren stood in an ovation.

Erica knew Warren remembered, even though he kept his eyes on the game. He was a sucker for HD television and the Wizards were playing the 76ers on the mega-sized flat screen. But after dealing with Brandon, Erica needed music. She pulled a five dollar bill from her purse, strolled over to the jukebox, and scanned for a song that would get the party started. Warren acted like everything was cool, but she knew her man: he wanted all of her and the book signing had taken longer than she promised. Bob Marley was the perfect remedy, and seconds later Erica shifted her hips to the sultry sound of "Is This Love."

I wanna love you and treat you right;
I wanna love you every day and every night

This was their song. They had danced to it on their one week anniversary at Café Creole in the West Village. Erica slid her stool closer to him and laced her fingers through his, humming with the music. Warren ordered a second round. The point guard for the Wizards shot a three-pointer to end the half. Warren pumped his fist and Erica moved in circles to the music. The beer had made her happy and she was singing the lyrics softly but out loud.

"Who're you rooting for?" Warren turned.

"The Sixers of course."

"Can't you ever root for my team?"

"I am on your team, just not the Wizards'," she leaned in and dragged her glossy lips over his cheek until he turned and kissed her back.

Bob Marley, the Wizards' victory, and three pints of Raging Bitch beer had Erica laughing brashly on the elevator ride to

Warren's apartment. The hallway was long and narrow with four beige doors on each side. Warren's unit was on the right and while he unlocked the front door, Erica's cell phone started ringing. Her mother's name flashed across the screen and Erica gritted her teeth. What could she possibly want now? Her mother knew better than to interrupt Erica's weekend with Warren.

"Yes?" came out sounding annoyed.

"If you weren't gonna send the money, you shoulda just said so," her mother hiccupped.

Warren closed the door and was fastening his fingers around Erica's waist, but she shook him off, mouthing that it was her mother.

"I walked four blocks in the pourin' down rain, with no long johns, and you know my arthritis in this damp weather."

"Ma, I deposited the money last night," Erica padded down the hall, closing the bathroom door behind her.

"Wasn't there and it's freezin' in here."

Erica opened the vanity and reached for her hair clip. She wasn't in the mood for her mother's drama.

"Okay, let me call the bank."

After ten minutes of holding, she was told that the money had been withdrawn from an ATM down the block from her mother's home. A persistent tapping worked her temples as she listened to her mother explain.

"Chile, I ain't crazy. I went down to the store; put the card in the machine, and nothing. Maybe the person behind me stol' it," clucking her tongue.

"Ma, you been drinking?"

"Pepsi is all. Just tired from that long walk. God as my witness I never got that money. Can you send it again?"

God was going to strike her Pinocchio ass down. Erica wasn't a fool. An enabler, yes, but not a fool. The money had been spent on a liter of Bacardi, four Colt 45s and a hard pack of whichever menthol lights happened to be on sale. It was the same story.

Erica shifted her weight against the pedestal sink listening to her mother ramble. Warren's white bathroom was spa-like, with jasmine-scented candles and stark white towels stacked in wooden shelves. Ordinarily, it was a room that relaxed her, but talking to her mother had her wound-up and irritated. When she looked at herself in the mirror she wondered why she even bothered. Her mother had celebrated her fiftieth birthday last year and Erica didn't understand why she couldn't get it together. Every conversation with her was the same, beginning with a need, ending with what she wanted, and Erica was exhausted.

"It's so cold in here, I'm wearin' my coat. 'Member that red one Aunt Mavis gave me with the big black buttons?"

She remembered.

"Well, Mr. Handy won't fix the heater without the money. Tues-dee's first of the month and I told you I'm selling my pills. I'll pay you then. Promise."

Promise? If Erica had a book for every time her mother broke a promise, she could build a library.

"I don't have it," she responded flatly.

"Come on Slim, I'll pay you back."

"Ma, I'm with Warren."

"He'll understand. Will take you ten minutes then I'll be outta your hair."

Erica tapped her foot against the floor.

"Come on Slim, I wouldn't ask if I didn't need it. I tried all of my friends but everyone I know is broke til Tues-dee."

It took effort for Erica to control her tone. "I don't know why you think I'm an ATM. I had to spend an extra seventy-five dollars to get here because I missed my train."

"Warren don't pay your way?"

"Ma, that's not the point."

"You right. Well just do it for me one more time. I'll help you with a little extra to get you through next week," she hiccupped again. "Thanks baby."

WARREN SAT IN THE leather recliner, working a soft cloth in and out of the front valve of his trumpet. A piano soloed in the background and a single tea light burned on the coffee table.

"Everything all right?" he looked up from his horn.

"Yeah," Erica said, fumbling with the buttons on her shearling coat. "I'll be right back."

"Where you going?"

"To the bank. Keep practicing, I'll be right back." She closed the door behind her with more force then she intended. Anger was percolating inside of her like a strong pot of coffee. Her mother was a damn leech and once again Erica had found herself trapped in her bloodsucking clutches.

WARREN WAS STILL CODDLING his horn when she got back to the apartment. Her mother had completely killed her buzz, and since she had a headache she was debating between ibuprofen and water or a glass of chardonnay. Then she opened the refrigerator and saw the frosty bottle. The chardonnay won.

"What do you want to eat?" she called out.

"I know you love Tex-Mex, so I just ordered. Is that okay?"

"Yeah, fine," she mumbled, uncorking the wine. Everything inside of her was tense and after a few sips she was still restless and decided to do a word search puzzle, a habit carried over from adolescence that she found soothed her nerves.

She reached for the top left kitchen drawer where she stored her book, but it would not open. She gave it a yank but the drawer only slid an inch forward, which surprised her because nothing was out of order in Warren's apartment.

He was Mr. Fix-it and organized almost to a compulsion. Vintage records were coordinated alphabetically, toiletries stowed in labeled baskets, shoes stuffed with shoe trees and stored in the original boxes, and take-out menus arranged by the specialty of cuisine. With the flat of her palm she reached inside and after a brief tug-of-war pried the culprit loose. It was a thick envelope that bore Warren's company seal and Erica knew what it was without opening it.

Warren was a software engineer by day and a jazz musician by night. They had only been dating a month when his father scored him the very lucrative position in D.C. When he left New York, he promised that it would only be temporary. But when the first six month contract ended, another one popped up.

Just then, Warren entered the kitchen whistling a tune. "Pour me some water, babe?"

The package had gained weight in Erica's hand and she didn't move. When Warren's eyes adjusted to the situation, he rushed to explain.

"I was going to tell you."

"Tell me what?" she stood.

"Brett just offered it to me on Thursday. I haven't really worked it out yet."

Erica opened the envelope and read over the conditions for the new contract. "Another whole year?" she tossed the papers on the counter.

"They want me to head the project, and the money is sick."

Erica had never cared about money and she reminded him of that. It was him that she wanted.

"But then you wouldn't have to work so hard. You know, with your mother and sister. Let me do this for us."

"Don't throw them in my face," she chided. "It's already been a year, now you want to make it two?"

"Move down here. You could start your own PR firm," he said.

"Why do you keep saying that? You know what I'm trying to do."

"Because it's logical."

The food arrived just in time.

Warren made small talk with the delivery guy and then returned to the kitchen with two bags in hand. "You want to eat in the kitchen or the living room?"

"I'm not hungry."

"You haven't eaten anything all day. Let's enjoy our meal and talk it over."

"What is there to talk about? When you left New York a year ago, you said it wouldn't come to this. Now I'm wondering how committed you are to this relationship."

"Like you can talk? You can't even make it a whole weekend without working. Selfish."

"I'm selfish?" Erica tightened the clip in her hair. "I'm just reminding you of what you said."

"Yeah, well things change."

"Oh, now you have the nerve to be pissed?"

Warren laid the tin container on the counter and removed the plastic lid, ignoring her.

Erica stepped in front, blocking his path. "If you aren't committed to being together then why are we even doing this?"

"What are you talking about? I didn't say that."

"Actions speak louder than words," Erica shouted.

"You are being ridiculous."

"Whatever." Erica couldn't think straight, so she walked off into his bedroom, closing the door behind her. On top of the headache, now her stomach was twisting in knots.

With all of the men walking the streets of New York, why did she have to fall in love with a man who lived and worked four hundred miles away? And loving Warren was an understatement; Erica revered him. There were times when they were together that she couldn't stop touching him—her hand on his forearm, a toe rubbing his calf, or a finger resting in his belt loop. So many nights at home alone she wondered what it would be like to just dissolve into him, breathing his air, and feeling his heart tick.

And there was no way possible that she could move. Erica had worked hard for B&B publishing for five years, starting as a publicity assistant, then becoming a full fledged publicist, publicity manager and now associate director of publicity. Her director was preparing for maternity leave, and Erica wanted to be named her successor. The promotion would make her one of the youngest ranked African-American women in the company. *Publishers Weekly*, the industry trade magazine, would do a story on her, maybe even *Essence*. She couldn't stop now and Warren knew that.

The bedside clock marked each second until Erica grew tired of listening to it. She opened the bedroom door and headed back to the living room. Warren was chewing on a bite of his steak taco. It amazed Erica how his appetite never failed him, not even in the midst of a major fight. She sat on the sofa with him, leaving lots of space between them, focusing on the potted plant in the corner next to the double paned window.

Warren had a green thumb and his houseplants were thriving. There was a devil's ivy with leaves hanging from the windowsill, two types of ferns full and luscious, and a pretty

African violet with big velvety leaves and lavender flowering. His whole apartment reminded her of something off of HGTV. It contained all the usual bachelor pad elements—the mega flat screen television, booming sound system and lazy boy recliner—but everything was high end with uncluttered lines.

When she looked down at the table, Warren had her quesadilla unwrapped and had scooped a bit of sour cream on top.

"Thanks," she said, cutting into the tortilla and taking a bite. They ate with their eyes glued on the television. Warren poured her a glass of wine and popped open a beer for himself.

When she finished the quesadilla, he pushed the remote towards her. "Want to watch a movie?"

"Sure."

Erica carried the empty containers into the kitchen. The contract was still on the counter. Disappointment washed over her, but before it felt consuming, Warren was there wrapping his arms around her and pulling.

"There's nothing in the world I want more than you. We'll get through this."

"But I'm tired of just getting through it," she said and her resistance made him hold her tighter, pressing his pelvis and chest against her until she retreated.

Warren unclipped her hair and ran his fingers over the curve of her neck, "You're my first round draft pick. Just trust me to run the team."

He was such a man. After spending most of her life without her father, and having an incompetent mother, Warren was just the rock that she needed, and that knowledge was sometimes as scary to deal with as the distance.

Chapter Three
Publicity 101

On Monday morning Erica dressed happy, in a taffy colored pantsuit and patent-leather peep-toe-heels. She brushed her eyelids with Glad Ginger, rouged her cheekbones in Bitter Bisque, and slid Pouting Plum over her lips. On the subway ride to work, she watched two lovers bump against each other with each shift of the train, enjoying each other as if no one was watching. A block from her office, a teenaged couple cuddled over a Styrofoam cup of cocoa, kissing and keeping warm. At the corner, a stooped man held the door to a diner open for his wife, waiting as she hobbled through. Every scene reminded her of Warren and how it seemed they would never have Monday mornings together.

But when she pushed the revolving door of B&B Publishing's building Number 416, those feelings were checked at the curb. Erica morphed from a red-nosed girlfriend into a powerhouse publicist who lunched with top television producers, influenced booksellers, and persuaded the opinions of erudite editors with the same fervor as a storefront preacher.

"'Morning, Iris," she waved to the receptionist who buzzed her in.

B&B Publishing had started as a family business before being sold to a British media company a year after Erica was hired. It was now first in producing the most *New York Times* bestselling fiction titles, and as Erica stepped over a box of books into the publicity department, she knew she had a lot to do with their success.

Erica had always loved books. Every Saturday morning, she would slip into a pleated skirt and soft leather shoes, and walk the three short blocks and two avenues to the Newark, New Jersey, branch of the library where all the librarians knew her by name. She'd check out five new titles, reading them whenever she could. During class, she had a library book tucked between the pages of a textbook. In the schoolyard she read while the other girls jumped Double-Dutch, chased boys, and played hand games. At night she wouldn't put the book down until she finished the last page, even if it meant reading by flashlight.

Ntozake Shange's *For Colored Girls Who Have Considered Suicide When the Rainbow Is Enuf* affirmed her black-girl struggle. Maya Angelou's *I Know Why the Caged Bird Sings* made her salivate for poetry. Then Terry McMillan wrote *Mama*, and it was the first time Erica had ever read a book twice. Her voracious appetite for reading was what drew her to publishing, and her passion for words is what made her successful.

Erica P. Shaw, Associate Director of Publicity, was stenciled in gold script in a black plaque fastened in the center of her door. Erica ran her manicured finger across it like she did every morning for luck. Inside of her closet-like office books were shelved in every possible corner and since there was no window, she hung a black-and-white framed photo of a pebble being tossed in a calm lake. It served as her daily reminder that the director's office with the view was within reach.

"'Morning," a watery voice called from behind her. Erica's shoulders tensed when she turned and saw Goldie Gardner, newly appointed senior editor of B&B's literary imprint, standing in her doorway. Work did not officially begin for another full hour and only Goldie would think this impromptu drop-in was appropriate. Erica hadn't removed her coat, checked her voice messages, or pressed play on her get-the-morning-started CD. Hell, she hadn't even poured a cup of coffee. But there stood Goldie with her limp hair, clutching a file folder to her chest, asking, "Do you have a review list ready for *Arranged Proposals*?"

She was referring to a debut memoir by Bollywood actress Chitra Jotwani. Karrington Press had published a similar memoir last year and the media hadn't been interested in the runner-up, but Erica couldn't say that to Goldie even though she longed to.

"I need to do another round of calls. I can have an update to you by the end of the day," Erica answered, opening her spiral notebook and writing it down.

"Well, if you're swamped, I can have my assistant make the calls," Goldie flicked her bangs out of her narrow face, and as she did Erica caught a whiff of her grassy shampoo, making her sneeze.

Goldie had only been with the company a few months, and after working on two other titles together, she was on Erica's "avoid-this-editor list." Publisher Genève Meyers-Sheppard had wooed Goldie from a competing house with a reportedly large salary. The deal had been "hot news" in all of the trade magazines and, as Grandma Queeny used to say, "The child is smelling her piss." Goldie knew damn well that Erica wouldn't let her editorial assistant make publicity calls, just as Goldie wouldn't let Erica's edit one of her books.

"We'll handle it," she smiled tartly.

"We really don't mind." Goldie leaned into the door frame. "This book is really important to me."

Every book was important to the editor who acquired it, and Erica's job as the publicist was to sell it to the media as the next best thing, whether it was or not. The telephone rang.

"I'll have the list sent down to you later," Erica replied. But when Goldie still didn't move, Erica answered the call on speaker, in a final dismissive gesture.

"Erica Shaw."

"HELLO, YOU HAVE A COLLECT CALL FROM ESSEX COUNTY FACILITY JAIL…" Erica clamored for the receiver.

"Is that an author?" Goldie's thin fingers hugged the floating heart necklace around her neck.

"I'll see you later," Erica stared schoolyard style until Goldie backpedaled out of her office.

"PRESS ONE TO ACCEPT THIS CALL."

The line clicked several times before she heard her mother's voice crack. "Er-ri-ca. It's Mom-ee."

"Where're you?" she whispered, though it was painstakingly obvious.

"The county. They 'rested us for shoplifting, but I ain't do nothing."

A numbing sensation brushed over Erica. Experience told her that the "us" was her mother and her longtime friend Bonnie, and that they had absolutely been stealing. Bonnie had been the canker sore in their lives ever since Erica could remember and was always leading her mother into a pile of manure.

"What do you want me to do?" she asked crossly.

"Bail me out," her mother cried, calling out a telephone number. "God as my witness, I'ma pay you back."

Her mother's fingers were as sticky as a wad of chewing gum. Most of the time what she took was worthless: trinkets such as crossword puzzles, pot holders and key chains from the Dollar store. Sometimes, she'd tuck greeting cards, spatulas and hair magazines between the pages of the supermarket circular. When she had the nerve to lift from department stores, it was earrings, pantyhose and sunglasses wrapped in her neck scarf and then pressed into the folds of her rubbery arms. Erica had warned her mother that these sins would catch up with her and now jail was her penance. Molten lava had spread through Erica's stomach and was bubbling up flesh.

Just a year ago, she had played the concerned daughter when her mother and Bonnie ventured on a casino bus trip to Atlantic City. The two of them had consumed too much of everything and like most drunks started fighting. Fed up, Bonnie took the bus home and Erica's mother staggered around the boardwalk looking for her, stoned and confused. The police finally picked her up, and dropped her off at the psychiatric ward of the General Hospital.

Erica received the humiliating call then and although she hadn't known Warren long, he rented a car and insisted on driving her to Atlantic City. When they got there, Erica had to sit next to her new boyfriend in a conference room filled with white-lab coats telling her that her mother had a substance and alcohol problem. She thought that Warren would bolt after that, but somehow the situation brought them closer.

She dialed Warren's number, but when his voicemail picked up, she remembered that he was in meetings. She called the bondsman.

"Bail bonds."

"I need to get someone out of jail," her voice thinned as she recounted the arrest story. The bondsman asked for her mother's date of birth, location and charges, and put Erica on hold.

"Her bail is set at ten grand," he came back to the line, "I'll need one thousand to get her out tonight, plus a thirty dollar filing fee."

As much as she loved her job, publishing wasn't Wall Street and she didn't sit on savings. Most of her expendable cash was spent on rent and general living. A small portion went into her 401k and an even tinier portion was stashed in an IRA that she wasn't risking for her mother.

"Thanks, I'll have to check my funds and give you a call back."

Erica moved robotically down the hall towards the ladies' room, her mind too warped to speak to the few early birds in their cubicles. But as soon as she rounded the bend, she ran into Edie Butnick, her very pregnant Director, wearing a screaming pink paisley headband. The morning couldn't get any better.

"Erica, just the girl I wanted to see."

"'Morning, Edie," she forced a smile.

"How did it go with Brandon this weekend? I'm not feeling plugged in."

"There were a few hiccups, but I took notes and we should be able to iron them out before he starts the tour."

"Can you email me his schedule, budget, and a quick recap before the eleven a.m.?" Edie's hand drifted over her protruding belly.

Erica said that she would, and then continued quickly to the ladies' room before her boss could add to the list. She rushed past the double vanity and into the last stall, where in a matter of seconds her entire morning came loose.

Chapter Four

Daddy's Girl

It was always her stomach that shut down first.

After her father moved out, Erica's mother changed her name. Not legally, but men started calling the house asking to speak to Jackie. In the beginning, Erica was confused, insisting that they had the wrong number. But they would keep calling until her mother picked up the telephone. Shortly after each call, her mother would burst into her bedroom tucking herself into her Gloria Vanderbilt jeans and smoothing her soft hair into an up do twist.

"Watch ya sista while I run to the store," she'd say, brushing a tube of dollar-store lipstick across her mouth, and then using it for blush on her cheeks. She was a pretty woman with a firm body and pleasing features, but it was her eyes that gave away her pain.

"When're you coming back?" Erica would ask, throwing up a little bit in her mouth.

"Right back, and don't answer the telephone. If it's me, I'll let the phone ring once, hang up and then call again," she'd say, bolting the thick wooden door behind her.

It was always the store and even though the bodega was a block away, the run could take her mother hours to complete. From the moment she walked out, Erica would feel her stomach spin, as if she were on a carousel ride that had suddenly lost control. To cope, she medicated herself with back-to-back reruns of *Welcome Back Kotter*, *Good Times*, *The Jeffersons*, and *Alice*.

Sometimes her mother would return with a greasy bag of fried chicken wings and soggy fries from the Chinese store, but most times she came home empty-handed, jeans soaked in urine and smelling like she had bathed in a bottle of Bacardi. Erica couldn't stand to see her mother liquored up and each night before bed, she knelt against her canopy bed with her bare knees pressed into the cold wooden floor, begging God to send her father back. She would seal her plea with The Lord's Prayer and two Hail Mary's, but as the seasons passed, he never came.

Then one day when she was in her mid-twenties she received a Thanksgiving card from him with a fifty-dollar bill Scotch-taped to the left side. It was simply addressed to E-Bird, his pet name for her with no return address. A few weeks later, he sent her a Christmas card with another fifty and a photo of his new family.

There were four people in the photo, clustered in shades of green like sprigs from a mistletoe: a thick-skinned woman with a gap between her teeth and tits the size of Texas, a young boy with crescent-shaped eyes and a smile that mirrored her own, a little girl with braids and rainbow beads. Her father's wavy temples had grayed, but his face held the same handsome sheen. Just looking at him conjured his waxy scent into her living room. The little girl sat in Erica's father's lap, sucking her index finger with eyes that screamed into the camera, "My Daddy."

The fifty-dollar bills came almost monthly after the first one but Erica never responded, choosing to forget about the bills collecting in the drawer of her nightstand. One day she planned to stuff the money in a big envelope with pictures of her missed dance recital, basketball games and graduations.

On the bad days, she wished that she could send him snaps of her terrified self; when the electricity had been shut off, and their spoiled food invited every rodent in Newark to camp out in their home. Or when her mother stole her elementary school's candy-drive money, and the principal scolded her daily in front of her classmates. Or when Ms. Frances, her babysitter's mother, refused to let her daughter watch Erica and her sister, and was kind enough to yell her reason from her screened-in-porch, just in time for Erica's business to reach the neighbors' table with dessert.

"'Cause that woman ain't never coming back," Ms. Frances puffed on her Marlboro Red, "and the Daddy ain't shit either."

THE ASSISTANTS HAD LONG finished their water cooler talk about their weekend hangovers and Erica's half-sipped coffee was stone cold. Peering at her online banking, she calculated her remaining bills for the month. Rent and cable were due at the end of the week. The company was late again with the check for her expenses, so she would have to pay AmEx and wait to be reimbursed. With a phone call, she could delay paying her student loans and her dry cleaning would have to stay put. But even with this, she was still short. Her sister, Jazmine, was away at Clark Atlanta University and Erica put a small allowance into her account every month. So when she picked up the telephone to call Jaz, it was more out of need to share information than to expect real help.

"Sha low."

"Is that how you answer the telephone?"

"Girl, I knew it was you. Caller-ID, duh."

"Your mother's in jail."

"Shut-up," Jazmine said, and Erica could hear the lollipop she was sucking pop from her painted red lips. She could picture her sister's bleach blonde fro, feathered and free, while she recounted the arrest story and how much they needed to get her out.

"She's so stupid," Erica finished.

"And you know she's in there freakin' out. Probably peed her pants."

"I hope not."

"Well I only have twenty dollars to last me 'til the end of the week. I would say call Daddy, but he doesn't have a cell phone and his wife cock blocks like a mug."

"You talk to Daddy?" Erica asked, stunned.

"Sometimes. He asks about you."

She felt a pang of jealousy over her sister forgiving their father and not keeping her side. Although she should have known Jazmine would talk to anyone who gave her money, she was still pissed. He left them for Christ sakes, and was raising a brand new family like they never existed.

"So what should I do?"

"Borrow it from Warren."

"I'm not a leech."

"You're fucking him aren't you?"

"Jaz."

"I'm just saying, what's his is..."

"I'm not Mommy. I don't ask men for money."

"Excuse the hell out of me," Jazmine shot back.

Erica hadn't intended for her words to sound so harsh. After all, Jazmine was the love of her life. It was Erica who raised her when her mother couldn't. Teaching her sister how to skate, use tampons, and helping her change her sheets when she wet the bed in the middle of the night. But watching her mother wait on Sugar Daddys, and still come up empty had made Erica fiercely independent, probably to a fault.

"You can't borrow it from anyone?" Erica pushed.

"Girl, I have robbed every Peter I know to pay Paul. But we can't leave Mommy in there overnight. She'll have a nervous breakdown."

"All right, don't worry. I'll figure something out."

Erica ended the call just as Prudence entered the office, her long brown hair pulled in a tight ponytail.

"Sorry to bother you, but Edie wants the follow up email on Brandon Sykes, it's almost eleven."

Erica minimized her online banking screen. "Tell her I got caught up on a call and it's coming now."

"Anything I can do to help?" Prudence asked, rolling up her long hair.

"Can you make another round of calls on *Arranged Proposals*? Goldie's breathing down my neck. Try and get a few definites."

"Absolutely." Prudence left.

Erica pulled together the information for Edie, and then called the bondsman and set the appointment. She knew where to get the extra money from, even though it crushed her.

Chapter Five

Play Something Nice

Warren sat in a corner conference room, stuck in his second operations' meeting of the morning, and although he was trying to concentrate on his manager's review of the monthly metrics, his mind kept reminiscing over Erica. When they were apart it was her scent that he missed most. Erica never doused herself in perfume but her skin was naturally fragrant with a mix of sprigs, water, something wild and bloomy. Tonight he would trace her fragrance on the pillow, trapped between the threaded sheets. But by Wednesday it would be lost. It had been only twelve hours since Erica departed yet Warren was yearning for her with a lump in his gut like it was the middle of the week. If not for the distraction of his weekly jazz gig, Mondays would be murky and mundane, and just knowing that later he would be on stage playing at Sweet Melodies made the day more bearable.

Warren loved Sweet Melodies. It was a well-known jazz club in the heart of Adams Morgan in D.C. and had been in the same corner location since the "Era of Bebop." Though the owners changed several times, the essence of the club remained the same: don't take the stage unless you're ready to jam. And every Monday night, Warren's band played house to these sessions. Once in a while, a musical giant blessed the stage and tonight it was the legendary saxophonist Bobby

Watson. Warren was such a fan of Bobby's that as a broke college student, he traveled all the way to Charlotte, North Carolina in the back of his friend's rusty Ford to see Bobby perform. The trip was the pinnacle of his junior year at Howard and since then he had collected all twenty-six of Bobby's albums.

Warren admired Bobby because he could move from soprano to alto to tenor, with the same blind precision that his late mother used in squirting mustard, pinching relish, and tossing mayonnaise in a bowl of homemade potato salad. Bobby had played with jazz legends Art Blakey, Wynton Marsalis, Max Roach, and Victor Lewis. Warren believed that when you shared the stage with a musician, you took a piece of them with you. He couldn't wait to earn his piece of Bobby.

"We're over budget," said Brett McDaniels, manager of software. "Alan, you'll have to cut back on overtime."

The five-person team was assembled around an oval-shaped table long enough to accommodate ten with Brett at the head, Warren and Blanche on the right, and Carl and Alan to the left. Everyone had their notepads opened and Warren could see Blanche doodling sunflowers instead of taking notes. An intercom telephone sat in the middle of the table along with built-in plug-ins for the engineers' laptops. The smart board hanging from the ceiling displayed Brett's power point presentation on the defects of last year's work.

Alan whined. "Why me?" He was middle-aged, thick-bellied and balding.

"Well, because last month you put in an additional fifty hours."

"I wasn't the only one," Alan retorted, pointing his finger over at Warren like a tattle-telling pre-schooler.

"You've got to be kidding," Warren leaned forward in his seat, but Alan sat across the table unfazed, chewing his stubby finger.

Since Warren joined the team, he tried to foster a relationship with Alan but was met with a cold shoulder and backstabbing remarks. Most software engineers were antisocial outcasts, the nerds who were picked on in school. Warren was the exception, which made people either love him or hate him. Alan fit the "geek" mold to a tee, down to his oily hair, constant sweat and the circulating rumor that he was a forty-year old virgin. Warren was jaw-breaking smooth, well-dressed and moved through the building with a blustering swank that Alan couldn't muster, not even on his birthday. Alan fell squarely in the "hate Warren" camp.

"Take fifteen." Brett closed his notebook. "We'll go over staffing and budget when we return."

Having a tooth pulled without novacaine would have suited Warren better than sitting through another meeting. This was already the third one on the same topic since Friday. Most of what they were discussing could have been settled in an email, but Brett pulled the team together so that he could caravan as the man in charge and his ego-tripping wore Warren thin.

RSCI was a leading software company that made advanced applications for mobile telephones, the first in the industry to come up with text applications. Being a software engineer came easy to Warren. He had always been good with math and problem solving and his team made product ideas come to life on short deadlines. Stan Greenwood, owner of RSCI, was a close friend of Warren's father and hired him directly. Stan believed that the company could transform text messaging industry-wide and was pumping a lot of money into their software division. When the finished product hit the market, the company was going public and Warren would receive shares in addition to his income. Certainly a lucrative deal.

"Got a minute?" asked Brett, just as Warren was exiting the room.

"Sure," he shifted his laptop case. Brett was the same height as Warren with pool-blue eyes and honey slicked hair. The joke around the office was that Brett thought he was a GQ model.

"What's up?" asked Warren.

"You're the last to sign. Something wrong?"

Warren could feel the presence of the unsigned contract crammed against his computer. He looked down at the carpet feeling Erica's disappointment. The last thing he wanted to do was hurt her, and he knew the distance was an obstacle, but he needed to make a living. Growing up, his father stressed how important it was for him to be financially secure. "Ain't nothing worse than a man who can't provide for his woman, son. Nothing."

Moving to New York would feed Warren's aesthetic soul, and cure the longing for her that had become as much a part of him as his music. He wished he could have it all. Erica was his muse, the reason his skies were painted blue. He wanted to share his whole life with her and the money from the stocks would be a wonderful start.

"I have it right here," Warren placed his case on the table and pulled the contract from an inside pocket.

"Awesome," said Brett. "Stan is going to be over the moon. He said that you were the key to moving this project forward."

Warren placed his case on the table, and before he could think more, he signed and dated the papers. "Looking forward to it."

Brett shook his hand and Warren tried to smile, but it fell short around his chin. For some, this position was a dream in the making. But Warren's dream was to sign a contract for a week of gigs at the world famous Blue Note in New York, with a sold out audience, and Erica sitting front row.

A THICK FOG SPREAD through Warren and his head felt like a twenty-pound weight. Scotch would level him out but coffee would have to do. The enormity of what just took place kept knocking against him. So much was on the line. Not only did he have to give this project his all, he had to do it while keeping his music moving, and his weekends free for Erica. He needed to call her. The conference room was just down the hall and as he rounded the corner to his cubicle, he saw Blanche leaning against the felt wall clutching a cup.

"Coffee, black like you like it," she sang with her melodic accent.

"You don't have to bring me coffee every day." Warren reached for his money clip, but she waved his hand away.

"You kidding? If you hadn't created the framework, I would have never finished my last layout on time. I ought to be doing more." Her sentence hung. Warren took the coffee.

Most of the guys in the office referred to Blanche as the Brazilian bombshell. Her hypnotizing voice rang in your ears long after the conversation. Her clothes were short and scant and she wore tall skinny heels even on dress down Fridays. But she didn't do it for Warren. He enjoyed a rounder ass.

"How was your weekend? Did Erica come down or you go up?" She made herself comfortable on the tip of his desk as her school girl skirt rested in the middle of her thigh.

"She came down. It was fun."

“Erica doesn’t exist,” chided Alan. A dollop of mustard caked his graying beard as he chewed on a sandwich.

“What’s your problem?” Warren cocked his head, not realizing that his fist had balled. Alan was so bitter that Warren could usually ignore his sly comments, but at that moment he was hotter than a steam roller. Deep down he knew this wasn’t the time, but he felt like punching Alan in the throat. Blanche must have recognized his rising temper, because before Warren knew what was happening she stepped between them, swishing her golden streaked hair, and straightened Alan’s tie.

“Alan is seeing the receptionist on the third floor. I saw them having lunch the other day.” Her blouse was unbuttoned down to her breastbone and she wore a thin gold chain. Leaning closer to Alan, she moved her hand from his neck and patted his cheek. As soon as her fingers left his face, Alan’s shoulders contracted and his skin flushed a fiery red.

“Oh, ooooh,” he said, his mouth puffing into a stream of Os, while his hips contracted forward. Blanche threw Warren a knowing look.

Alan turned his back as Brett walked up, clapping his hands. “Kids, fifteen minutes is over, back to the conference room.”

Alan darted down the hall towards the men’s room and Warren never made his call.

Chapter Six
I Wish I Could

It was dark when Erica got off the PATH train at Penn Station. Even though she was born and raised in Newark she had spent so many years in New York that she felt like a stranger. She maneuvered through the pedestrian traffic past the bookstore, the wine and spirit shop, the newsstand, and McDonald's, pinning her handbag to her side, never forgetting that it was filled with her father's fifty dollar bills. Now because of her mother's trouble her dream of throwing her father's money back in his face would never be.

Train stations brought all classes of life together; suits with hired cars curbside, commuters chugging down that last cup of coffee before heading home to children and chores, and the down-and-out loiterers who hogged the wooden benches until police ordered them to move on. Erica was one who hurried, pushing through the sliding glass doors and onto the street, not stopping until she reached the taxi stand. A heavy-set woman with a curly-do and airbrushed nails motioned her into the next cab.

"Where to?" the driver asked in a thick West Indian accent as she slid across the splintered vinyl seat. The car smelled like a half carton of cigarettes and Erica hoped the smell didn't get trapped in her hair. She read off the address while letting the window down some. The fresh air calmed her nerves, which had not stopped buzzing since her mother's morning call. She couldn't wait for this to be all over.

Outside the tinted window, Broad Street stumbled by with packed bus stops, vendors selling the latest bootleg DVDs and mixed CDs, knock-off designer purses, tube socks and children's trinkets. Young mothers in tight pants negotiated prices as their babies sucked on pacifiers, kicking their feet against plastic-covered strollers.

When the driver made a left onto Bergen Street and headed toward Central, Erica counted five liquor stores in a twelve-block radius. Fatty fast-food restaurants occupied every third corner with large signs advertising dollar menus. The homes were rundown but shackled with wrought-iron gates. Housing projects were named after African-American heroes like Betty Shabazz, Malcolm X and Shirley Chisholm, people who deserved higher recognition for their American achievements than dilapidated tenements. The debris blowing down cracked streets was as common as the young men hugging the corners in oversized coats, jeans fastened below their waist, and Timberland boots. Even the trees look sad.

"Thanks," she paid the driver. He sped off before she reached the front door. Chivalry was so dead.

The bail bonds' office was a standard storefront with a red-and-white striped awning and thick bars over the two windows. The street was eerily empty and Erica was relieved when she was buzzed inside. At the end of the short hall a man dressed in a velour running suit waved her in. He was younger than she had expected.

"I'm Chris," he said with a warmness that put her at ease. The office was sparse with a gray metal frame desk on the right and two faux leather chairs. An old boom box sat on top of one of the file cabinets and Erica recognized the song playing low. The walls were ecru and bare except for the poster of Martin Luther King, Jr., holding his inmate number taped with the quote, "If you bend your back people will ride your back. If you stand up straight can't nobody ride you."

The quote hit Erica with a pang. When she was seven-years old, she would go to work with her father in his garage every Saturday. Each week he brought her a crispy fried bacon and egg sandwich that she would eat while sitting in the driver's seat of whichever car he worked on. Careful not to spill crumbs. The same quote was pinned to her father's bulletin board and it was one he repeated often. Her hand dropped into her purse and caressed the wad of fifties.

"We have a problem," Chris took her coat. "In addition to the bail we discussed earlier, a detainer for your mom popped up in Irvington. Turns out she has some unpaid traffic tickets."

Her mother had lost her driver's license years ago.

"How much is it?"

"Five hundred with no ten percent."

"What does that mean?" Her hand covered a cough that came out dry and rattled.

"It's cash only, which means you'll have to pay the whole thing."

Erica's armpits began to sweat. "Why didn't you tell me this over the phone?"

"It just popped up before you arrived. I can still post bail for the shoplifting charge but the jail won't release her until the detainer has been satisfied."

Erica didn't know what to do. This situation had already caused her to split her soul in directions that troubled her pride. She had left her job an hour early, was spending her father's money that had accumulated in her drawer, and now she had to call Warren for the difference. Although he wouldn't hesitate to help, she still hated asking.

Music was already swirling in Warren's head as he clicked off his desk lamp and shoved a file in his satchel. At the last minute Brett had called another meeting, this time with the hardware team to discuss design options. Now he was running late for his gig at Sweet Melodies, but if traffic was on his side he could still make curtain. His band had never had a musician of Bobby Watson's caliber sit in before and Warren couldn't wait to share the stage.

"'Night, Gladys," he waved to the evening receptionist as he crossed the travertine floors of the main lobby. Erica's ringtone went off and he reached for his phone.

"Hey, baby," he sang.

"Where are you?"

"Heading to the club. Bobby's there tonight. What's up?"

"My mother is in jail," her voice cracked.

"What? Why didn't you call me? Where are you?" he stopped in front of his building, but the air was so chilly he was forced to keep walking.

"In Newark. At the bail bonds. I can pay the bail but some ticket came up for another five hundred."

"Whatever you need, baby. How come you didn't call me earlier?"

"I did but…"

"You should have left a message," his voice was rising, and before she could respond, he apologized. Erica put him on hold and he could hear her talking to someone in the background. It bugged him that he couldn't be there to help figure things out.

"There's a Western Union on the corner but they close in thirty minutes. Do you have time to stop?"

A fierce wind spun up, licking Warren's face. He knew that if he stopped he'd never make the show.

"Can I send it first thing in the morning?"

"She won't get out if I don't pay the detainer and I'm not leaving her there overnight."

"What about my credit card?" he slid behind the wheel.

"Honey, it's cash only. Forget it, I'll figure something out."

"Let me speak to the bondsman."

"I said don't worry about it, I'll handle it," she said, her tone embarrassed. "I don't want you to miss your performance."

"Erica, put the man on the phone," he retorted, leaning on agitation. A few seconds later Warren heard a man's voice and they talked about what he needed to do.

WIRING THE MONEY HAD sucked up a full hour. When Warren walked into the club his band was well into the second set, jamming with a young trumpet player from Southeast. He didn't see Bobby anywhere. The place was packed with Monday-night regulars but Warren wasn't in the mood for small talk. The bar was shaped like a horseshoe and Warren found a seat in the curve.

"What's up, Sissy?" he said, greeting the regular bartender over the music.

"Hey, handsome. What's your poison?" she smiled, resting her hand on her curvy hip. Sissy's skin was the color of cognac and she wore a black Cleopatra wig that was as much a staple at the club as she was.

"Glenfiddich, neat. Bobby still around?" He leaned in over the music and could smell her wig spray.

"No, honey, he rushed out of here about ten minutes ago, said something about teaching a class first thing."

It was just Warren's luck. A chance of a lifetime lost in a puddle of responsibility. Sissy returned with his drink.

"What happened to you? Boss working you like a runaway slave?" she chuckled.

"Something like that," he said, dipping his head. Warren downed his four ounces and headed for the stage.

Chapter Seven

Game Time, Jersey Girl

Erica lounged on the bright orange futon with her feet tucked under her. "I'm home."

"You took a taxi, right?" asked Warren. Live music was playing in the background, and Erica could hear the chatter of different voices resonating at once.

"I had more than enough left over," she said, feeling sheepish. "Thanks."

"I need to keep you safe."

Even with the distance, Warren overwhelmed her with devotion and mere talk couldn't express how sustained she felt.

"How's your mom?"

"A mess, but at home. Did you make the show?"

"Naw, but it's cool," his voice dropped and Erica felt his blow.

"I'm sorry."

The music got louder. "Look, you've had a long day. Get some rest. I'll call you in the morning."

"Promise?"

"Kiss, kiss."

Erica held the phone against her breast long after the line died, too riled up for bed. A glass of wine would have been sedating, but her cabinet was dry. So she sat staring at the exposed brick wall in front of her. It was one of the best features in her one-bedroom apartment. It wasn't newly refurbished like a lot of the Harlem apartments, which had attracted a mix of young, white, and foreign professionals. But for Erica, the place was a perfect fit. With gleaming hardwood floors, oversized windows, a tiny kitchen cove, claw foot bathtub, and original moldings and trim throughout, the space had an old school feel. Her unit was at the front of the house, so it was flooded with natural sunlight. Adjacent to the window was a three-tiered bookshelf leaning heavily on its side bursting with books, some from childhood. Magazines and manuscripts were stacked under the glass coffee table. On the surface of the table were two used tumblers, a dry cleaning receipt, and a word search book stuffed with a pencil. Erica grabbed the book and started flipping.

It was important for her to pick the right subject when selecting a word search. The topic needed to capture her mood. Exotic islands, Cadbury candies, Celtic string instruments, sea animals. She settled on the islands. First word Bora Bora. Eight letters and she was sure the word was either upside down or backwards. It was backwards, jackpot. Next the Cayman, easy. Daukuskie Island, tricky, but she found it diagonal, right side up. Circling each word was like pulling the lever on the slot machine and winning. Chi ching. She moved through the puzzle, ending on Vancouver Island. The next puzzle she chose was Goddesses of the World, and the sound of lead scratching the page became her lullaby.

TUESDAY NIGHT SHE WORKED late and so did Warren, so their conversation was quick.

"How was your day?"

"Missed you."

"You more."

"Dream about me."

On Wednesday to pass the time, she took a free African dance class with her neighbor, Tess. That night, she and Warren fell asleep whispering and breathing on the telephone. When Friday finally arrived she couldn't contain her excitement and dialed Warren first thing.

"Don't be late. I have a surprise for you."

"I hope it includes nudity," he teased.

"You're such a dirty old man," she called back.

"With a fine ass woman like you, can you blame me?"

Erica felt her face blushing and promised to see him soon.

After their long week apart, Erica was really looking forward to relaxing courtside at the Nets/Wizards game with him and she planned to look incredible while doing it. Her biweekly paycheck dropped on Thursday and after work she had her shoulder-length hair pressed and curled. The nail salon was her next stop. She sat for over an hour getting her eyebrows waxed and nails polished. Finding the right look for the game wasn't easy either. After scouring the shops along Avenue of the Americas in the West Village, she finally scored a pink Nets baby tee and a pair of skinny jeans that fit like they were sketched on.

At work, she camouflaged her evening look with a two-buttoned blazer and ballerina flats, saving her stiletto boots for game time. All morning she slaved over a press release. For lunch, she sat in the cafeteria forking down a salad, but the afternoon sauntered on like a stubborn heat wave. The office was insanely quiet for a Friday, and after dashing off an email to one of her authors, she decided to call it quits. But then Warren called saying that he was running late.

"I thought you were leaving early?"

"I should've been finished by now but the program I'm working on has some sort of bug."

"Will it take long?"

"No, I just need to see if the problem is on my end or with the developer's program."

"I hope there's no traffic," she was trying not to pout.

"Once I verify that it's not my error, I'm on the road."

"K, meet you out front."

When Warren dropped the receiver in the cradle he noticed Blanche hovering over him. Their cubicles shared a common wall and she was leaning on it like she wanted to chat.

"Everything all right in paradise?" She picked invisible lint from her French puffed sweater. Her lips were painted fuchsia, her hair pulled to one side.

"Debugging. Should've been out of here thirty minutes ago." He flicked his wrist and pushed back his sweater.

"Quick favor? Could you grab me a few backup disks from the supply room? Whoever stocks them puts them way out of my reach."

Warren cut his eyes.

"Being petite is such a handicap," she said, cupping her chin with her palms.

"Fine," he mumbled, figuring it would be quicker to grab the disks than find someone else to do it.

Blanche waited until Warren turned the corner and slid around to his desk. Reaching into her skirt pocket, she pulled out a disk and inserted it into his computer. Within three seconds the screen froze and she sped back over to her side.

Warren whistled on his walk down the hall.

"Here," he handed her the box. Time was ticking, and if he moved quickly he could at least get to the game by the start of the second quarter. Rolling back his sweater he tapped the keyboard, but after a few strokes realized the program wasn't responding.

"What the hell?"

Blanche popped her head up. "Need help?"

"Did you see anyone touch my computer?"

She shook her head.

"The program is non-functional. This is bullshit."

But there was no time for him to figure it out, he had to call IT. The operator told him that someone would be right up, but that always meant twenty minutes. Warren dropped his head in his hands. Nothing this week had gone according to plan.

"Since you're going to be around, want to put in for Chinese?" Blanche called from her seat. Warren wished she would just leave him alone. He thought about leaving and dealing with the consequences later but, to his surprise, a young lady from IT arrived.

"Please fix this quickly," said Warren, offering her his chair.

Chapter Eight
Distant Lover

Blanche forced an egg roll and coke on Warren as he was hustling out the door, but he couldn't eat anything. His appetite and thoughts were only on making the game. After a few tries, he persuaded Erica to leave his ticket at will-call, promising to meet her inside by halftime. But that didn't happen either and for the third time that day he served her with bad news.

"Where're you now?" she shouted, battling the noisy crowd.

"There was an accident on the turnpike. I'm doing like ten miles per hour," he yelled, aggravated.

"The Wizards are down…" she said and he could hear the roar of "Defense" before the call dropped. Warren tried phoning back but didn't have a signal and threw his mobile against the dashboard. Frustration became his roadside companion.

WBGO-FM pumped through his hi-tech sound system but even his favorite jazz station failed to mollify him. From exit 5 to where the New Jersey Turnpike split traffic crawled at a mind-dulling pace. Once he passed exit 8A, three truck lanes opened on the left, ending the gridlock. For the remainder of the ride, Warren's speedometer stayed on 80. But he was still late. When he pulled into the arena's parking lot, boozed-up fans were pouring into the street waving Nets banners celebrating like it was the championship. Warren stopped an older man wearing a Wizard's cap to find out the score.

"Damn fool hit a three-point shot at the buzzer," the man said, unfolding his portable cane. While he complained about the referees, Warren caught sight of Erica and his stomach turned to slush. She was here. His baby. The one he drove two hundred and thirty-two miles to see in traffic, with no water, no stops, just highway, and a feverish yearning to touch her face. Erica was his cure-all and even with thirty-feet between them he felt amazingly well.

On thin heels she glided, swinging her hips and smiling. Warren opened his coat to her.

"Hey, babe," she mashed her body into his with her cheek brushing his chin. While they rocked and touched hello, Warren's hands slid down the slope of her ass, which felt like marshmallow, spongy and plush, and he held it with both hands as he pressed into a kiss. Her mouth tasted melony and, like a glass of champagne, it went straight to his head.

"I can't believe you missed the whole game. It was so damn exciting," she tilted, and the glow from the street lamp made her brown eyes sparkle. Warren got lost watching her.

"What?" she traced his nose.

"Just missed you," he said. "Where's my surprise?"

"Oh, that," flashing a toothy grin. Erica took two steps back. Keeping eye contact, she slowly unzipped her waist-length jacket.

"Is this X-rated?" He looked around to see if anyone was watching, but everyone who passed was either shouting about the Nets or rushing to their car trying to avoid the inevitable traffic.

"You tell me," she flirted, spreading her jacket and flashing him. The Nets tee stretched across her curves, and it took Warren a few seconds to realize what she was doing.

"You're so corny," he snickered.

"And your team stunk. I was so close I could have been the towel girl." She pretended to shoot the ball.

"I heard they won at the buzzer." He took her hand, helping her into the car.

"And it was oh so pretty," she threw back.

Warren rounded the vehicle and hopped into the driver's seat. "The Nets got lucky, is all," he put the car in reverse, merging with the departing traffic. "I can't believe I missed it."

Erica reached across the console for his trumpet hand, caressing his calluses. "I'll make it up to you," she said, kissing each finger.

TRAFFIC INTO THE CITY was minimal and they made it to Lafayette Street with ease.

"There's someone coming out," Erica pointed and Warren swerved, ducking in front of a yellow cab for the parking space. It was a tight fit, but after cutting the wheel twice he was in.

"Wish you could drive like me?"

"Whatever," she said, checking her reflection in the mirror. After clipping his mobile to his waist, Warren got out and walked to the nearest parking sign. He had received too many tickets in New York City and needed to confirm the space was legit. Satisfied, he went back for Erica. It was chilly, and they walked the three blocks with their arms wrapped around each other.

The entrance of the Moroccan-style lounge was dim, but when they crossed into the main area the room was draped with white, sheer curtains. Mini stuffed sofas sat in shades of oranges, purples and reds, with round mahogany tables. A glow of candles lit the way as a hostess in a ruffled mini showed them to their cushy corner booth. It was still early by

New York standards, so the place was mostly empty. Warren ordered a round of drinks.

"What happened at work?" She flipped through the menu.

"Damn program stalled."

She gave him a blank look. "And the contract?"

It was just like Erica to lead into the weekend with business, but Warren wasn't ready to discuss the unpleasant obvious, so he reached for her chin and told her she looked beautiful, over and over until her face flushed.

"Gorgeous." He leaned in, letting his nose linger over her throat and ear until she stirred in his arms. Bending their bodies towards each other, their foreheads touched and their fingers laced.

The waitress dropped off the drinks and they ordered dinner. Middle Eastern instrumental music had started playing in the background and on the big screen near the bar a belly dancer, dressed in purple and gold, undulated her hips while twirling a veil between her fingers. They watched while sipping.

"I've always wanted to learn to belly dance," Erica shared.

"So take a class. I'll pay for it."

She touched his thigh.

The hostess escorted in two other couples and Warren could see a DJ off to the side setting up equipment.

"Is this going to turn into a club?" he asked.

Erica nodded. "I hope so."

Their food arrived and they shared red snapper and lamb with a tangy yogurt sauce while conversing about their week apart. By the time their dinner plates had been cleared, the Middle Eastern music faded, a few couples had sauntered onto the dance floor, and it became difficult for them to talk over the music. The DJ was spinning and mixing a string of top-twenty songs and even though they played the same tunes on the radio every hour, there was something electrifying about hearing music full-blast through high-definition speakers.

Erica excused herself for the ladies room. When she returned she was wearing a linguini-strapped camisole cinched at the waist.

"What happened to the Nets?"

"Time and place for everything." She slid against him. Warren had ordered another round of drinks and she tipped her wineglass. A few beats later, she was throwing her hand in the air.

"This is my song," moving her head to the beat. "Let's dance."

"I'm good right here," Warren sipped. He wasn't big on dancing, but Erica would move her body to anything.

"Come on, please," she pleaded.

He shook his head.

"If you won't, I'll find someone who will." She scooted out of the bench and moved past him. Her jeans fit her curves like a wet suit, and Warren grabbed her hand before she got too far.

On the floor she snapped her fingers and popped to the beat while Warren kept up a basic two-step. Then a popular reggae song by one of the Marley brothers came on and the crowd lost its mind. A few lighters flickered in the air while couples danced liked they were at home alone. Gyrating her hips, Erica turned around and backed into Warren's pelvis. Then he placed his fingers around her throat and gave a light squeeze. She moaned, closing his hand tighter.

Sweaty and aroused, Warren breathed, "It's time to go, baby." Clasping onto his belt loop, she followed.

ERICA STUMBLED INTO HER bedroom, pulling a pack of baby wipes from her bedside drawer. Warren was in the bathroom and she quickly freshened-up the key areas. Feeling tipsy, but not quite drunk, she removed her boots and slipped into a pair of ultra high heels that Warren had picked out for her at an adult novelty shop on St. Mark's Place in the East Village. They were stripper shoes and she only wore them in the house to entice him. The heels were six-inch glass platform with thick red patent straps across the toes, and when Erica spread her feet into them she felt herself transform.

The curls were gone and the roots of her hair had frizzed out on the dance floor. Since she couldn't comb the hair, she gave it a fluff and wild tug until she looked like a red-headed lioness. Clicking her heels against the wood floors she moved into the living room. The table lamp against the window was turned up just enough to keep the mood. Warren entered from the bathroom drying his hands on a paper towel. His pants were unbuttoned and his arms looked like two strapped guns against his white tank. They had stopped for a six-pack on 125th Street, and she could smell the fragrance of his anticipation as he handed her an uncapped bottle.

"Nice shoes."

Warren moved to the futon and sat gap-legged like he was preparing for a show. The moon was high. Al Jarreau sang low. Seduction like this could take them all night.

"Take your jeans off." His voice entered her like a sex pill. But Erica lingered near the brick wall sipping her beer, smiling.

"Excuse me?" she teased. Thirsty chill bumps sprouted along her forearms as the straps of her cami slipped to her elbows. Patience was one of Warren's strong suits, and he gulped down his beer while waiting for her to serve up his request.

Swaying her hips to Jarreau's "Ain't No Sunshine," Erica could feel warmth bubbling between her legs. Resting her shoulders against the brick wall she let the music move her. With her eyes closed, her hands glided over her breasts and then drifted down to the V of her thighs. The snap of her jeans cracked open as she pulled her ribs in tight while pushing the zipper down. Red lace panties peaked through the open slit of her pants. Warren's bottle clanked against the table as she used both hands to peeled back her jeans and push the material down to her knees. He watched her as if in a trance. With her jeans around her ankles, she moved her ass slowly to give him the view an ass man like Warren longed for. She sensuously made figure eights in the air.

"Damn baby," escaped his lips and Erica felt egged on. The beer had revved her past tipsy but she managed to get the jeans off and platforms back on. Erica was a traditional "good girl," so she knew that Warren enjoyed it when she completely let go and went all the way to the other side.

"Bring that sweet ass here," he commanded, and again the timber in his voice went through her. Slower than the music Erica dragged her heels across the floor, careful not to wobble away what she hoped was a sexy picture. Then Warren was reaching for her, and she was in his lap. His tongue spread and traveled, causing Erica to drizzle like a neglected scoop of ice cream, and Warren, master of her body, didn't waste a single drop.

Chapter Nine
Jammed

The sticky sweetness of their fluids permeated the air. The cotton bed sheets were stretched to exhaustion. Styrofoam containers with soggy sprigs of parsley and salty fries littered the floor. Warren had propped three pillows behind his head and was reading a news clip on his laptop. Erica rested at his elbow flipping through a copy of *Travel & Leisure* magazine. College basketball served as their backdrop. Saturday's sun had come and gone.

"I think this stock is going to perform," he turned his computer screen toward her.

Erica nodded with as much interest as she could muster before rolling onto her belly. "What should we do tonight?"

"I wanted to head down to Smalls so that I could shed. Haven't played much this week."

"Good, I need some air." Finding a clip on the side table she pinned her wild hair. Warren closed his laptop, hung his long legs over the side of the bed and then made his way to the bathroom. The room was lilac with a full frosted glass window facing the tub and looking out over the alley. Once he had the shower running Erica followed him in, carrying two plush towels.

"Thanks, baby," Warren slapped her on the ass.

"Don't start nothing," she pulled back the shower curtain and gestured for him to go first. Warren made room so that she could stand closest to the showerhead. The water was very warm, instantly steaming her skin. Erica soaped the cloth and handed it to him. His lips were on the small of her neck.

"You are so hot," he breathed. "Damn, my woman is fine," he rubbed his pelvis against her booty.

"Hmm," she let her head fall back. Warren moved the sudsy cloth up and down her back and then around to her breasts and midsection.

"You ain't trying to go to the club tonight," she backed against him while wetting a second cloth. Lathering it with liquid soap she turned to face Warren and moved the cloth from his ears to his shoulders and then brushed both thighs. When she let her hand rest on his manhood, pleasure flashed across his face.

"We're going," he kissed her deeply. "Just stealing an appetizer to hold me over." He tongued her ear.

"Okay then, trumpet boy. Dip your head," she removed his hands from her waist and switched places so that he was in front closest to the water.

Erica shampooed and rinsed his hair, making sure all of the suds were off their bodies and down the drain before she shut off the water. Wrapping him in a towel, she led him into the bedroom where she oiled his skin, paying close attention to his feet.

"You need a pedicure."

"I have you," he said when she was finished.

"Whatever," she switched her hips, purposefully giving him something to smile about as she went to her closet to search for something to wear.

Warren tore his eyes away from her long enough to rummage through his tote, though the outfit choice for him tonight was obvious.

Most musicians have superstitions, quirks and rituals that they perform before taking the stage. Warren's drummer always wore mismatched socks. His pianist: gold bracelets on each wrist with his baseball cap twisted backwards. Warren dressed in black from head to toe and rubbed a drop of frankincense on his throat and on the crown of his head. The dark clothing was his invention; the frankincense his late mother's.

Warren's mother Alma had grown up in the swamps of Louisiana. She believed in voodoo, church and essential oils, and was always rubbing Warren and his older sister down in something. Peppermint was used for upset stomachs, clove for teething babies, lemon increased circulation, and lavender helped with a good night's sleep.

As a classically trained pianist, his mother shared with him her love of music. Warren was taught piano at four, banged on the drums at seven, settling on the finger pattern of the trumpet by ten. Weekly music lessons gave way to recitals, all unattended by his father, who refused to acknowledge Warren's musical gift.

"My son won't end up a needle-pushing junkie. Warren's getting a good job," he'd say. And that was how Warren came to earn his Masters in computer engineering. But what his father didn't understand was that Warren's music was more than a hobby. Playing his instrument was like a choice between living and dying slowly.

With just a sprinkle of frankincense in his palm, Warren could already feel the balsamic oil seep into his skin. Erica walked over to him as he tied his shoes on the sofa. She had decided on wearing a red sweater dress. Her beauty sucked up the oxygen in the room.

"Pretty."

"Handsome," she winked, holding out her wrist with a bracelet she wanted him to fasten.

WARREN LOVED JAMMING BECAUSE it separated the men from the boys. At any given time there could be as many as ten, twelve musicians on stage with four playing the same instrument. The choice was either play or be played and Warren never fell victim to the latter, especially at Smalls, a well-known jazz club in the West Village where the top musicians in the industry came to flex their genius.

Smalls stayed open all night and there were photographs on the wall of Miles Davis, Charlie Parker, Betty Carter, McCoy Tyner and Sonny Rollins, who all sharpened their skills on the very same stage.

"Look who's traveling on the wind." A fair-skinned man wearing a black beret limped toward them. "Come to jam?" His voice was raspy like he smoked two packs a day.

Warren held up his horn case and the men slapped five.

IN THE TEN MINUTES that it took for his name to be called, Warren closed his eyes and visualized warming his instrument. It was a talent he had picked up playing in the band at Howard University. Once on stage, he tipped his horn to Erica and waited while the pianist counted.

"One, two, a one, two, three."

The quartet played a standard, "Never Let Me Go." Roy Hargrove had redone the song on his third album and Warren knew the piece well. During his solo, Warren spit the notes. Even when he stumbled on the wrong note, it was right. Musicians rotated in and out, other brass instruments jammed with him and against him, but time didn't tick. Warren played like a man possessed until his lips swelled with the satisfaction of a familiar kiss.

WARREN'S BLACK SHIRT WAS soaked through and he left the stage feeling like Superman. At a bistro table in the corner, Erica was slouched over asleep with her head resting against the cushiony padded wall. He had played so hard that he hadn't realized that she had slept through it. In the chair next to her, he rubbed her hair softly.

"What time is it?" She opened her eyes and ran the back of her hand over her mouth.

"Seven."

"You played for five hours straight."

"It felt like five minutes."

"Good, honey," she readjusted her dress and stretched her arms overhead.

Two busboys were clearing off the table and she could smell the bucket of water with bleach and disinfectant.

"You hungry?" he asked, helping her into her coat.

"Think the Pink Teacup is open?"

"Should be." Warren gave the man with the limp a pound and told him he'd be back soon. Once they made it up the stairs and out onto the street, Warren draped his arm over her shoulders. The sun had risen but was cloaked behind pregnant clouds. Warren could have used his sunglasses to help adjust to daylight but they were in the car.

"You were snoring louder than the music," he teased.

"Whatever, I don't snore. How long did you think I'd last?"

They walked three blocks over to the Pink Teacup, a soul-food restaurant that had been in the same location on Grove

Street for five decades and owned by three generations of the same family. The restaurant was painted pink inside and out with black-and-white celebrity photos hanging from the walls. Because it was early, they had their choice of window seating. The waitress dropped off menus they didn't need with fresh squeezed orange juice and a saucer of homemade biscuits.

Erica watched Warren. He had that far-away, detached look in his eyes and she could feel her body counting down the minutes until he had to leave. The weekend had once again gone too fast and she was sick of saying goodbye.

"Why don't you stay one more night and leave first thing in the morning?" she tried.

"I wish, but there's so much work waiting for me."

"Have you signed the contract?"

Warren's eyes flashed down at her and she could see the wheels turning in his head, like he was choosing his words wisely.

"Is it a secret? My life is affected by this, too." She became impatient.

"Yeah, I signed," he confessed.

"Why?" She wanted to pound the table with her fist. Her cell phone rang from inside her clutch. It was trapped in a pocket being smashed by her wallet, keys and lip gloss. After taking everything out the caller-ID flashed that it was her mother. She silenced the phone. This was not the time for one of her silly emergencies. Erica was having a crisis of her own.

Warren reached across the table. "I'm telling you nothing will change." But what he didn't understand was that Erica craved change. She wanted every day with him, all night, and no more filler.

The waitress returned to the table with the heaping plates of steamy food and Warren ordered more orange juice. Erica watched a couple who had just walked in pushing an infant stroller. The man smiled with the goofiness of a new dad as he looked for a place to stow the stroller.

Salmon croquettes and cheesy grits were her favorite, but when Erica looked at her plate she felt nauseated. Nothing ever deterred Warren from eating and he explained while stabbing a bit of fried chicken and a slice of waffle with his fork. Erica's disappointment suddenly gave way to anger.

"You just don't want to move," she pointed.

"It's not that, honey, but I need to make a living."

"New York is a major city. I find it difficult to believe you can't make a living here."

"This opportunity that they're offering me is huge. Trust me, I want to be with you too."

"If you wanted to be with me, you would." She pushed the food around on her plate. "Well, at least your dad is happy."

Warren swallowed hard. "What's that supposed to mean?"

Erica watched the rosy cheeked mother scoop her swaddled baby from the seat, sliding the child beneath her shirt, and said nothing.

Her silence seemed to have ticked a nerve with Warren because he ground his teeth and said, "If I hadn't signed, we'd be broke."

"Why is it always about money for you?"

"Because we have bills. And you," it was his turn to take a jab. "You have your mother. I'm sure that was her ringing your phone."

Erica's fork clanked against her plate.

"I know you aren't bringing my mother into this. Don't worry, you'll have your money next week."

"It's not about the money."

"Well apparently it's not about love or we wouldn't be having this conversation, again."

"You are so fucking unbelievable," he reached into his pocket for his money clip, peeling off enough bills to cover the check. "Must be nice thinking that the earth revolves around you."

"You are one to talk," Erica tossed back. She gathered her purse, slipped into her own coat and followed him out. At the door, she glanced back at the couple, wondering how she and Warren would get from where they sat to happily ever after.

OUTSIDE, HE WALKED TOO quickly up Seventh Avenue while Erica struggled to keep up in her heels. Her toes were pinched, a misty drizzle had started to fall and she didn't have anything to cover her head. Warren walked several paces in front of her and Erica cursed him in her head.

"Why are you walking so fast?" she shouted.

"'Cause I know you are cold."

"Well, slow up."

Warren turned to wait for her, but he didn't grab her hand. When they reached his SUV he rounded the car to the front window, checking for a parking ticket. The rain had started to drop and the breeze was bone chilly. When Erica stepped into the SUV the slit of her dress flew open exposing her thigh, and it was so unlike Warren not to notice.

Their argument continued up the West Side Highway.

"If you don't want to be with me just say it," Erica tossed.

"You still haven't told me how we're supposed to live? Off you?"

"That and your music."

His laugh was bitter. "Get your head out of the clouds, Sweetie; I just played all night long for free."

"Well, when I become director…"

"Your mother's hand will be in your pocket and you'll still be too chicken to tell her no."

"You are such an asshole."

"And you're a selfish bitch."

Warren footed the gas hard crossing 125th Street and Frederick Douglass. Anger had been trickling into his skin like fluid through an IV.

"Who do you think you are talking to?" She whirled around in her seat as if just slapped. "I'm not some ho off the street."

"Just shut the fuck up."

"You shut up and show me some damn respect," she said, continuing to pull him in a back and forth match determined to get the last word.

Warren found a space right in front of her building. Erica jumped out of the car first and stormed up the front steps of the building. Warren waited in silence while she fumbled with her key. When they reached her apartment, Warren went straight to her bedroom and started shoving his clothes into his bag. He was so mad he didn't even fold them.

"What are you doing?" she stood in the doorway.

"Leaving."

"Why?" Even though they were fighting, she didn't want to spend Sunday without him. How had it gotten this far?

"Because I need to get the hell away from you." He threw his bag over his shoulder and pushed past her to the living room, scanning the area to make sure he had everything. His laptop sat on the coffee table and he quickly shoved it in his bag.

"You haven't slept all night. You can't drive to D.C." Erica was standing in front of the door.

"Move," he looked past her.

"Don't do this," she softened.

"This past Monday I missed one of the biggest gigs of my life providing for you and you still find something to complain about." He flicked his hand in the air. "The fuck out of my way."

"No," she crossed her arms. Warren was in her face and breathing hard but she couldn't let him go. "Just stay so we can talk about this."

"I said move."

She didn't budge. He asked her three more times, but she held her ground. Warren was smoking hot. Erica really knew how to push his buttons.

"Get," he shouted and then without thinking his fist swiped at the table lamp, knocking it to the floor. Porcelain pieces split into jagged edges and the bulb flicked yellow before flashing out.

The whites of his eyes had darkened, "I don't want to see you," he pointed his finger in her face and fear sliced through her like scissors. He pushed past her, leaving the front door wide open.

"Bastard," she yelled after him, and then picked up a magazine and flung it at his head, just missing. "Go to hell."

Warren's footsteps pounded down the four flights of stairs as if he was angry with the linoleum.

Erica breathed back tears, looking at the broken piece of her lamp at her feet. The porcelain pieces could have cut her legs or her feet. They had never fought so vehemently before, and even though he took his anger out on the lamp, it felt very much like he was trying to punish her. While picking up the pieces to see if the lamp could be salvaged, she couldn't help wondering if this was how the violence between her parents had begun.

Chapter Ten
The Cusp

Erica's parents married in the parlor of her grandmother's house on a watery day in January. It was the mid-seventies and her mother, Gweny, was twelve weeks pregnant. She stood in a white full lace gown with two button gloves fastened at her wrists. Her father wore his good black suit and shiny wingtip shoes. Bottles of homemade wine, corn liquor, and crème ale were set up on a card table with paper doilies and plastic wedding cups. At seventeen Gweny wasn't old enough to drink, but her cousin ignored legalities, mixing together wine and beer, which they called boilers. She sipped, laughed, and forgot for one night that she was pregnant.

Women had babies in her family but very few married. The ones who did ended up cheated on, abused or abandoned. Growing up Gweny didn't have one positive example of marriage and family, so young and without instruction she picked her way through her own marriage and motherhood with the baton of failure looming overhead. It almost felt as if failing at it was her destiny. Her husband was a decent provider but his new auto mechanic business often kept him away from the house, leaving her alone with two small girls born twenty-two months apart. Confidence was never Gweny's strong suit and with no help and her little ones to care for, depression had an easy time finding her on the kitchen floor scraping up peas, in the basement doing the laundry, and on the sofa crying softly over the constant smell of shitty diapers. Her life proved to be a repetitive guilt trip. She longed for an escape from her mundane existence, and found it in Bonnie, a mistress disguised in housewife's clothes, who one day at the neighborhood bar handed Gweny freedom in a fancy glass.

At first the change in Erica's mother was subtle. She began oversleeping, and forgot little things like changing the clocks for daylight savings time. The laundry started to pile up and it seemed as if they were eating their dinner from a can more often than not. She was known to run their house on a familiar schedule and like all children, Erica thrived on predictability. Gradually her mother started losing track of time and Erica found herself being picked up later and later from nursery school, until one day she was the last child. The memory was as strong to her as the smell of ammonia, and she could remember waiting on the industrial rugged stairs, wringing her fingers in her four-year-old lap, trying to quiet the urge to poop.

"I'm so sorry," her mother said the first time it happened, bursting through the double doors fussing with her dark sunglasses, while muttering a stream of excuses. After helping Erica into her scarlet wool coat, she carried her down the stone stairs without paying the late fee. Erica's ponytails flapped in the wind as she wrapped her arms and legs around her mother, searching for that familiar scent. Inside the car, the stitched vinyl seats were toasty because she had left the engine running, but Erica wanted her mother's attention and cried that she was still cold.

With her mother hanging out and her father's short fuse it didn't take much for their house to fall into a place of conflict. Her mother would come home late and her father would be waiting for her at the door screaming about money missing from his wallet.

"You got a babysitter here every night. Why can't you stay home?" he'd roar and the violent moments would stay stamped in Erica's mind no matter how hard she tried to wash it away: him turning the kitchen table over, splashing her mother's blouse with spaghetti. In the living room, he hurled a rotary telephone at her, bruising the skin around her eye, and Erica didn't know if she should help or hide. In the bathroom, her mother's arm went through a window and Erica fretted that the neighbors would hear. Upstairs, in the long hallway was where her father dragged Gweny by her ankles kicking and screaming and, as she watched, Erica worried that her mother would get a splinter.

Soon her parents stopped sleeping together and her mother became Erica's burden, moaning and turning in the canopy bed that she had once loved, but now hated to share.

OVER THE NEXT FEW years Erica constructed a shell around herself, searching for her mothering elsewhere. She was a likable girl and had no problem finding nurturing in her favorite card-cataloging librarian, bubbling camp counselor, sugar-faced lunch monitor, or doting classroom teacher. These women were generous with cleavage-filled hugs, nourishing smiles and tongues that spun encouragement. And from the moment Erica stepped into Claire Downing's sun-drenched corner office, Claire became one of Erica's women.

President and executive director of B&B's publicity, Claire Downing was the epitome of corporate professionalism. As one of the highest ranking women in publishing, Claire's experience spanned close to twenty years. She was credited with building the career of the most successful authors in the history of the business. Her petite five-foot frame commanded respect. When her velveteen voice opened up in a room, everyone listened.

The chemistry between Erica and Claire was apparent in their first meeting together. Erica was delighted to have the chance to work with a woman who reflected her own ambition and she decided right away to do whatever it took to work side by side with Claire. But that plan came to a halt the moment Edie Butnick, vice president and director of publicity, strolled in with her long legs and narrow eyes, sucking up the air like a parched potted plant.

"You'll report directly to Edie," Claire introduced the woman as her right hand and Erica soon discovered that just as the Christians believed that the way to God was through Jesus Christ, in the publicity department the only way to Claire was through Edie.

From Erica's first encounter with Edie it was apparent that they were as likely to get along as oil and water. Edie looked down her nose at Erica and had a tendency to talk in a condescending voice that Erica found offensive. She was a knit-picking control freak who didn't hesitate to call Erica at home on things that could be solved the next morning. Worse, she was constantly removing Erica from projects she started and giving them to other publicists to finish. Whenever Edie pulled one of these stunts, she explained that she was putting Erica on books that were a higher priority to the House. This would have been flattering coming from Claire, but from Edie it just aggravated the issues between them.

So on that Monday morning after her blow up with Warren, Erica heard a light tap on her office door and was astonished and surprised to see Claire breeze in. Women as high up on the chain as Claire never visited their subordinate's offices, and Erica sat up taller in her chair to greet her.

"Good morning," Erica smiled.

"Always here early." Claire's designer sling backs carried her to the empty chair in front of Erica's desk. The soft wool coat she wore was opened and the fluorescent overhead light twinkled against the gumball diamonds dripping from her ears, throat and ring finger. Erica touched the hem of her gray sheath dress. It was one of the more expensive pieces she owned, and she was happy that she was well dressed for this impromptu occasion.

"How was your weekend?" she asked Claire.

"Busy, Reverend Black is holding a major conference down in Atlanta and I've been on the phone with his people all weekend hammering out details. It's a big deal even though we just found out about it." Claire gave Erica a knowing look.

"Anyway, everything is set—the press conference, dinner, and a satellite tour. Black will be promoting the *Powerful Men* book and audiotape. His office wants us there for show. No one from editorial is available and Edie can't travel, so I'm taking you."

If pigs could fly there would be one buzzing around in her office. Erica couldn't contain her disbelief.

"Don't look so surprised." Claire pushed a file across the desk towards Erica. "You know you are my go-to-girl. This trip should be interesting."

"Thanks so much. I'm looking forward to it," said Erica, and before she could add to the conversation Claire was on her feet cruising out on the same air she sailed in on.

She called over her shoulder, "We'll meet again after lunch."

Alone, Erica pumped her fist in the air. Her insides were turning as she got to her feet, dancing a hip-shaking jig. This was it. The opportunity had finally come for her to prove herself. She had been pulled in on the Reverend Black campaign, a coup in itself and the sweet strawberry on top was that she was going to Atlanta with Claire. Just the two of them, without Edie breathing her dragon breath down her neck. What would she wear? Her mind was working through her wardrobe as she flipped through the folder that Claire had given her. For the tiniest moment, she had forgotten that Warren hadn't called last night when he got home nor had he phoned her this morning. It had felt like her entire life was intact. Then, on page three, she saw scribbled in Claire's curvy handwriting that the trip was scheduled for this coming weekend. Erica fell back against her seat.

Why was she even surprised? Nothing ever came easy.

Chapter Eleven

Dad Knows Best

As soon as Warren skidded away from the curb, he knew that smashing Erica's lamp was wrong. He hadn't meant to lose control, but it pissed him off that Erica didn't even try to understand his position. Why did she always insist on making the fight him versus her, when really the fight was them versus the distance? And where was all this pressure coming from? In the year and few months that they had dated, the couple had never missed a weekend. Didn't that speak to his dedication to her?

The light drizzle elevated to a windy storm, and the rain splattered against his windshield on the ride down the New Jersey Turnpike. By the time he crossed the Delaware Memorial Bridge, he had run out of adrenaline. The tasteless cup of coffee he had picked up at a bodega on 135th and Madison sat cold and abandoned in the cup holder on his right. Sleep deprivation caught him by the toe, and he wrestled his vehicle into the parking lot of the Rest Area. His SUV had tinted windows, so he climbed into the spacious backseat and made a pillow with his scarf. Lying there, he thought about how many times he and Erica had made love in that very spot.

It was like a weekly ritual for them. They would carry their portable chairs to Central Park's Summerstage with mixed drinks disguised in soda bottles. When the show was over, they would giggle their way into the backseat for a steamy romp. The windows would fog and the air conditioning could never cool their flaming bodies. Warren wanted that time back, when every moment flowed with effortless ease. He drifted to sleep with those memories rolling through his head. Two hours later, his cell phone vibrated against his hip. It was his father. Warren straightened up in his seat.

"Sir," he cleared his throat.

"Son, how are you?" his father's voice boomed.

"Fine. Heading back from New York."

"Maybe we could do an early dinner or something when you get into town."

Warren looked at the clock on the dashboard. "I should be home in about two hours."

"Great, I'll be at the Willard."

THE VALET ATTENDANT OPENED the driver's door and Warren stepped out in front of the Willard hotel, two blocks from the White House. He was still wearing his all black ensemble and was pleased that it was wrinkle free. Walking through the lobby, Warren passed the hand-crafted fireplace, china flower vases and sofa tables. The hotel was a bit gaudy for his taste with all of its Persian rugs and antique chairs, but it was his father's favorite place to dine.

Inside the Willard Room Restaurant, his dad was already seated at a center table, bent over the Sunday Post drinking a cup of coffee, looking very much at home.

"Son," he rose, pulling Warren into a hug.

"Afternoon, Sir."

Warren took the seat opposite him and opened his menu. The pianist sitting at the baby grand started to play a composition of Bach's. Warren knew the tune well because the composer had been one of his mother's favorites.

"How was your trip?" His father looked up. Maynard Prince was a youthful-acting older man with a full head of salt and pepper waves. His skin was the same rich brown as Warren's, but he stood an inch shorter. He wore a navy blue suit with a canary yellow shirt opened at the collar and a gold link chain that had been his grandfather's around his neck.

"It wasn't bad. Traffic was easy."

The pointy nosed waiter approached the table. "Good afternoon, can I interest you in something to drink, Sir?" He sounded nasal.

"Dad, you ready to order? I'm starved." Warren hadn't eaten since his breakfast with Erica and with all of the fighting, it hadn't stuck.

"Just the lobster bisque," he said. Warren ordered grilled shrimp and lamb sirloin.

The waiter took the menus and disappeared.

"Stan called me. Congrats on the extension."

Warren felt the smile start down in his belly and drift up to his face. His father didn't dole out praise often, and he was glad to be on the receiving end.

"It's a big step for you." He tossed his newspaper aside. "So I can't understand why you were the last to sign?"

Warren draped his napkin across his lap, hating that his father knew everything that happened at work. It was one of the downsides of the job. Snitches were everywhere.

"I was just trying to figure some things out with Erica and the music."

"What's there to figure out?"

"She wants me to move to New York."

"And do what?"

Warren hesitated. "Concentrate more on my music."

"Son, please. Don't start that starving artist, hippy bullshit." His father flipped his vintage watch around on his wrist.

The waiter appeared with an iced tea for Warren and fresh coffee for his father.

"With your new contract, you are making more money than any of your friends. Keep climbing that ladder. Stan says sky's the limit."

But at what cost to his soul, Warren thought, chewing the side of his lip.

"Trust me," his father continued, as if answering his thoughts. "Erica doesn't want some man depending on her for a glass of water. That gets old real quick."

The waiter dropped off the first course and Warren plunged his shrimp into the drawn butter.

"Have you dry cleaned your tux for Friday night?"

Warren looked blank.

"Son, tell me you have not forgotten about the 'Man of Honor' dinner this Friday. I bought a table for your coworkers at two hundred dollars a plate."

With everything going on, it had slipped Warren's mind. "I'll drop it off tonight."

"You really must stop waiting until the last minute to do things. There's no room for error."

Warren knew that all too well. The main course was served and, as his father chatted over the details for Friday, Warren's mind wandered over to the piano.

Chapter Twelve
The Waiting Game

Once two nights passed without a call from Warren, Erica started to fret over their last conversation. Perhaps she was pushing him too hard. The fight had been one of the bigger ones and the broken lamp a first. This space they were in made her antsy and she had a good mind to call out the next day and head to D.C. They needed to straighten things out, especially since she had to work that weekend. But with so much preparation needed for Atlanta, she didn't have the gall to ask Claire for a day off. This was corporate America, where a certain protocol was demanded. Work came before everything: sickness, death, vacation, maternity leave and most certainly a long distance love affair. The job was always number one. She decided a call would have to be enough to fix things. But after four rings she got his voice mail, and didn't leave a message.

On Tuesday morning, she sat at her computer trying to distract herself with a manuscript from one of her favorite mystery authors. The sales team wanted to reposition the author with the hopes of driving up sales. Erica's job was to comb through the manuscript for clues on how to angle the new novel to picky media outlets that wouldn't otherwise budge.

Her assistant buzzed. "Warren's on line two."

Relief and anxiety fought for space as she answered the call.

"Hey." His voice sounded normal.

"How come you haven't called?"

"I had lunch with my dad Sunday and last night was the jam session."

"That's never stopped you before."

"Yeah, well. I've been thinking."

"About?"

"Don't cut me off," he said a little too sharply. "This conversation that we keep having is moot. Instead of us arguing over me working another year, let's figure out how to get more time in to make things better."

It wasn't what she had expected. Her emotional strings had been pulled. "You're right," her voice was faltering.

"Are you crying?"

"No."

"I want to be with you, girl, but this is not a ten-city publicity tour. Things aren't always going to fall according to your plan."

"Okay, Honey." Erica's line blinked. "Hang on, Warren." She blew her nose and then flipped over. "Yes, Prudence?"

"Lillian's on line three. There's a major snowstorm in Denver and she's worried about her signing tonight at the Tattered Cover."

Erica went back to Warren. "I have to take this call."

"Okay, but before I forget, can you leave work early on Friday? My dad is being honored for his 35 years of military service."

"What? How come you haven't mentioned this before?"

"I forgot," he offered, but since they had just made up she tried not to get upset, even though whenever she had a function she gave Warren plenty of notice.

"Claire asked me to go to a conference with her in Atlanta this weekend."

"Now you're working weekends?"

"I was going to see if you could meet me. I'm staying at the Ritz."

Another one of her phone lines flashed and she really needed to go. "Babe, we have to finish this tonight. I'll ring you as soon as I get home."

IT WAS ALMOST NINE o'clock when Erica got in from work. When she reached her floor, she could smell something buttery. Tess, her sister-girl from across the hall, was home, which meant that something was on the stove. Erica knocked.

"Sha-low," Tess greeted from the doorway. She was tall and thick, wearing her surplus like none of it was extra. A maroon mushroom wig covered her head and her eyelash extensions were at least a full inch long. She was a lounge singer so Erica was accustomed to seeing her in costume.

"You sound like my sister. What smells so good?" asked Erica, pushing past Tess into the apartment. Diana Ross' *Greatest Hits* was playing. Tess was Diana's biggest fan.

"Little something."

"Nice wig."

"You like? Thinking about wearing it to my tribute. Does it look like the one Diana wore in *Mahogany*?"

Erica nodded her head in agreement while removing her coat.

Their apartments shared the same floor plan, except Tess' faced the back of the house. Since she didn't get as much natural light as Erica did, she had amassed a quirky collection of lamps, stacking them in every other corner. Without asking if she was hungry, Tess dished up two plates heaping with rosemary mashed potatoes, French cut beans and oversized turkey wings smothered in gravy. Erica sat across from her at the dinette covered in a printed kente cloth and told Tess about the conflict with this weekend.

"You know I'm a hopeless romantic, but are you kidding me? This is totally the break you've been waiting for," Tess fanned her large breasts.

"And I bought a new suit last week that would be perfect. It's just..."

"Warren will be fine, and two weeks ain't the end of the world."

"You're right." Erica pushed her plate aside. Tess was a true southern girl, and her comfort cooking reflected all of the heavy ingredients.

"Sugar, Tess Rodgers is always right." She reached for her pack of cigarettes and lit one. "Glad you're saving room. I baked a pineapple upside down cake."

"You spoil me," Erica reached for the lit cigarette and took a long drag. She only smoked with Tess, who fired up another.

"We can eat dessert and watch a Diana movie?"

Erica flicked the ashes. "I'd love to, but I need to go home and deal with Warren. Can I get the cake to go?"

Tess pouted.

"I promise to stay next time, Sweetie. I'll even watch *The Wiz* and you know how I feel about that long ass movie."

"It's Diana at her best," proclaimed Tess, and the two hugged the way true girlfriends did.

Across the hall, Erica dialed Warren's number. Her living room seemed to be collecting dirty laundry, papers and book galleys by the hour. While the phone rang, she removed her work clothes, unclipped her too-tight bra and slipped into one of his sweatshirts.

"Hello," Warren answered.

Her eyes were closed and she pictured him with his arms wrapped around her.

"Babe?"

"Just picturing you here," she said.

"Yeah, I'm missing that fat booty, too."

"That all you miss?" She took a fork and stuck it into the cake.

"What're you eating?"

"Tess baked." Breathing. "You cool with this weekend?"

"Not really."

Erica put down her fork. "I can't get out of it. Edie's too pregnant and Claire said I'm next in line."

"That's nice."

"So you understand?"

"Yeah, it's cool. I know you've been waiting for this."

"I'll send your father flowers first thing."

"Okay." Warren told her about the applications program he was working on but had to put her on hold. When he came back to the phone, Erica was skipping down memory lane.

"Do you remember the first time you told me you loved me? I was in the kitchen, washing the dishes and when you said it, I dropped the plate."

"That's because you didn't love me."

"I was in love with you by the second week," she confessed, "doodling your name on my work pad, putting little hearts around us."

"So you've always been corny?"

"Just soft on you."

"Well, I remember the first time you took the train to D.C. to see me. The weather was still warm, you showed up in a pair of cut-off's, flip flops and your hair wild. I thought I hit the jackpot when I saw you."

"Really?"

"Yeah, man. So beautiful."

Erica twirled the edge of her sweatshirt. "Do you remember the first time we made love?"

"In your apartment."

"You were nervous and fucking the shit out of me."

"Did I hurt you?"

"Don't get all bigheaded. I was just a little sore."

"I don't hurt you now," his voice mellowed an octave.

"You didn't Saturday," she whispered.

"Take your clothes off."

"Huh?" And when he didn't respond, Erica put the telephone down and stretched out of her layers. "Are you naked too?" She could hear him fumbling around.

"Yeah."

Erica walked to her bed and propped the phone on the pillow next to her. On nights like these, Warren always found slumber before her and for the next hour she let the sound of his breathing lull her into sweet dreams.

Chapter Thirteen

Absence Makes the Heart...

It had snowed two inches in D.C. overnight. Warren's leather boots crackled against the gritty salt scattered around the employee parking lot. Although the temperature had dropped below thirty degrees, Warren didn't hurry away from the cold and the chilling air felt good in his lungs. He breathed in as much as he could stand before walking into the office building.

When Warren got to his desk, he thought about calling Erica. All of the sudden he was nervous about attending the dinner alone, and if there was ever a moment for her to take one for the team tonight was the night. His father was receiving the highest military honor for thirty-five years of service and it would have made Warren's world to walk in with his woman on his arm. Since he was trying hard to be understanding, he wouldn't beg. So he put the phone back into its cradle and turned his attention to an unfinished computer program.

"Going to lunch, cowboy?" Blanche popped her head over the cubicle wall.

"Yeah," said Warren, saving his work on a disk and slipping it into his pocket. Since that night when his computer inexplicably froze on him, he didn't trust leaving any valuable work around.

"I'm starving, I don't know why I keep skipping breakfast." She rounded the wall between them with her red wallet in her hand.

"It's the most important meal of the day," Warren replied.

"But a girl needs to hang onto her girlish figure," she winked. Blanche followed Warren down the hall and they caught the elevator to the cafeteria. The lunchroom was crowded as usual, but the food stations helped with the flow of traffic. Warren walked to the sandwich section for a turkey wrap while Blanche went in the opposite direction, grabbing a pre-made salad. Warren paid for both, following Blanche to a seat by the window overlooking the ice pond.

"Thanks for lunch." Blanche tossed her hair over her shoulder.

"You going to the 'Man of Honor' dinner tonight?" he asked, making conversation. Stan, with his military background, went to the dinner every year and as a thank you for his support, Warren's father bought extra seats for some of the company's key employees.

"I wouldn't miss it." She took a bite of her salad. "Is Erica coming?"

"No, she's working in Atlanta this weekend," he said, trying to sound casual, but the look in Blanche's eye told him that she didn't buy it.

"So, you don't have a date?"

He shook his head.

"Well that just won't do. You and I will go together," she finished.

"Blanche, I'm fine. You don't have to go through any trouble."

"It's no trouble. My date cancelled this morning, so it's a win-win."

He hesitated.

"Your father is being honored for all of his years of service. We can't have his son walking in alone."

At least she got it.

"So, I'll meet you in the lobby of the hotel at seven."

THAT EVENING WARREN ARRIVED at the Fairmont Hotel on time and as planned Blanche was there waiting for him. She was dressed in a black beaded halter dress, with her blonde streaks pinned into a loose twist.

"Hey you," said Warren, extending his arm out to her, but she threw him off by kissing his cheek.

"I took a cab over. Do you think you could give me a lift home?"

Warren nodded.

Dinners, charity events and award ceremonies had been a fixture in Warren's life for so long that he wore his black tuxedo like a comfortable uniform. His hair had been cut hours before. The shoulder pads in his jacket gave his arms and chest an added layer of bulk, not that Warren needed it. Blanche's heels echoed on the black-and-white marble floor as they walked through the airy lobby to the reception hall.

Inside there was a six-piece band playing a ballroom tune that Warren could play with his eyes closed. It was one of the first pieces that he had learned in the band at Howard and he hoped the musicians would kick it up a notch before the night was over. The reception hall had high ceilings with thick crown moldings and oversized chandeliers. White-gloved staff members swept through the room balancing silver trays filled with half-full wine glasses. Guests dressed in their formal best made polite conversation to colleagues, whom they would later dish dirt about that night over their bedroom pillows.

Warren's table was situated opposite the band. His father was already seated, with his secretary, Shar, by his side. Although Shar had worked for his father for more than ten years, Warren hadn't expected her to be there and certainly not as his father's guest. Her skin was the color of oak wood and she wore her hair in a short relaxed style popular for ladies in her late-forties group. She was a pretty woman. A different pretty from my mother, he thought to himself. Warren pecked Shar's cheek and shook his father's hand.

"This is my coworker, Blanche."

Shar looked quizzical.

"Erica's away on business," he finished.

His dad gave Blanche a once over. Warren knew his father's facial expressions well enough to know that he thought Blanche was hot. The room was filled with friends and acquaintances of the family and once Blanche was seated, Warren excused himself to offer hellos. When he returned dinner was being served.

"How's the salmon?" Blanche leaned in. Warren told her it was fine, dutifully asking about her chicken.

"Perfect. Marinated in a lemon crème sauce," she said, while placing a piece on his plate without asking. The gesture made him think of Erica, who loved to share.

Once the dinner dishes were cleared, the band took a break, allowing the DJ to play a soft waltz. The dessert buffet was set up with dishes so eye-pleasing and elaborate that it was difficult for people to choose. Warren and Blanche continued to exchange pleasantries regarding the food over a fig marmalade tart. Then the master of ceremony took his place at the podium.

The MC wore a navy blue dress uniform, adorned with three medals and four ribbons. He was such a short man that he needed a wooden stepstool to reach the microphone. A mole the size of a grape hung from the edge of his chin. Two long hairs curled downward toward his collarbone. But when he cleared his throat and spoke, the peculiarities of appearance were immediately excused. The booming power in his voice made it obvious that public speaking was his calling.

"The 'Man of Honor' dinner is a celebration of the military's finest and most distinguished men. As the Army's Chief of Staff, Maynard Warren Prince has served our country for more than 35 years," he said, spending the next ten minutes listing the honoree's accomplishments. When he concluded, Warren was the first on his feet leading the room in a fierce applause. His father raised his hand in thanks as he walked to the podium with a smooth stroll that came with confidence, experience and age. Standing close to six feet, his body was lean with just a trace of mush around the middle. His hair was brushed back in a fit of tight curls.

"Thank you," he said, raising his large hand again, but as the applause continued, more people got to their feet. Soon the entire room was standing and he waited for the excitement to die down. After dabbing his handkerchief across his forehead, he began offering his acceptance speech—a healthy mix of wit and charm. The audience responded by laughing in all the right places.

When he returned to his seat, Shar was the first to greet him. Warren was next. "I'm proud of you, Sir," he said, pulling his father into a hug.

"I have something else to announce tonight and I hope you'll be equally as thrilled," he said with a wink, but before

Warren could ask, his father had lifted his champagne flute and tapped it with his fork.

"May I have your attention?" he said, just loud enough for only their table to hear. "I've been waiting all night to do this." His father blushed, and the red in his cheeks caught Warren off guard. He couldn't remember seeing his father so open, especially not in public.

"Last night, I asked Shar to be my wife. And I'm happy to announce... she said yes." He reached for Shar's hand and the three-carat solitaire glowed like he had handpicked a star. It was Shar's turn to redden.

"The wedding is in a month and you're all invited," he said, giving Shar a full kiss on the mouth.

Another first for Warren, he couldn't recall his father ever showing his mother any public affection and the shock of it all stampeded through him like a stable of spooked horses. His mother had only died six months ago after a quick battle with cancer. How could his father have moved on so soon without breathing a word of it to him? Blanche touched his bicep.

"I need to get out of here," he whispered to her, and after mumbling something that resembled congratulations to his dad, he headed for the door.

Chapter Fourteen

One Night Stand

Warren drove quickly to Blanche's townhouse in Georgetown, dipping into potholes and bends in the road like a staggering drunk. They had been silent for most of the ride.

"Glad Alan didn't show," Blanche said, attempting to break the silence in the car.

"Yeah, he would have been annoying." Warren chewed the inside of his jaw as he made a left onto her block.

"It's the third house on the right," she pointed. The street was narrow with cars crammed on both sides. Warren double parked in front of her house. He was so caught up in his thoughts about the night that he didn't hear Blanche until she repeated herself for the third time.

"Earth to Warren."

"Sorry."

Turning in her seat, her dress opened around her thigh. "I said would you like to come up for a drink. You look like you could use a friend."

A friend was what he had in mind but Blanche wasn't it. A Ford pick-up honked a horn behind him.

"Look, I'm blocking traffic. Maybe another time," he said, looking through his rearview mirror. "I better go. Thanks again for coming."

Blanche pushed the heavy car door open, but as she moved to get out of the car she dropped her purse. The clasp came undone and the contents spilled all over the seat and floor.

"Sorry," she mumbled with her head in the floor. The Ford honked again.

WHEN BLANCHE FINALLY CLOSED her front door, Warren peeled off down her street. It had been almost a year since he stopped smoking marijuana, but after his father's news, sitting in his living room in a foggy, purple haze was all he wanted to do. Driving faster than he should have, he cranked up the volume of his sound system. The grimy rap lyrics from a New Orleans artist spilled from his mouth as he rhymed along. The clean sidewalks and thriving businesses of Northwest turned into dilapidated housing projects as he headed for Southeast D.C. He knew that his partner James would have a stash. He always did.

When Warren reached the front of James' building, he dialed his buddy's number. James didn't have a working front bell. Once they connected, Warren got out and made his way up. James was the drummer in Warren's band. The two had been close since college.

"What's up, Prince? You look good, son. What's the occasion?" James leaned into Warren for a half hug, half handshake and snapped his fingers.

"Nothing, just a dinner for my Dad. I was in the neighborhood and thought I'd stop by for a sec."

"Well, I'm glad you did. Come on in. I was just listening to some old Dizzy. You know how I do." James closed the front door. The white T-shirt he wore had "Free Mumia" typed across the chest and his long dreadlocks were tied behind his head. Warren removed his shoes as was the custom. James was bent on keeping his coconut-colored carpets clean.

The apartment had an artsy feel to it. The walls were decorated with paintings that James had splashed together himself. None of the stuffed furniture matched as a set, but somehow it all meshed well. Warren unbuttoned his tuxedo jacket and plopped down on the plaid sofa that doubled as James' pull-out bed.

"Dog, I can't stay long. I just stopped by to see if you had some bud."

James flicked his tongue against his teeth. "Thought you quit."

"Just relapsing."

Smiling, he disappeared behind a red and gold shoji screen. "Don't they test your piss at work?"

"Yeah, but it's cool," said Warren, drumming his fingertips on his thigh. He wanted to dump his problems on James but felt too anxious to talk. His horn would suit him better.

James wrapped the grassy bundle in Saran Wrap, covering it with aluminum foil. "This good?"

"Plenty. Thanks, man," and the two slapped and pounded, the black man's universal sign of brotherhood.

As soon as he walked into his apartment, Warren took the phone off the hook. He didn't feel like being bothered by anyone, not even Erica. He rolled the weed, puffed, and when he started to float, he reached for his horn. Just the weight of his trumpet on his lips made the pressure in his throat subside. It was like he could breathe again. The first few slow notes cried over the loss of his mother, because he still woke up some mornings forgetting that she was gone. His tempo picked up and in marched Erica and their complications. His father's news was next and the resulting sound was so incredible that he had to stop playing to write it all down.

Chapter Fifteen

More Like Claire

"Stay close to Reverend Black during his signing. Fanatics show up at these events," Claire said to Erica as the chauffer-driven car pulled into the circular driveway of the W Hotel.

Erica nodded while Claire rattled off last-minute instructions: the correct color of Sharpie pen, how to flap the books, and the Reverend's preference for Dr. Pepper with plenty of ice. The prep continued into the entranceway of the hotel where a stout woman in a yellow hat waved for their attention.

"That's Alana, Black's personal publicist," Claire led.

"Praise the Lord, Claire. It's so good to see you." Alana wrapped her blubbery arms around Claire's petite neck and once Erica was introduced, she was hugged too.

"I'm so glad y'all made it safely. God is sure enough good." Alana clapped her wiggly hands and as she led the way to the Reverend, Erica couldn't help watching her large hips shake like a bowl of Jell-O.

When they arrived in the private holding room, the Reverend was seated behind a large table with his bulky bodyguards flanked on each side. All three men were dressed in fashionable suits and the Reverend looked just as he did on television and in pictures. A fair-skinned man, easily categorized as a pretty boy with features best described as fine. Deep natural waves swept through his auburn hair, and his eyes shifted between shades of hazelnut and gray. Erica had always found him attractive but didn't understand the fuss until he took her hand and shined his signature smile.

The Reverend's teeth were like a bracelet of freshwater pearls with each tooth filed in perfect succession, partially hidden by lush lips that spilled from his mouth like poetry. As his smile began to fade, Erica glimpsed a gold-faced crown that hinted at a less-than-Christian past. Yes, she could see why folks were smitten.

The book signing was held in a large reception room with a line that twisted itself anxiously in knots and clusters with people who had traveled both near and far to meet their beloved Reverend. They brought with them children who needed anointing, marriages desperate for prayer, illnesses to be healed, and sinners whose souls needed saving. When the Reverend entered the room, you would have thought that Jesus Christ had arrived. Women began fanning themselves like they were in a breezeless church packed with sweating bodies, and men waved hands shouting hallelujah.

The Reverend was gracious, signing every book placed in front of him, including the Holy Bible. Pictures were snapped, hands shaken, foreheads kissed, bodies blessed until the last customer was satisfied. When the signing was over, Claire sent Erica back to the hotel to confirm the media portion of the itinerary for the next day. It was late and she didn't expect anyone to answer, but it was important to leave messages with her telephone number should something arise. When working a publicity campaign everything had to move like clockwork, there was no room for a mistake.

For the evening dinner, Erica changed into a simple black scoop neck dress that was fitted at the waist and stopped an inch above the knee. It was one of her favorite work dresses and went well with a pair of black and white zebra-striped heels. She gathered her red hair up into an elegant twist, which left Grandma Queeny's earrings dangling from her lobes. After sweeping a light blush across her cheeks, she grabbed a white patent purse and made her way to the elevator.

The Atlanta Grill, a sumptuous steakhouse located in the center of the Ritz-Carlton hotel, was where Erica had arranged the private dinner. Before the other guests arrived, she wanted to be sure that everything in the room was appointed as she had requested. Indeed it was. Erica checked the place cards against her seating chart to make sure everything was right, and talked to the head waiter with last minute instructions on how to cater to the Reverend's whims. When she felt confident that everything was right, she slipped her phone from her purse and called Warren. After two rings, his voice mail picked up.

"Hey, it's me. I hope things are going well. Atlanta is lonely. Call me."

Moments later, Claire swept in with the Reverend and his six-member entourage which included his publicist Alana, the two macho body-guards, a deacon from the church, his head consultant and a personal assistant. His wife was not present. Claire looked radiant in a short gold suit with big jeweled buttons. Onyx dripped from her neck and wrist. Everyone found their assigned seats with ease. Claire sat next to Reverend Black and Erica across from her.

The Reverend held the floor through most of the dinner, telling funny stories about his early experiences preaching at the age of twenty.

"The town was so tiny it's not even on the map," he smirked. "I got the calling early, but I had a hard time getting folks to follow me."

"Well, God is sure enough good because now we have over fifty thousand members at our Church in Pensacola coming from as far as Mobile, Alabama every Sunday," Alana chimed.

"Amen," was heard all around the table. One waiter refreshed drinks as another served raspberry sorbet and lemon meringue pie, as was the Reverend's request for dessert.

"Thank you," he dipped his fork. "One thing I can't ever get use to being on the road is those citied fancy desserts. I'd take a pie baked by Mother Meadows every night of the week."

More mumbles of amen.

Between bites, the Reverend leaned into a private conversation with Claire and then turned his attention back to the table.

"Miss Erica, I want to thank you so much for all of your help today. Claire tells me that you were hand-picked to work on my campaign, and that you are a star."

"Claire is the star. I'm just fortunate enough to be able to reflect a little of her light," Erica replied graciously.

"Well isn't that sweet. Bless your heart, darling. Reverend, I'm going to excuse myself," said Alana, pushing back from the table. "I sure don't need any dessert. Claire and Erica, you have done a lovely job and I can't wait to see you at the seminar tomorrow."

"Indeed." Claire waved.

When the others started saying good night to the Reverend, Claire leaned across to Erica. "Let me get him to his car, and I'll meet you in the lobby lounge to wrap things up."

ERICA WAS SEATED ON A Queen Anne sofa with a paisley print by the fireplace when Claire bustled in looking flushed. The room was warm and lazy with only a handful of patrons scattered around the bar.

"Did I miss something?" asked Erica.

"Nothing. Black is just too much," she chuckled softly. The bartender took their order and Claire poked her hand in her handbag, coming up with a cigarette.

"Mind if I smoke?" she brought the lighter to her lips without waiting for a response. "It's a nasty habit. My husband thinks I've quit, so this will be our little secret." Claire fanned a bit of smoke. "Only Edie knows. God, I'm going to miss that woman."

"She is something," Erica replied neutrally, but the truth was that Edie couldn't leave fast enough.

The bartender returned with a glass of chardonnay for Erica and brandy for Claire.

"With Edie leaving, I'm going to expect big things from you." Claire sipped, leaving a faint cinnamon kiss around the rim. "Where do you see yourself in five years?"

Erica didn't hesitate. "My goal is to grow with the company. I love what I do at B&B and I envision myself climbing the ladder while mentoring the junior publicists on our team."

"I can see that in your eyes. The sky isn't even the limit for you. You've got real talent, kid."

"Thanks, but really it's because I've worked with such an awesome team." Erica tried to keep her head from swelling with the pressure of so many compliments as Claire studied her. "What about your boyfriend? Is he still in D.C.?"

"Yes, we see each other every weekend." Her wine tasted like citrus and pears. "This is the first weekend we've missed."

"He must be so disappointed."

Erica didn't mean to confide in her boss, but Claire had such an easy way. "It's tough."

"Is he the one?" Claire continued, and the intimacy made Erica giddy. Of course Warren was the one, she had known the moment he followed her out of the Iridium jazz club in New York, insisting that he could hail her a taxi cab.

"He is," smiling at the memory.

Claire flicked her cigarette ash in the tray, as she watched the flames from the fireplace prey on unassuming logs. When she spoke again her voice was husky and low.

"Don't make that man wait too long. You'll look up and twenty years will have passed, and you'll have no idea where all the time went. It's easy for work to become your everything—-spouse, children, free time." Claire finished her drink in one gulp, "just be mindful of the time."

They had gone somewhere new and Erica didn't know how to respond. A silence lingered between them before Claire spoke again.

"Why don't you catch a late flight out to D.C. tomorrow? I can do Sunday church without you," she offered.

Stunned, Erica stuttered, "Ar-re you sure? I'm more than willing to stick it out."

"I know you are. That's why I'm telling you to go." Claire lit another cigarette, then said in a voice that was barely audible, "my husband's used to it."

Chapter Sixteen

Honey, I'm Home

Erica didn't know her flight had been canceled until she reached Hartsfield-Jackson airport in Atlanta. At the counter, the clerk explained that her only option of getting out that night was to fly to Miami for a connection. Desperate to see Warren, she agreed. But when she called to give him the news, the home line was busy and his cell phone went to voicemail. She batted away the fleeting thoughts of unfaithfulness. Warren had never given her cause for concern, but it troubled her that she couldn't get in touch with him.

When she arrived at Reagan National airport, it was much later than she had planned. Tired and worn thin, she eased into the backseat of the taxicab hoping that Warren was at home. She gave the driver the address and pulled a compact from her handbag to touch-up her lips. The anxiety she felt wasn't comforting, and when she finally stood in the hallway at his door, one of Grandma Queeny's sayings slapped against her ear.

"When you think you surprising a man, nine out of ten times, you're the one left wide-eyed."

She turned her key. The flat-screen television flickered while a shampoo commercial played on. A pizza box lay open on the coffee table with five untouched slices and several ends of crust. Warren was on the sofa rounded in the fetal position wearing only his underwear. Erica could smell the scent of marijuana in the air. "Hmm, I thought he'd quit," she thought to herself.

Warren had been a typical weed-smoking musician when she met him. He had even persuaded her to try it a few times, but it made her too hyper and it never became something they shared. When he accepted the job at RCSI, he had no choice but to stop because of the drug testing. He hadn't lost his way once since, even when his mother died. Something serious must have happened to make him break now.

"It's me baby," she pushed her hip into his waist, squeezing next to him on the sofa. Warren opened his eyes and the sleep on his face made him appear boyish. When his focus adjusted, his expression widened to a smile.

"You're here," he grabbed her tight and they rocked and touched.

"Why's the phone off the hook?"

Warren stretched out his legs, yawned and then struggled to stand while uttering something about practicing. But it didn't sit well with her. The living room was completely out of place. His trumpet wasn't in the case, which he was religious about. Two pairs of shoes without their shoehorns were scattered and a pile of sheets were crumpled in the lazy chair. Warren was a neat freak by nature and the disorder puzzled her.

"How did you get here?" he broke into her thoughts.

"Claire let me leave early," she reached for a cold slice, but he took the pizza from her and offered to warm it.

The cheese from the pizza was heated but wasn't hot, and while she nibbled on her slice Warren flipped the television from TNT to ESPN trying to decide on a game. He was too quiet, making her wonder if he was still mad at her.

"How was the dinner?" she tried.

"Cool." His lips curled but his eyes never left the TV.

"What's wrong? You don't seem happy I'm here."

Warren twisted the cap to his water bottle. "My dad's marrying Shar."

"His secretary?"

"In a month."

"Damn," reaching for his knee. "You okay?"

"My mother hasn't been in the ground a year. I knew he'd move on, but shit. And it would have been nice if he'd talked to me first instead of making a fucking announcement in a room filled with people." The thick vein in his forehead pressed against his skin.

Erica stood up. "Get dressed."

"What?"

"Let's take a walk. You need some fresh air and I'm stiff from the plane."

"You hate the cold."

"I'll layer up."

TEN MINUTES LATER, THEY were walking down thriving U Street where some of their favorite restaurants and bars lived. Erica was especially fond of Ben's Chili Bowl when she wanted comfort food and Patty's Boom Boom when she needed to let her hair down, drink a rum punch and dance.

"How come you never wear gloves?" She grabbed his hand, and he shrugged.

Warren had on his three-quarter heavy coat, a skullcap and trendy boots. Erica had changed into a pair of flats and wore her mint green scarf and its matching hat low and tight. It wasn't just cold, it was freezing and the party street wasn't as crowded as usual.

"I'm glad you're here," he squeezed her around the waist, and they walked two more blocks before he opened up.

"Losing my mom, there's like a hole inside of me the size of a cantaloupe. I can feel it every single day. My dad doesn't feel that?"

"I know, I remember honey," Erica had taken off a whole week of work to be with Warren the week of his mother's funeral. She had even helped write the obituary.

"Maybe it's different for him." They stopped on the corner of 9th Street while waiting for the light. Dance music was blasting from the top floor of Nellie's sports bars, and Erica could hear the patrons shouting their fun.

"He was probably so used to being taken care of that he can't be without a woman," she added.

"I can't be without you," Warren turned and cupped her chin, "no other woman would do."

She kissed him and ran her fingers across his cheeks. "I was miserable thinking I'd have to go two weeks without you."

The light changed and they turned off U street, dipping down a side street. In front of them was an old school bar that dodged the gentrification of the neighborhood. The neon sign flashing in the window reflected an era that had since passed. On impulse, Warren steered Erica through the front door. It was an older crowd and the barmaid didn't smile when she took their order. A pool table was positioned toward the back. A jukebox sat across from it and someone had played Curtis Mayfield's "Pusher Man." Two middle-aged women with sagging breasts and thick waistlines danced together in the middle of the floor while three men watched from their barstools. Warren took Erica's hand while they sipped vodkas splashed with cranberry juice and continued about the events of the dinner. "And when he made the announcement, he was looking at me like I was supposed to be happy. Meanwhile, my world is turned upside down. And I feel like a punk for saying it."

Erica wrapped her arms around his waist.

"Sorry, I'm just rambling. Tell me about Atlanta."

"Nothing much to tell," she said, filling him in on the Reverend, his entourage and her conversation with Claire.

They drank another round. Alcohol had a way of making things better.

One of the men sitting at the bar played "Reasons" by Earth, Wind & Fire, and Warren surprised the hell out of Erica by asking her to dance. It was the first time he had ever done that in public and she shuffled to her feet.

"My dad played this song out when I was growing up," he whispered, pulling her to a dark spot by the window. While their bodies responded to the music he sang in her ear, "Kissing and hugging and holding you tight."

Erica rested her head on his chest, savoring the sound of his soul's breath against her ear. The layover, connecting flight, and hassle to get to him was all worth the pleasure of a single slow drag in a dinky local bar.

When they got back to his apartment, Warren flipped through his vintage records for Earth, Wind & Fire. Erica lit every candle that she could find, placing them along the windowsill, table and kitchen counter. While the sounds of the seventies serenaded them, Erica undressed Warren. Kissing his lips, she undid his belt, letting his pants fall to the floor. Pressing into his pelvis, her hands searched his chest, and then relieved him of his sweater. Black boxer briefs were all that was left, and as she thumbed them down, she licked every bit of skin that was within reach. Warren moaned for more attention and she knew by the way he whispered her name that he was ready. A passionate urgency welled between them and when they couldn't make it to the bed, they used the floor.

THE NEXT MORNING ERICA didn't want to get up, so Warren spooned her while stroking her hair. "So lovely."

"Such a lie. What's for breakfast?"

"You've been sleeping awhile. It's lunchtime, baby. I can order you something, or we can eat cold pizza."

"Cold pizza." She forced herself to sit up, then stood in front of the closet mirror. Her red hair was tousled and her lips dry. She pulled on her white, fluffy bathrobe before meeting Warren in the kitchen where he was making coffee. His chest hairs pressed flat against his bare tea-colored skin.

"Why do you have to leave me?" He handed her the Book section of the Sunday newspaper.

"'Cause Claire knows I am here, crazy."

"So cancel the flight. I'll book you the last train out."

Erica smiled, swatted him with the newspaper and agreed. They spent the afternoon in T-shirts, passing the newspaper back and forth, dozing in and out of sleep, and occasionally taking in the various basketball games on the screen. He took her one last time in the shower and they both hoped it would get them through the week.

WARREN PLACED HER CARRY-ON in the trunk and once he closed her door, she flipped on the seat warmers. Nestled into the buttery leather chair her foot kept hitting something spongy.

Reaching down she picked up a condom, extra-large and flavored. Her nerves sank like an iceberg. She and Warren hadn't used condoms in months.

"What the hell is this?"

He glanced over, while backing out of the parking space. "I don't know."

"Don't give me that shit. Where did it come from?"

Warren looked again, searching his memory, "Blanche must have dropped it." They rode down U Street.

"Blanche?" Erica racked her brain for why the name sounded familiar. "That girl from work? What was she doing in your car dropping condoms?"

"I gave her a ride after the dinner Friday night."

"Why? Did her car break down?"

"She was sort of my date," he said, regretting the way the words sounded as soon as they left his mouth. Erica's toffee skin turned the color of eggplant. Rushing, he explained that the whole department had been invited and that he and Blanche just sat together.

"Did you fuck her?"

Warren laughed. "No. You sound insane." They were at a stoplight and he turned to face her. "Babe, she must have dropped it when her purse fell open."

"Why didn't you mention this before?"

"I forgot," he shrugged.

"You don't forget important shit like your father being honored for all of his years of service and that you took some bimbo from work instead of me," she said, without taking a breath. "Now the little whore thinks she has a chance."

"Would you calm down? You don't even know her."

"Apparently, it's you I don't know." Erica turned up the volume on the stereo.

Warren turned it back down. "What's that supposed to mean?" It was his turn to flex, but she refused to give up her position in the argument. Her butt had grown hot and she flipped off the heater. Trees sped by with streets that she had driven several times with Warren but everything seemed different now, duller with no sheen. When Warren pulled in front of Union Station, she got out of the car and rounded the trunk, but he was there before she could unload her luggage. Every organ in her body felt cracked. She wanted to sucker punch him.

"Stop looking at me like that. I'm not cheating on you," he folded his hand around the handle of her bag. Warren wore a black baseball cap and a thermal shirt, his leather jacket flapped open, but he didn't close it. "Look, I wouldn't waste my time running up to New York if I were," he stepped closer.

Erica paused. She hated that she was already thinking about forgiveness. "You should have told me," she said softly.

"But that's my only crime," he took a deep breath. "I swear on my mother's grave that nothing happened." Another first and when Warren reached for her chin, she knew she could believe him.

"Come on, baby, I don't want to end another weekend arguing. Especially over this bullshit," he pleaded, touching his lips to hers, but when he tried parting them with his tongue she pulled away. Grabbing her luggage, Erica hurried toward the double doors of the station with Warren staring after her.

Chapter Seventeen
Foolish Me

From the moment Erica slipped her key into Warren's lock, she had sensed that something wasn't right. The weed smoking, chaotic disorder, and phone ringer turned off could have easily added up to him cheating, but Erica didn't know. So far his loyalty was as clean as freshly laundered shirts and up until that point he gave her no concern for worry. But what was worse, Erica couldn't even begin to picture her life without Warren. If he were cheating, then what? Did she start over or swallow the affair like a tart tonic? These thoughts turned over in her head while walking the aisles of the train searching for an empty seat. For the first time, Erica understood why some women didn't investigate when they thought their man was cheating. It was much easier to look the other way. Because to be in it—knee-deep, faced flat in it—breathing the stink of your own failure was gut-wrenching.

Usually she found riding the train comforting; the chugga-chug of the engine, the cushiony window seat, the long bridges, crystallizing bodies of water, and the multiple colors of piney vegetation. But on this trip Erica's chest throbbed and the passing scene did nothing to stop her crippling thoughts.

There was no way that the condom just "slipped" from Blanche's purse. Baby girl had that planned from the moment she stepped foot into Warren's car and what made Erica furious was that he was being so naïve.

Through the reflection of the glass window, she could see Blanche's face, eventually remembering her well. They had met at last year's company Christmas party. Model thin, oversized eyelash extensions, teeny clothing, chatty, blonde patched hair, mole on left nostril, sing-songy voice, flat ass, Thumbelina feet, and the ability to shine in a room filled with straight, successful men. Women like Blanche didn't drop anything accidentally.

By the time Erica arrived in New York her temples were tender from overthinking, and she couldn't see straight. So she hailed a taxi, and it was in the backseat of the car that the blues found her. Biting down on the collar of her sweater, she tried sending those feelings away. As they passed through Times Square, Erica couldn't believe that she had put her job in jeopardy by going to D.C. Sure Claire had told her to go, but she should have declined, saying that work was much more important. How was she supposed to climb the corporate ladder if she was busy chasing Warren? Then out of nowhere, the next thought hit her so hard she bolted straight up in her seat. What if this weekend had been a set-up from Claire, testing her dedication? Well, then Erica had failed miserably, and she felt even heavier as she tugged her luggage up her front steps.

The telephone message light was blinking when she entered her apartment; two from her mother, one from Edie, and the last from an irritating author complaining about the thread count of his hotel sheets. Erica wasn't in the mood to deal with work yet so she called over to Tess' to see if she wanted company. When she didn't get an answer, she surprised herself by dialing her mother.

"Hey, Slim," she answered on the second ring. "I been calling you all weekend."

Erica explained that she had been away.

"What's wrong?"

"Nothing."

"Don't tell me nothing, girl. I can hear it in your voice."

It always amazed Erica how well her mother could read her, even over the phone. It was like some sixth sense that she had or a radar that always zeroed in at the right moment. Erica rewarded her by recounting the story.

"So whatcha gut saying?" her mother was munching on something crunchy, probably salt and vinegar potato chips.

"I don't know."

"You know."

"No I don't," Erica yelled back, but her mother was unfazed by her outburst and spoke even softer. "Then you ain't listening. Slim, push past the anger and feel Warren. You know his heart. 'Cause you're in it."

When did her mother get so smart? Erica pulled her chenille throw up to her chin and wiped the tear now slumped in the corner of her lip.

Chapter Eighteen

Not Trying to Fool You

Falling in love with Erica had been like coming down with a terrible bout of bats in the belfry. There was no escaping his feelings when it came to her. In those first few weeks, Warren remembered being consumed by the raw scent of her skin. She rarely wore perfume, but it was her natural scent that made him feel like a crazed mammal. During that first summer, they had spent every single day together until he left for his job in D.C., and up until her trip to Atlanta they had been together every single weekend. So it was hard to understand what was going wrong.

Thank God it was Monday, and when Warren pushed through the entrance of Sweet Melodies, he whistled along with his favorite Wynton Marsalis tune. Dark-haired waitresses in loafers and leggings hastened around the lounge taking orders. There was Sissy, the bartender, chatting it up with the patrons. Warren's band was hosting the weekly jam session again and just being in the room relaxed him. With his horn strapped across his chest, dressed in his black uniform, he strolled through the crowd soaking up praises from the regulars until his head had comfortably ballooned. This momentary brush with fame pleased Warren, and tricked him into believing that all was right with the world, if only for a few seconds. On stage, James sat tightening his drums.

"What up, Black man," James stood and pulled Warren into a half hug, half handshake. "How was the bud?" A drum screw sat between his lips and it flopped up and down like a cigarette.

"Just what the doctor ordered. You always come through."

"Solid."

"Wanna grab a beer?" James shrugged, following Warren to the bar. He was shorter than Warren by a head, but the same dark complexion. Tonight he wore a bright orange T-shirt with "Free Sudan" typed across his chest.

Sissy pitched two lagers on the counter for them and as she sashayed the length of the bar in a yellow slouchy dress, James followed with his eyes.

"You know she's too old for you," Warren teased.

"I'd still like to taste that," James reached for his beer. "You see how she was looking at me?"

"She looks at everyone like that," Warren said, and after a long gulp of beer told James what was on his mind: his father's announcement at the dinner and the problem with Erica.

"Think of it like this, at least someone's taking care of your dad."

Warren admitted that he hadn't looked at it that way.

"And Erica? Man, you two are made for each. You probably just need a change of scenery."

"It does feel like the honeymoon is over."

"Well I have just the place," said James, reaching into his back pocket for his wallet, producing a tattered business card. "My snow bunny took me here for my birthday. This place will cure anything."

Warren turned the card over in his hand, thinking that James just might be on to something. When he got home he called Erica. The line was busy, and he knew she took the phone off the hook to get back at him, but what she didn't realize was that he was an effective stalker, so he just kept calling.

After two sleepless nights, three calls from Warren, a full word search book completed, a pint of butter pecan Häagen-Daz ice cream, a bottle of Shiraz, a few shots of vodka and four pieces of catfish fried hard, Erica finally picked up the phone when he called that Wednesday night.

"Stop fighting with me over bullshit," he said.

"Learn to keep the bitches at bay."

"Can't help it if I'm good looking."

"And charming."

"You think I'm charming?"

"I'm talking to you, ain't I?"

Warren laughed at her slick girl tongue.

"So you're coming up this weekend?"

"I'll be there before you know it," he answered, and he meant that literally.

Chapter Nineteen
The Cleopatra Room

Warren was on the road heading to New York before he decided to tell Erica his plan. It was a surprise, a risky one, but it was time for some spontaneity to spice things up. James had provided the lead on the Pocono Mountain resort, which inspired Warren to research the best restaurants, antique shops, and hiking trails for their weekend. Blanche agreed to cover his projects at work, so the only thing left to do was call Erica and invite her.

She answered the phone. "Erica Shaw."

"What're you doing?"

"Looking over a satellite tour," she replied, sounding distracted. "Where're you? What's that noise?"

"I'm on the highway, heading up to see you."

"Stop lying," she giggled, but when he didn't recant his statement, she laughed out loud. "You serious?"

"You need to take tomorrow off. We're going away for a long weekend."

"Oh my goodness. Warren."

"We need this."

"I know but..."

"We'll get what you need along the way."

"Honey, I..."

"See you at seven," he said, powering off his phone.

The arrogance of Warren both infuriated and excited Erica and at that moment she didn't know which emotion took the lead. He could be so damn cocky, assuming that she could just take off from work at the kick of his heel. She had responsibilities. People depended on her. Projects needed overseeing. But as soon as she stopped fussing with Warren in her head, she gave in to the excitement.

They were going on vacation. A nice long, quiet weekend with just the two of them and, knowing Warren, it was someplace romantic. The last time he took her away, they spent a week in a sleepy little shore town in the Outer Banks where Erica had barely dressed and stayed drunk off the scenery. Though she hoped this getaway didn't involve a bikini because her body was not summer-ready. Tapping her pen against her pad she wished she had scheduled a wax, plus her nails could use a fresh coat of polish. But there was no time for vanity. She needed to get focused if she planned to leave on time. She made a must-do-list to stay on track. Thank God Edie was out and she could put in her personal day via email. After that she needed to finish up a satellite tour, meet with Prudence, and then carry the Kessler manuscript with her to read over the weekend.

At 7:01 Warren called from the downstairs lobby. With her work bag packed, she stopped in the bathroom to touch up her lips and give her lashes a quick swipe. Her tweed pants and brown riding boots were nice, but she wished that she hadn't spilled the oily salad dressing on her turtleneck. Because even though she had blotted it twice, the stain wouldn't let go.

Outside, Warren leaned against his shiny SUV dressed in an ivory shearling and matching Kangol chewing on a toothpick.

He made the simplest gestures look sexy and her breath stalled at the sight of him. If only she had her camera. Hurrying towards him, her tan swing coat rustled and her bone-straight hair blew.

"You think you're so slick," she smiled up at him, while pulling a few stray hairs from matting in her plum lip gloss.

He kissed her cheek. "It's the only way to get on your calendar." Then he took her bag, helping her into the car. Once he was behind the wheel, he brushed her thigh. "You look beautiful, baby."

"Sweet." She held his hand from her seat.

Traffic was heavy, and despite the fact that Erica's office was a few blocks to the Holland tunnel, it took over thirty minutes to get out of the city. Once they reached Route 80 though, the ride was tranquil. Erica could feel the stress in her shoulders unwind, like calm fingers on knotty laces. Even in the dark, she was comforted by the silhouettes of evergreens, oaks, pines, and maples.

Warren had made a playlist of different versions of "Wild is the Wind," and they had a private listening party on the drive.

Erica was digging the scratchy vocals of Esperanza Spalding, asking Warren to play her version again.

"I knew you would like her. She's a beast on the bass."

Erica let the music take over, and when it ended she wanted to hear it once more.

"No, junkie. Nina's next." Warren let the song play.

The piano started with a down-tempo belly crawl, slowly introducing her melodic, manly voice.

"Esperanza sounds good," said Warren, "but Nina Simone's version is heavy, soulful." He paused and Erica could see his mind working out the notes. "Yeah, she touches me in a place that only the most accomplished singers can reach," he said, turning the music up so high Erica felt her senses awaken. The clarity and sound did something to her heart.

"Singing like that is a skill that comes with aging," she offered finally. Warren looked at her like she was pure love.

Erica cracked her window just enough to let some of the breeze flow into the car and mix with the renditions of David Bowie, George Michael, Amel Larrieux, ending with Cat Power, a singer she hadn't heard before. Warren was up on everything.

"I don't think men do the song justice," she said, admitting that Cat Power's breathy voice and folksy sound had her mesmerized. Cat took the vibe back to jazz.

Erica grew up on the music, her father had as many jazz albums as Warren, and used to quiz her on what instruments she heard when he played his tapes in the car. It was almost funny that she was having a similar experience with Warren.

THICK CHUNKS OF GRAVEL crumbled under the tires as he pulled into the couples-only resort, and from the headlights, Erica spotted two fawns scampering for the woods. When she stepped out of the car the air was wonderfully exhilarating. She felt like dancing.

"I hope you like it," Warren said, leading her from the reception area down the beige-and-gold hallway where pictures of snow-capped mountains and shy forest animals covered the walls. He was carrying a duffle bag, and told her that he had lifted her toothbrush and some hair products from his bathroom. Erica squeezed his hand in anticipation while waiting for him to use the key.

"Welcome to the Cleopatra Room," he grinned while pushing the door open, where a seven-foot champagne-glass whirlpool greeted them in the center of the living room.

"Wow," she whispered.

To the left was a wood burning fireplace and further in sat a heart-shaped plunge pool. The suite was bigger than her entire apartment, and although the features were over the top, she more than appreciated the effort.

"Hon, this is awesome. You are the sweetest to go through so much trouble for me."

"There's more," he led her into the bedroom, pulling her onto the rounded king bed. When she looked up, she couldn't help but smile at the celestial ceilings.

"It's like sleeping under the stars."

Warren opened his mouth over hers. "You like?"

"I do, I do, I do," she hugged his neck. Being with him was all she needed. The rest was extra.

"Hungry?" Warren backed off the bed, disappearing into the next room without waiting for a reply. When he returned he handed her a glass of Prosecco and explained that a seafood platter and salad was on the way.

"To a great weekend," he clinked.

"To my thoughtful man," she chimed.

"Now, let's try out that tub."

Erica followed him up the metal stairs and dipped her toe, but Warren jumped right in. After a few minutes she eased the rest of her body in while the steamy water sloshed between them. Champagne-like bubbles gurgled from the core of the whirlpool's glass and splashed against their bare skin. The warmth felt wonderful, but after a while the moisture began drawing up her hair. When she started twisting it off her shoulders, Warren told her to leave it down. He moved closer, his big round eyes holding hers, looking like he wanted to possess her.

"I don't want to fight anymore," she said with her fingers working the nape of his neck.

Warren responded by positioning himself in the fold of her arms. "I've missed you."

They sighed and spooned.

THE FOOD WAS DELIVERED and after about ten minutes there was very little evidence that it ever existed. Drawn butter had dripped into Warren's chin and Erica used the sleeve of her terry robe to sop it. Their bellies satisfied, Warren poured a second round of Prosecco.

"Brought Boggle," he said.

"Well let's get it on."

He set up the game in the living room near the fireplace while Erica went into her bag for paper and pens.

"I hope you brought the dictionary," she called.

"Don't worry, I know how you like to cheat."

The two were fiercely competitive at all games, but Boggle was their number one battlefield. Erica thought she was the smartest at the game because she manipulated words for a living, but Warren claimed he was king because of his MBA.

After three rounds, the king was winning, prompting Erica to complain that the fireplace was making her too warm. Slowly she removed her robe.

"Are you trying to distract me?" he reached over and lifted her left breast.

"No, just hot," she swatted his hand away, quickly flipping the hourglass for another intense round.

Warren found two five-point words, and was the first to reach fifty. He was a showy winner, pumping his hands like he had just won the World Series. His confident gesture aroused her. It was something about the way he dropped his head to the side and gave her that crooked grin that made her leave her robe and find his lap.

Warren never turned her down, but before she could start something, there was a knock at the door. They exchanged looks, before he moved to answer it, allowing Erica time to put on her robe.

"Excuse me, Mr. Prince," she heard a man's baritone voice, but couldn't see past Warren. "I'm sorry to bother you but your phone line was down and we've just corrected the problem."

"Thanks for letting me know."

"There is an urgent message that came in for you from Ms. Blanche Laurent." He handed Warren a slip of paper.

Anger pricked Erica's skin.

"She said for you to please call immediately."

Warren thanked the man and closed the door.

"How does she know we're here?"

Warren ran his fingers over his damp hair. "She's covering for me on my projects. Something must be wrong." He went into the bedroom to use the phone.

Pulling her robe tighter, Erica moved toward the empty food platter, scrounging the garnish for a piece of celery. She needed something to settle her nerves. Blanche, again? She drained the bottle of Prosecco of its last drops and tried to concentrate on the lemony fizz of the Italian sparkling wine, rather than eavesdrop on the conversation going on in the next room. But no such luck. Warren's voice was gaining strength by the minute.

"You can't handle that? That's why I asked you to cover for me." Pause. "I gave you the password, just go into my computer." Another pause. "You have to be kidding me. I'm more than five hours away. Stan asked for me? Well, didn't you tell him I was on vacation?"

The last pause was the longest, and Erica knew what came next. Backing her chair from the table, she walked to the bar and poured them both a glass of water. His call ended when she entered the bedroom. Warren sat on the edge of the bed, his robe loose over his tree-trunk thighs.

"What's up?" she handed him the glass.

"Damn imbeciles. They act like they can't do shit without me." He held the drink.

Erica watched the worries cross his brow. She already knew what he was thinking.

"Would you be mad..."

"I'll go with you," she replied, and when the relief spread across his face, she knew she had made the right decision. For this to work, they both had to learn how to press apples into a smooth sauce, as Grandma Queeny use to say.

"I have to be in the office by tomorrow afternoon for a mandatory meeting with Stan. It's my fault, I should have planned this better." He brought his head to his hands.

"Honey, it's fine." She put her arm around his stout shoulders. "This will still be our special weekend. I'm not going to let anyone ruin it," she said.

Especially not Blanche, she thought to herself.

Chapter Twenty
Throw Down

Warren and Erica left for D.C. early the next morning and, as soon as they arrived in his office, they encountered Blanche, arched over the water cooler with her flirty skirt boldly displaying too much leg.

"You made it," she said, folding her lips over each syllable like she would a spoonful of sugar. Her eyes were leopard's hazel and her streaked hair moved as if guided by a fan. She was at least three inches shorter than Erica. She was also two sizes smaller. And when she spoke, the smile on her face never reached her eyes.

"Nice to see you again," Blanche held out her hand.

"You too."

Before driving down, Erica had done her best to pull her look together, but standing beside Blanche she knew she had failed. Her curls frizzed from the hot tub, and even though she had brushed her hair into a bun, it had only helped a little. The slacks and shirt she wore groaned under the pressure of having to stand up two days in a row, while the small stain from yesterday's lunch seemed to have tripled in size.

Warren moved a tattered box out of the extra chair in his cubicle, motioning for Erica to take a seat. Blanche disappeared behind the wall separating their desks, and returned clutching a cup.

"Black coffee. Just like you like it," she said, handing it to Warren. Erica wondered if this was their daily routine.

"I'll have a cup," she injected.

"Oh, the cafeteria is on the eighth floor," Blanche pointed towards the elevator. Warren offered to get it.

"It's fine, babe. Just concentrate on your work so we can get back to our weekend." She smiled like it was a private conversation between them.

But at the elevator, she felt so insecure.

The cafeteria was empty, except for a few caffeine junkies stealing an extra cup. Erica took her coffee to a corner table and dialed Tess.

"What's wrong?" Tess' voice was caked with sleep.

Erica explained the situation. Sparing no details, she started with the surprise trip, Blanche's call, ending with the coffee comment. "She's a chickenhead dressed in fox's clothing. What should I do?"

"Nothing."

"Nothing? That's the best you can do?" Erica's knee jerked against the table, causing her coffee to tip. She balanced the phone on her shoulder while mopping up the spill with some napkins.

"If Warren wanted Blanche, you wouldn't be at his office. Don't give her power, Sugar. You're holding all the cards."

Right, thought Erica. Of course Tess was right. She pushed back from the table in search of the ladies' room. It was time to pull it together.

When she got back to Warren's cube, there was a note taped to his computer telling her he had gone to a classified area, so she busied with checking emails. Moments later, Blanche appeared.

"Warren sent me to check on you," she smiled evenly. Erica's eyes stayed on the computer as she mumbled that she was fine, but Blanche didn't take the hint and leaned over the cubicle.

"Sorry you missed the 'Man of Honor' dinner. It was really something."

"I've been before," Erica typed without missing a stroke.

Blanche shook her hair. "Warren took his dad's engagement hard. Good thing I was there, he nearly fell apart."

A ringing sounded in Erica's ear and before she realized what she was doing, she was on her feet, her full attention on Blanche.

"Thanks for seat-filling, but I've got it from here," she said as quickly as a one-two punch.

Cosmic forces must have been on their side because just then Warren appeared.

"Ready," he said, looking from one woman to the other. Erica nodded and allowed him to help her into her coat. Mustering grace, she told Blanche that it had been a pleasure seeing her again, then took Warren's hand and walked away.

Chapter Twenty-One

Song Cry

In less than 24 hours, Warren had driven from D.C. to New York, to the Poconos and then back to D.C., without more than a few hours sleep. His big weekend had been a waste of time and more money than he wanted to count. But Erica was the one with the attitude. She slouched against the corner of the apartment elevator as if it were her plans that went sour.

"What's wrong with you?" he asked.

"Nothing," she replied flatly, but he knew the tone and went through the motion of asking until she answered.

"I just didn't realize that you sat right next to Blanche," she said finally.

"We're on the same team."

"Mighty familiar preparing your coffee black just like you like it," mocking the woman's accent.

Warren shook his head. "Everyone in the department takes turns getting the coffee."

"Yeah, maybe. But how come she was the only person I saw up your ass?" she eyed him, and as he unlocked the door, he told her she was overreacting as usual.

"Am I?"

They were standing in the kitchen and Warren could smell three bananas rotting in the fruit basket on the countertop.

"We work together. What do you expect me to do?" He reached for a beer.

Erica rolled her eyes. "You are way too naïve."

Her spoiled demeanor pricked at his skin like porcupine quills, but he didn't feel like arguing. All Warren wanted was to drink a beer and zone out with his feet up in front of the tube. But as he claimed his spot on the sofa, it was clear that Erica had other plans. She stood blocking his view in what he liked to call her war pose; feet four inches apart, fingers stretched across the back of her hips, chest thrust forward and lips pursed into an upside down u.

"I know her type," she countered.

"What the fuck do you want from me?" He picked up the remote control and tossed it across the room as the thick vein in his forehead stretched to the size of an asparagus stalk.

"For you to stop being so stupid. First you take the whore to your father's dinner without telling me and now the bitch is bringing you coffee like you two are a damn married couple," she answered. "Get with the program."

"There isn't a program, except for the imaginary one in your head," he said. "Now move, so I can find the Wizard's game."

Erica didn't budge and her defiance further annoyed him.

"She can't be trusted," she raised her voice, remembering the unused condom she found in Warren's car.

"Fine," Warren stood. "I won't trust her. I'll even tell her to stop bringing me coffee if that makes you feel better. Now move." He stepped closer.

"You care more about the stupid game than my feelings," she spat, popping the thin lid holding his anger. Warren didn't plan to hurt her. He just wanted her out of the way, so he grabbed her by the wrist and pulled her away from the television until she was falling backwards into the lazy chair.

"Sit down and shut up," he yelled. "Damn you talk too much."

"Don't you put your hands on me," she jumped back up and into his face fearlessly. They stood glaring at each other when the telephone rang. Warren broke the eye contact and moved to answer it, and before he could say hello he heard her mumble, "It had better not be Blanche."

Warren hoped for all their sakes that it wasn't.

"Hello."

"Son, what are you doing home?"

Just the sound of his father's voice made his stomach feel like he had been caught playing hooky in grade school.

"I took the day off, Sir," he answered, and without giving Erica another look, continued down the hall to his bedroom. He was gone for over ten minutes and when he returned, she was sitting on the sofa with her legs folded under her Indian style. A manuscript was opened in her lap. The television was tuned to a sitcom, but as Warren moved toward it, all he could hear was his heart beating against his chest like a tom-tom drum. Hidden in a wooden box beneath the VCR was the last of the weed, and after his conversation with his father the joint was exactly what he needed.

"What did he say?" Erica broke the silence between them.

"He asked me to be the best man at his wedding," Warren opened the box.

"What did you say?"

Pinched between his lips, the white boy bounced like a pogo stick. "He's my father. What you think I said?" he found his lighter. "The rehearsal dinner is next weekend. It would be nice if you were there."

He was being nasty and she decided not to fan his fire. With only two nights left of their "special weekend" she wanted to go back to loving each other, so she made her voice like peach fuzz and told him she would be there. Then she surprised them both by reaching for his joint. Warren hesitated, but then passed it to her. After two hits she coughed like something was caught in her throat.

Warren tapped her back. "What are you doing?"

"What are you doing?"

They looked at each other, and Warren sipped on the joint twice more.

Erica scooted from the sofa and went to the kitchen for some water. It didn't take much to get her high and she soon felt a cloudy confusion that made her light-headed. She had only smoked to deaden the fight, and as the drug took over, a barrage of thoughts flickered through her head like a child's 3D viewmaster.

The argument hadn't really been about Blanche; it was more that Warren wouldn't admit that the girl had a thing for him, and his unassuming blindness made her want to choke him. If he couldn't see through Blanche then he was easy prey, and she would beat a bitch down before she let some heifer gobble up her man. Erica laughed to herself. The weed had her feeling brazen. But then the viewmaster clicked, and in strutted fear.

Warren reached for the heavy brass latching and unhooked the case containing his horn. He moved through the first notes as if rediscovering a lost lover, plunging but restraining at the same time.

Perspiration pressed around his forehead, crept down his cheeks, settling in a pool on his neck, soaking his shirt. He felt it all—death, disappointment, the longing, the loving—and it all weighed on him with a heaviness that was becoming too regular to stomach. Then out of nowhere, he heard Jay-Z rhyming in his ear. *I can't see 'em coming down my eyes, so I gotta make this song cry.*

Warren's song howled.

And Erica heard it, because she was crying too.

What was happening to them?

When the music ceased, she went to him. With care she removed the trumpet from his hand and took it apart piece by piece the way she had seen him do so many times, and placed each part carefully into the case. Lifting him to his feet, she held his hand and led him back to the bedroom. The shades were down and the room was pitch black, but Erica knew her way to the place that always made things better.

Between the satiny sheets, they held, clung, rocked and trembled, apologized, kissed, begged and promised, eventually falling asleep with their bodies drenched in the weightiness of their long distance world.

IT RAINED ALL DAY Saturday so they took it easy, ordering take-out and watching movies. On Sunday Erica led them into their end of the weekend routine, by frying some eggs and buttering the toast. Warren handed her the book section of the Post and spread the business section for himself. Gospel music floated from the stereo on the kitchen shelf. They seemed relaxed and comfortable with each other once again, but as Erica nursed her coffee, she knew there was still too much left unsaid. A bandage had been put on the wound. But the wound really needed flushing and to be stitched. At the rate they were going the slightest bruise was bound to make the gash open and bleed. Unfortunately for her, the news she would receive the next morning at work was going to be that bump.

Chapter Twenty-Two

New Assignments

There was an unspoken hierarchy when it came to the seating in Claire's office. Edie, the director, claimed the pillow-stuffed chair at the right of Claire's desk. Even when she was absent, no one dared to venture into her seat. Publicists sat on the beige woven sofa and the assistants folded themselves against the carpeted floor. Claire always stood behind her vanity-sized desk, making her small frame seem larger. Today she wore a tan suit with her hair styled back, showing off emerald studs. It was nine in the morning, and despite having three children at home and an hour-and-twenty-minute commute from the suburbs, Claire's face was fresh and ready for the start of her ten-hour day.

"Edie had the baby. A girl, seven pounds six ounces," she announced, pausing briefly for the room's reaction.

"Wow."

"That's awesome."

"It is great," she said, and with the wave of her hand silenced the side conversations. Erica sat speechless. She hadn't expected it to happen so soon.

"I've had to make a few assignment changes to compensate for Edie being out of the office. Amy, take the Barnes' campaign. We've just added Dallas/Fort Worth to the tour. Erica, LaVal Jarvis is in town lecturing at Hunter College this Saturday. I know you've expressed interest in this early on, and now it's been bumped from midlist to top priority. Go to the lecture and find something we can sink into. We need him to feel like we are rolling out the red carpet for him."

Erica dropped her head, pretending to take notes, but she was really cursing under her breath. How could this happen to her again? This Saturday was Warren's father's rehearsal dinner and once again she had to be the carrier of crappy news.

WARREN TOOK IT BETTER than she had hoped over the phone, but what Erica didn't realize was how much the upcoming nuptials had Warren tripping. James had given him another bundle of weed and he had been puffing hard every night. It was the only way he could fall asleep, and even then his mother kept coming to him in his dreams, sitting in the drawing room at her piano with her fingers poised, but the music never came. Someone was sobbing.

Chapter Twenty-Three

Going to the Chapel

Warren hurried through the parking lot of Tabernacle Baptist Church. Tabernacle was Warren's family's home church. His mother had been on the Board of Willing Workers, and served as choir director for more than twenty-five years. Warren used to attend church in spurts, but he hadn't been since his mother's funeral seven months ago. Returning for his father's upcoming nuptial was odd, but as he walked through the heavy church doors and was greeted by the strong fragrance of lemony wood polish, he buried his feelings under the smile he offered his dad.

"Son," they met in the drafty foyer and his father pulled him into a hearty embrace.

"Sorry I'm late. I hit a little traffic," Warren offered as he straightened from the hug.

"Shar's late too and your sister's not going to make it back. Said she couldn't stop filming." He looked disappointed. Warren's older sister Billie was a filmmaker working in the Sahara Desert on a documentary.

"Where's Erica?" his father looked past him.

"Working."

"Again?" he gave him a questioning look, but Warren didn't meet his gaze.

"Why is rehearsal a week before the wedding? Isn't it usually done the night before?"

"Pastor Davis is going out of town and it's the only time he can run through the ceremony. Shouldn't take too long."

"Makes sense."

"Are you all right son?"

"Yeah," he looked towards the sanctuary.

His father patted his back. "Well let's go inside, I want you to come meet Shar's boys."

The main sanctuary of Tabernacle Baptist had been built in the early 1900s, but despite the cathedral having undergone restorations a few years back, the church still held onto its original oversized stained-glass windows, high arched ceilings and hand-carved wooden pews that fanned the center aisle like angel's wings. The floor was carpeted in a bright royal blue that never looked worn. At the front of the church the two boys were huddled in the front row.

"Bernard, Jared, this is Warren," his father introduced, and the timbre in his voice made the comic book shared between the boys quickly disappear. The organist began to play a recognizable hymn. Pastor Davis entered through the side door chatting with the church's Treasurer.

"Boys, you'll have to excuse me. I need to have a word with Pastor Davis before we begin." His father strolled off, leaving the three alone.

The young boys were the same reddish-brown, dressed in navy slacks, white polo shirts and gray vests that bore the Point Academy school crest. An uneasiness passed through Warren, and as he placed his hands in his pockets, he confirmed that the boys attended the Academy.

"Yes Sir, I'm nine years old and Jared is seven," answered Bernard, the older one.

"I'm almost eight," whined Jared.

"Well you're seven now," his brother called back.

Jared pushed his foot against Bernard's knee, and instinctively Bernard popped him hard over the head like a mother would a disruptive child.

"Ow, why'd you do that?" Jared pouted while the tears gathered.

"Boys," said Shar, pushing past Warren and snatching them both by the collar. "Cut out this foolishness and show the Lord some respect." She narrowed her eyes and the two sat still with their hands in their lap.

"How're you, Warren?" she turned, bending her cheek towards him for a kiss.

"Fine, thanks," replied Warren as Pastor Davis clapped his large hands, beckoning everyone to begin.

Once the rehearsal had concluded, Pastor Davis sent Warren down to the fellowship hall to make sure that it was empty before he closed for the night. As Warren cranked closed an old kitchen window, he heard voices traveling from the ladies' lounge just across the narrow hall. He didn't intend to eavesdrop but the rhythm of their talk lured him in.

"Now, he know he wrong paradin' them children round, talking about 'here are my stepsons.' Everybody this side of South Dakota know them boys his," said the first voice.

"It's a crying shame," said the second. "After all Sister Alma done gave for this church."

Warren stiffened at his mother's name.

"Chile, please, dat woman knew what was gon' on. She just looked the other way. God rest her soul."

"The older one is the spitting image of Warren when he was that age."

"And to bring them to this church. Umph, it's an abomination 'gainst God, praise his holy…" The lounge door swung open and just like that Warren was nose to nose with big-boned, monkey-face Sister Clara. Her counterpart, Miz Bertha, was so close that the two hippy women collided and Warren could smell rosy talcum powder.

"Warren, baby," cried Sister Clara, holding onto his wrist to steady herself. She looked at Miz Bertha for help, but before either of them could muster up something to say, Warren ran.

It was a crazy reaction he knew, but once he put one foot in front of the other he couldn't stop. He tore out of the side door through the church grounds picking up speed on 13th Street. Faster and faster his knees bucked the wind, but he couldn't outrun the memories that flooded him.

His father always had women.

Warren flew down Pennsylvania Avenue, headed over to 14th Street running in the direction of Southeast Washington. Ten, twelve, twenty blocks he ran without pausing to take a breath as the wind whipped at his flesh, making his skin chapped and raw. The pain felt good until his lungs heaved under the pressure and he was forced to a jog. When he finally stopped, his palms pressed into his knees as he tried to catch his breath, and a forgotten newspaper wrestled with a soda can at his feet. For five minutes he stood under the streetlights in front of James' five-story brick apartment building before he had enough wind to yell for him. He had left his cell phone in his car back at the church.

A figure moved behind the second-floor curtain, and then the front window rattled open.

"Dawg, what up?" James hung out the window, and when Warren didn't respond, he threw down the key.

HIS STUDIO WAS WARM and Warren quickly stripped off his suit jacket, removed his tie and parked his shoes in the corner. He could already feel his feet swelling under the pressure of running so many miles in narrow dress shoes. James was a good friend and knew Warren well enough to know that his story would unfold over time, so instead of asking the obvious, he offered him a smoke.

"Pick your poison," James opened a shoebox for Warren containing rolling papers, Dutch cigars and a smoking pipe.

"Dutchie," Warren leaned into the folds of the sofa, allowing the piano playing of Thelonious Monk to soothe him. "Where'd you cop this album?"

James split open the cigar and removed the tobacco, replacing it with marijuana. He was known to have the best vinyl collection in the band and the Monk album he was playing was a rare find. After licking the cigar leaves back together, James sealed the blunt with his lighter and lit.

"If I told you, I'd have to kill you," he took several hits from the blunt.

"Puff, puff, give," barked Warren, reminding his friend of the rules. As James passed the blunt, he knew the time was right to ask Warren what happened. Blowing a cloud into the air, Warren sighed heavily, not knowing where to begin. So he started with Erica.

"What's the problem?" James dusted a few stray ashes from his "Stop Segregation Now" T-shirt and sat back in his seat.

"She doesn't want to quit her job to be with me. I can't quit my job to be with her and all of a sudden the distance isn't working," said Warren, catching him up on the foiled trip, her missing the rehearsal and the space that kept growing.

"Erica's one of the good ones. Just hang in there."

The blunt traveled back and forth between them and once Warren was good and high, he was able to divulge what he overheard at the church.

James coughed. "How do you know that's not just gossip? Church women can be catty."

Warren shook his head, "It's eerie dude, but I felt that shit, soon as I laid eyes on those cats. You know how hard it is to get into Point Academy? I went there and only because of my father's connection. Shar's a fucking secretary. Who's she connected to?"

"Your daddy," James tilted his head.

They had smoked the cigar down to a roach and James offered him the last hit. Warren pulled on it from each angle, giving up when his fingertip burned. He readjusted the pillow at his side, feeling good and high. The memories came.

"Yo, when I'm completely honest with myself, and really allow my brain to breathe, I knew this shit was coming."

James settled back in the armchair opposite Warren. "What you mean?"

"I must have been about ten or eleven. It was an accident really, right after we moved to Chesapeake. By then we had lived in six states in ten years. This was before he was appointed chief of staff, and bought the house on Colorado Avenue. I was always the new kid in school who talked funny, 'cause I picked up accents every time we moved and they were all meshed together. Carrying my horn everywhere didn't help either."

"I didn't have that problem. Anyone who could play the drums at my school was automatically cool."

"Well, I did. The schoolwork was a breeze, so I skipped class a lot. We never lived on base because my old man was too proud for the subsidized housing. I had only been at the school for about a month when I cut class to check out a new Kung Fu flick that everyone was talking about."

"Which one?"

"I don't remember the name but it was a Bruce Lee flick. I didn't have any money so I was planning to sneak in through the back door. Then I spotted a brown Oldsmobile Delta 88, with the same sandy vinyl top as my father's. The motor was dead, and it was the only car parked.

"Yo, I remember creeping through the lot pretending to be Spiderman. The dumpster smelled like a week's worth of sour relish or some shit. It didn't even dawn on me that it could be my father in the car because he was supposed to be in Florida at a special training. Really, I was just goofing off."

James reached for the pack of cigarettes on the coffee table and put one to his lip. "Go on."

"Man, I crept up on the car and when I looked into the window, that fool was sitting in the front seat snaking his tongue inside the mouth of some dark-skinned woman with his hands yanking back her flimsy blouse."

"Get the hell out of here."

"I saw her tits and everything. I was too stunned to move, and he was grunting and telling her shit that men say when they're trying to fuck. Then all of a sudden the woman opened her eyes and stared at me with this look that said, beat it kid. So I did. I made it across the parking lot in time to catch an elderly couple exiting the movies and slipped into the theater between them."

“Have you ever told that story before?”

“Naw, ’cause I spent the next decade of my life convincing myself that it didn’t happen. How the hell could my father poke a woman in the same car my mom used to pick up the groceries?”

“Shit happens, man,” offered James.

“Yeah, I guess.”

Chapter Twenty-Four

Rich Ma, Poor Ma

Erica knocked her hand mirror off her desk, and without looking, she knew the glass had split in two. If her Grandma Queeny were alive she would have said, "Honey, prepare yourself for seven days of mishap, 'cause they sure to follow."

But it was only Monday and Erica couldn't afford a week of bad luck. Since she had missed the wedding rehearsal on Saturday, Warren's demeanor was distant and she felt like an ass for not being there for him. But she had to let Claire see that she was capable of filling Edie's shoes. No matter how much she hated having to choose between her career and her man, her career had to take center stage right now.

But this fact didn't keep her from longing for Warren in the shower, and daydreaming about him over her morning coffee. Most times, she only pretended to listen to her colleagues in staff meetings and working lunches. She felt unsatisfied and unsettled and wished there was a simple way to have it all. How do other women do it?

Her intercom beeped. It was Claire's assistant. Claire wanted to see her right away, so she put her personal thoughts aside and walked down the hall.

"'Morning," Erica lingered in the doorway waiting to be invited in. She wore a magenta wrap dress, hair loose, and make-up just right.

"I got a call from Goldie Gardner this morning. Harriet Lake wants you to accompany her to Los Angeles for the NAACP Image Awards at the end of the week." Claire looked up but her fingers were busy.

"This weekend?"

Claire nodded. "She has two tickets and doesn't want to go alone."

"Couldn't we send an escort? I have to go to a wedding on Saturday," Erica's stomach tightened.

"Are you kidding? Harriet would have a fit. She asked for you."

Harriet Lake was a high profile historian who always got her way. She was the daughter of a prominent Civil Rights leader and went around the country telling their family story. Her memoir spent twenty weeks on the *New York Times* best-sellers list, and there was serious talk of Harpo Productions buying the movie rights. Goldie Gardner was Harriet's editor, and Erica needed to avoid confrontation with her at all cost. Goldie was in Erica's office when her mother called from jail and she couldn't afford for that story to surface.

"You'll be back before Saturday. The awards are on Thursday and Friday. Where's the wedding?"

"D.C."

"Fine, take a red-eye to D.C. Just do whatever to keep her happy. The last thing we need is for her to call Genève on this and you know she would."

Genève Meyers-Sheppard was the Publisher of the company, and if Harriet complained to her than Erica was scorched toast. Translation, this trip was not up for discussion.

Walking back to her office Erica was at least grateful for the red-eye getting her to D.C. before the wedding. Shar had decided to forgo the rehearsal dinner since they had rehearsed a week earlier and was planning to spend the night before with her family in private. So perhaps Warren wouldn't be as cross with her for coming in the morning on the day of the wedding. It was another band-aid and one she would have to live with, but after two weeks without Warren she needed to see him first. How, she wondered, rounding the bend to her office. D.C. was so far. And then, like the flip of a switch, the plan to meet that evening in Philadelphia hatched in her head. It was a crazy idea, but it was all she had. There was a drought between them, and she was thirsting for the smallest details of Warren. Within seconds she was closing her office door and dialing his number.

Warren answered, "Hey, babe."

"What's happening?" After a bit of sweet talk Erica told him her plan.

"What're you, horny?"

"I just miss you," she said. "Come on, let's be spontaneous."

"Okay."

"Serious?" She hadn't expected it to be that easy.

"I have a lot to tell you too," he said. "Shit is really hitting the fan."

"What happened?"

"Just wedding stuff, but I'll tell you in person. Can you be there by eight?"

Erica told him she could.

"Great. I'll send you an email with the hotel details."

She loved how her man always took charge.

For the rest of the morning Erica plowed through her work, conscious of getting out of the office on time. Around lunchtime, the front desk called her.

"Yes," she answered.

"Your mother is here," replied Iris, the front desk attendant.

Erica's mouth dried.

"Should I send her back to your office?"

"No, I'll be right out," she said, biting down on the inside of her jaw. The broken hand mirror was turned face up on her desk and Erica picked it up and slammed it into her wastepaper basket.

While walking from her office to the lobby, Erica prayed that her mother was sober. On the other side of the double glass doors, her mother sat in the far left chair. She wore a wool coat two sizes too large, a yellow knit hat and black oval sunglasses.

"Hey, Slim," she staggered to stand. "Surprised to see me?" Erica dipped her body toward her mother's for an obligatory hug, backing away before she was smothered.

The receptionist pretended to work, but Erica knew she had an ear cocked toward the exchange.

"I need a favor."

"Can you take off those sunglasses?" Erica whispered, and when her mother did, she didn't know which was worse: the dark glasses that made her look like she had something to hide, or seeing her bloodshot eyes, red-rimmed with her breakfast beers.

"Wait here," Erica instructed and by the time she returned with her coat, her mother had slipped the glasses back on. An unlit cigarette dangled from her knotty fingertips as she shifted from one foot to the next.

"Put that away," Erica hissed in front of the elevator. Her mother was fiddling with her knock-off purse when the doors chimed open and Claire Downing cruised through. She was the last person Erica wanted her mother to meet and when they all stood face to face Erica prayed that the floor would swallow her whole.

Struggling to stick on her publicist smile, Erica cleared her throat and made the introduction.

Her mother dropped the cigarette in her purse, wiped her hand on the front of her coat, and then extended it to Claire. "Nice meeting you. Erica talks 'bout you all the time."

"Well, you've raised a lovely young lady," Claire said, shaking her mother's hand. "She's the star of our department."

"That's my daughter," her mother sang, breaking into a wide grin. The way she took credit for an accomplishment that she had nothing to do with burned Erica. Claire moved on. Once they were alone inside the elevator her mother mumbled, "I embarrass you."

"No, Ma." Erica fumbled with her leather gloves. "What's the emergency?"

"Doctor says I've an inflamed stomach. My Medicaid ain't working for some reason and I need the prescription today."

Silence.

"You know I wouldn't have come to your job if it wasn't serious."

Yes she would have. "Next time, call."

They exited the elevator and crossed the large marble lobby.

When they reached the sidewalk, yellow cabs zipped down the three-lane street. Erica asked her mother if she was hungry.

"Naw, just ate."

Since she was outside Erica decided to grab her lunch and ushered her mother down the block toward the delicatessen. But she spotted Bonnie's white Trans Am parked just a few feet away and the sight of the woman in the car took her someplace she'd rather not go.

ERICA DIDN'T QUITE REMEMBER when Bonnie entered their lives. But once she came on the scene, everything changed. Bonnie was unmarried, unemployed and childless, and her presence caused her parents to argue.

"You so far up Bonnie's ass, you can't do shit else," her father would yell before storming out of their home. When he left for the final time, the two women became inseparable. Her mother's attention to the household felt like an afterthought.

There was one particular harsh winter Erica would never forget. The gas had been turned off and her mother hadn't been home for two days. She and her sister were hungry and cold with only a kerosene heater and blankets to keep them warm. Erica knew her mother was at Bonnie's, but their telephone had been disconnected months before. Tired of waiting, she and her sister scrounged drawers and sofa cushions for loose change. By the time they had gathered enough money, it was dark out. But Erica bundled up her younger sister and they walked the five Newark blocks to the nearest public phone. Bonnie answered, passing the phone over, and just the sound of her mother's voice caused Erica's hard shell to crack. What kind of mother would leave her children?

"The gas is off, we're cold and there's nothing to eat. Come home now." Her strong voice had parted into a childish whine, and as the tears stung her cheeks, she hated herself for being so needy.

"You wanna say hello to Bonnie?" Her mother tucked the crisp bills into the pocket of her pea coat and Erica already regretted giving in to her.

"I know you 'on't like her, but she's my only ride."

"I gotta go," Erica shifted away from the memory.

"I'll pay you first of the month." Her mother extended her arms for another hug, but Erica stepped out of reach. All her mother ever had to offer her was hugs and the pretense of some deep love that Erica never felt.

Since Erica was a girl, all she wanted was for her mother to take her shopping at the mall. It wasn't a tall request. Every girl she knew went with their moms on Saturday afternoon and Erica would have loved giggling over a malted shake with her mother in the food court. But it never happened. What Erica received instead was promises of money that was supposed to come from faceless men. There were the long lies and endless embarrassment: the Easter Sunday, when she had to tighten the blinds and be still, so that when her friends came to take her to church, they'd think she wasn't home. The man never came with the Easter clothes money. Or on Christmas, when she would have to invent a list of new things she'd received, when in reality, her mother had sat them down the night before explaining that the tree would be bare. Erica guessed that the Christmas money man never showed up, or if he did, her mother had squandered the cash on her habits. It was frustrating that her mother didn't have a job like the rest of the women on their block. Even Ms. Precious worked and she was blind in the left eye.

While crossing the street, it dawned on Erica that throughout her life she had been waiting for her mother to have her "Ahhh ha" moment and change into the respectable, available, working-class mother that she wanted. After all of these years she was still hoping.

Her mother shouted after her. “Love you, Slim.”

And as Erica dodged between traffic, she wondered which lie was bigger—her mother paying her back or that she actually loved her.

Chapter Twenty-Five

Not Love, but Circumstance

Erica had no overnight bag when she arrived at the Wyndham Hotel at Franklin Plaza in downtown Philadelphia. Her leather tote was stuffed with a new pair of panties and a pantsuit she purchased from an inexpensive boutique along Broadway.

Although the reservation was in Warren's name, she was the first to arrive. Their hotel suite opened into the living area, facing the flat-screen television. The heavy taupe drapery was pushed open, exposing a terrific view of the Philadelphia skyline. The stars looked like crystal droplets suspended against blackness. On the coffee table was a woven basket filled with exotic cheeses, colorful fruits, fancy mixed nuts and tea biscuits tied together with a heart-shaped balloon and the words "I Love You" stenciled in metallic gold. Erica was tickled by the gesture; Warren knew her well.

The plan was for them to meet by eight, spend the night together and wake for work before dawn. But Warren was late, and that made Erica nervous. In the bathroom mirror she checked her reflection several times, fingering through her red hair, adding shiny mascara, dabbing away eye shadow and glossing up the pout of her lips. It had only been nine days since she last saw Warren, but when he finally walked through the door with his cell phone tucked at his ear, cap pulled low on his head, face filled with that crooked smile, brows thick and full, cashmere coat swinging behind him, and his pinstriped suit revealing nothing of his long day, she felt herself lean forward, like a baby who wanted up. It was in his arms that she felt the warmth of his breath and the coolness of his cheek as they tangled themselves around each other. Swaying like driftwood, their bodies moaned sweet nothings to each other through the barrier of unwanted clothing.

Warren made the drinks: Scotch neat for him, red wine swirled for her, and they sipped while catching each other up on the day. "Distant Lover" by Marvin Gaye crooned from the clock radio and Erica held her hand out to Warren for a slow drag. The power of him had already begun gathering between her legs, but she wanted her heat to last until the cry of the morning birds. It had been too long, and even longer if Erica counted when it was good, normal. She needed this. They needed this.

Spinning her and then pulling her close, Warren dipped Erica and hummed the melody in her ear. His voice was hot on her throat and the sensual hard-day-at-work scent drifting from his body made her nipples warm. She wrapped her arms around his waist and tugged on his belt. The moment could have gone on like that forever, but then Warren opened his mouth, and the spell they had created completely shattered.

"Before I forget, my father needs me at the church Friday night. What time are you getting in?"

Erica blinked, not meaning to stutter but did, "F… first thing Saturday morning."

He dropped his hands and Erica tried explaining. "I have to go to L.A. for the Image Awards, but I'll be back in time for…" but then Warren shocked her into silence by swiping at the radio, making it crash to the carpet.

"Unfucking believable. So that's what this is all about. I should have known." Anger mucked the whites of his eyes.

"What?" she asked, feeling as dumb as the word sounded. Warren threw back his drink and moved from the bedroom to the living room.

"So you thought you could fuck away missing my father's wedding."

"No. What are you talking about?"

"You are such a brilliant bullshit artist. I can't believe I didn't see this coming."

"That's not fair."

"Fair? Well what is? It certainly isn't fair that I no longer fit into your plans."

"I didn't say that," she wrung her hands.

"It's never in what you say, Erica," said Warren. The fury in his eyes was palpable.

Over the last few weeks, Warren had been through more than she could even imagine. And when Erica offered to meet him in Philadelphia, it was a relief. She had been his life support for so long, going two weeks without her in the midst of so much chaos made life unbearable. Warren needed Erica. He needed to be close and feel her skin against his if only for a few hours to rejuvenate his soul, so that he could get on with things. Now she wasn't even real to him. Who was this selfish girl standing in front of him? He could hire a hooker to be more available than Erica, and that was the thought that burst the pimple.

"I can't do this anymore," flew from his mouth and he clinched his teeth, choking down the urge to take his words back.

The phrase hung in the air for so long that a few moments passed before Erica really felt the prick from the sting. But when it hit her, it was like a full blast of steamed gas.

"What the fuck are you talking about?" She searched for his eyes, but when he wouldn't give them to her, she dug her fingernails into his arm.

"Stop." He shook her off.

"You stop. This is bullshit."

But his chest sank in defeat. "This hasn't been working."

"That doesn't mean we stop trying. I love you. Don't do this." She reached for his arm again, but this time he pulled out of the way.

"Stop, Erica. Just stop it."

But she didn't, and came at him with a flying fist that he grabbed midair.

"It's too late. Just stop."

"The fuck you mean it's too late." She was shouting but didn't seem to care, and before she could come at him again, Warren picked up his briefcase, mumbling that he was sorry it had to end like this.

"Good luck in L.A. and with the promotion. I really hope you find what you're looking for," he offered, and without a second glance closed the door behind him with a soft thud.

ERICA HAD EVERY INTENTION to run after him but her feet wouldn't move. It was as if a sudden paralysis had come over her. The patter of his footsteps had died, and the elevator must have chimed half a dozen times, while the "I Love You" balloon rocked from side to side mocking her.

"Warren," she called finally, surprising herself with the desperation of her voice, and then she opened the door and ran after him. The elevator was moving too slow, and if she wasn't on the twentieth floor she would have taken the stairs.

In the lobby, she searched the restaurant, the bar and every lounge chair scattered throughout the floor.

"Where's the parking garage?" she asked a bell hop in a red and black uniform. He pointed her to the right. Now she was running like her life depended on it, with wild tears dampening her cheeks. *Don't do this Warren*, she repeated over and over again. Opening the door to the parking area, she saw two men dressed in identical uniforms. One had a cigarette behind his ear.

"Did a man come for a red Yukon Denali? Tall guy, brown skin, long coat," she started describing, not caring that her face was surely blackened with mascara.

"Yes ma'am. Pulled off a few minutes ago," said Mr. Cigarette, while the other reached into his breast pocket for a tissue. It was then that the cold from the cement registered, and Erica realized that she had left the hotel room in her stocking feet. She asked the man if she could have his cigarette, allowing him to light it. Hugging herself on the metal bench, she inhaled hard as the men rushed back and forth, moving cars.

The scent of motor oil made her think of her father, and just like that she was back in her house on Monroe Street in Newark, standing barefoot on the shiny hardwood floors. Her ten-year-old shoulders pressed against the frosted-glass vestibule door, blocking her father from leaving, and like then, the man she loved with everything still went.

PART 2

I used to want the words "she tried" on my tomb-stone, now I want "she did it."
Katherine Dunham

To be a great musician, you've got to be open to what's new, what's happening at the moment. You have to be able to absorb it if you're going to continue to grow and communicate.
Miles Davis

Chapter Twenty-Six
Monroe Street

Erica could remember the day her father walked out on them. Jazmine had stayed home from school that morning with a sore throat, so she dawdled in both directions alone. It was a brisk autumn afternoon, and tri-colored leaves covered the lawns of her neighbors as she sauntered from her after-school stop at the library. Even though it wasn't late, the sky was getting dark; the Sunday before Erica had turned back their clocks to observe Daylight Savings Time. It had been her job to adjust all of the timepieces, but the one in the kitchen was too high, and she had to wait for her father to take it down. Ms. Hauptmann was her teacher, and she was just settling into fifth grade hoping that the pimples rising on her cheeks were just a passing phase. She had a crush on Javier, a Puerto Rican in the sixth grade, and she was fantasizing about what it would feel like to kiss him when she slipped the key from around her neck and unlocked the front door.

The soap opera *Guiding Light* was on, and Reva and Philip Spaulding were laughing about shaking up a blue blooded party. But their glee didn't have any effect on her mother, who was sitting limp on the peach floral couch. She was still wearing her nightgown, the sheer blue one that she wouldn't part with even though the hem had come loose against her left knee. Her eyelids were puffy and her hair was soggy against her forehead. Her shoulders sagged away from the sofa.

"What's the matter with you?" Erica kicked off her oxford shoes and tightened the band around her bushy ponytail.

"Nothin'," her mother uttered, but her hand shook as she stretched the remote and turned down the volume. "How was your day?"

"What's wrong?" Erica could feel a heaviness pressing down on them like thick smoke.

"There ain't no easy way to tell you this. I already told Jazmine." Her mother kept her eyes trained on the hardwood floor.

"Tell me what?"

"Your daddy's moving out."

"Huh?" The six Now and Laters Erica had sucked down on the way home felt like gallstones in her belly. "What're you talking about?"

"Leavin'," her mother's voice broke and fresh tears fell. "I 'on't know where. He'll be here in a little bit to get his things."

"So you have to make him stay." Erica clenched her fist.

"Girl, I can't make that man do nothing that he 'on't want to do. You might as well go start your homework. Ya sister's upstairs lying down."

The first floor of their home was railroad style, so Erica had to pass through the dining room to get to the breakfast area where she did her work. As she unzipped her book bag she heard her mother moving the seat cushions of the loveseat. Then she heard the cap twist. The tilt and sip to her mother's lips was silent but Erica knew she was drinking, and resentment burned through her chest like a smashed bottle of hot pepper sauce.

It was her mother's fault that her father was leaving. If only she would act right, stop running the streets with Bonnie, get a job, try harder so he wouldn't get so angry. Erica tugged on her ponytail and wondered how they would survive without him?

She idolized her father and wanted to be just like him. Whenever she asked him a question he knew the answer, never needing to go to a dictionary to look up the spelling or meaning of a word. It was him who sparked Erica's long-time affair with reading. Once a month, he took her to the black-owned bookstore on Broad Street in Newark, picking out books on slavery and black historical figures.

"Don't ever stop learning," he would say while explaining the material to her at a level that she understood.

Every Saturday she worked with him in the garage tallying up receipts, mopping oil and sorting auto parts. Over turkey sandwiches stuffed with sour cream potato chips, they discussed poetry by Langston Hughes, Claude McKay and Sonia Sanchez. Jazz was always playing in the shop and her father would stop her in mid-sentence, asking, "What instrument do you hear?"

"Trumpet?"

"Close, alto sax, baby," he'd tease, ruffling her hair. Their relationship was easy and free. They were thick as peanut butter, two halves of the same whole. Erica was his main girl. So this business of him leaving had to be a lie and Erica decided to pretend like her mother hadn't said anything at all

At the table, she turned her attention to the fraction worksheet that Ms. Hauptmann assigned. But after two problems, the equations bled into each other. She couldn't concentrate because her stomach hurt and her ears were cocked for the sound of her dad's tires rolling into the driveway. Every noise made her jump: a basketball bouncing, teenagers talking mess, horns honking, neighbors calling their dogs in from the yard. Her nerves were muddled and tangled and she knew the only thing that would calm her was a word search puzzle. So she pulled her book from her bag and started seeking words associated with the desert.

Three puzzles later, his key turned in the door and Erica was out of her seat, running to greet him.

"Daddy," she shouted, throwing her arms around his waist. She was growing like corn stalk and her head reached the top of his chest. As he kissed her forehead she could smell spearmint on his breath. When he pulled away his manila-colored face looked oily and long. His posture, which was usually so erect and poised, was droopy and unsure. Something was indeed wrong.

"Did your mother tell you?" The tweed cap he wore was so low Erica could barely see his brown eyes, and his navy work jacket had a bleach stain on the elbow patch, because her mother was terrible at laundry.

"Tell me what?" she feigned innocence.

"I told her, but she need to hear it from you," her mother's voice invaded their privacy, and Erica cut her eyes up at the ceiling wishing her mother would just disappear.

"You can't do nothing right," he grumbled on his way upstairs with Erica on his heels like a loyal puppy. She followed him down the long hallway to the back bedroom that used to be her parents' but was now just her father's because her mother slept with her. The tattered suitcase that she and Jazmine took to Grandma Queeny's house on weekends sat at the foot of the bed, and the old zipper stretched and groaned under the weight of his wardrobe.

"Where are you going, Daddy?" Erica asked when he reached under the bed for his second pair of work boots. Even with the evidence in front of her she still refused to believe.

"I'm moving into the apartment on top of the garage."

"But why, Daddy?"

He sat heavily on the edge of the bed and removed his cap. A misty sheen had gathered in his eyes. "Things haven't been right between your mother and me in a long time."

"So, she can keep sleeping with me. I won't complain. Just don't go," she whined and he opened his arms to her. Erica fell against her father and clung to him so tight it was hard for her to breathe. They rocked for what felt like forever and all of the fear that had been rising since she walked in from school poured out.

"Ta... take me with you."

"I can't, E-bird. Girls need their mother," he squeezed her shoulder. "I'll still come get you on Saturdays to work at the garage. Nothing will change." He rose to his feet and picked up the heavy bag.

"But it will."

Erica pleaded with him down the long hallway and on the stairs. By the time he set the suitcase down in the living room, she was beside herself, and had thrown her skinny frame and blocked the entrance to the vestibule door.

"Come on baby, I'll be back soon," her father promised, but his words held no value and when Erica moved from the door she threw herself on him again. The commotion must have woken up Jazmine because she ran down the steps. When she saw what was going on she joined Erica's tantrum. Both girls carried on with fever. Jazmine was on the floor holding his legs, and without thinking Erica kicked the suitcase over and stomped it with her foot.

"Enough," her mother intervened. "Girls, you can't cage a man who wanna be free."

"What are you talking about, Gweny? You ain't got no cause to speak. This is on you," he pointed his finger.

"You're the one leavin'," she replied, and her sad eyes hung heavy and the room fell quiet.

Erica was thinking about the Jets season, which had already begun. How could she watch a football game without her father? Right before Thanksgiving, they would turn their attention to basketball. They didn't have a favorite team, so they rooted for coaches and players. That year, they were going for the 76ers.

"What about the game? You promised to take me to Philadelphia," Erica screeched.

Her father rubbed her back and then wrapped his callused hands around the suitcase for the final time.

The air was humid and stuffy when he kissed her cheek goodbye, the tears so blinding and hot, she didn't even feel his lips. Watching him through the white screen door, Erica held Jazmine's hand while tattooing a picture of her father on her heart. She strained her ears for some type of music, something to remember him by as the engine of his Chevy Impala turned over. But there was none. The car pulled away from her life as silent as a hearse heading for a funeral. Erica was left unprotected, and fully in charge for the first time. She was 10 years old.

After her father's departure, Erica's mother didn't leave the house for days. She sat crossed legged in her queen-sized bed, in that same blue nightgown, chain-smoking menthol cigarettes, her dingy bedroom covered in a constant film of smoke. She was drunk all the time. It took Erica a week before she found all the secret locations where her mother kept her stash: in the wedges of the sofa, between the top mattress and box spring, behind a picture frame on the mantel, on the bookshelf covered by a book, or under music sheets in the piano stool. On the tenth day, when the gown was soiled and her mother had begun to smell like spoiled squash, eight-year-old Jazmine ran the bath until it was brimming with soapy water, and Erica summoned up her strongest voice.

"Ma, go get in the tub."

Their mother mumbled something incoherent, so Erica and Jazmine flipped back the crusty comforter and pulled her from the bed. Between her pillow and the wooden bed frame was another bottle, and while Jazmine watched over her mother in the tub, Erica went to the kitchen and poured what was left of it down the drain. After washing and braiding her mother's hair, Erica changed the linen, aired out the room, and then fixed egg sandwiches and fried bologna for dinner. They ate on T.V. trays in front of the set.

As the weeks drifted on, her mother slept later and later. It became Erica's job to wake and dress her sister for school. Most days when the girls returned home, their mother was either in the bed where they had left her or gone. If she was out, there was no telling when she'd return, because she never left notes and they didn't have a telephone. It could be an hour or days, and that scared Erica just as much as the mice hiding in the dark crevices of their home.

Her mother owed everybody money. Since the telephone was disconnected, men often came banging on their front door, unannounced to collect her debt. When this happened Erica and Jazmine ran what they called "code badman," a system they devised to keep the visitors from knowing that they were home alone. Whenever the bell rang, the girls would creep into the basement and see who it was through a small floor window.

They wouldn't dare move until it was clear that the person was gone. It was always a man looking for her mother, and once Erica heard a guy threatening her through the mail slot, calling her a bitch and shouting that if she didn't have his money when he came next week, "I'm a slice that pretty little face."

Petrified, Erica disconnected the doorbell, and later threw up in her sleep. Nights alone were unnerving. Jazmine would sleep in Erica's bed, with the television playing all night long. Most times their stomachs were empty.

As an adult searching for forgiveness, Erica came to the conclusion that her mother couldn't help who she was. Gweny had come from a long line of poor women, who raised their children as single parents, and chased away the Section 8 blues with twenty-four-ounce cans of malt liquor, Newport cigarettes and prescription pills. None of the women in her mother's family worked. Instead they found clever ways to live off of the government. They soothed themselves with soap operas, artery-clogging foods, street drugs and number-running, while passing their dysfunctional baton down to their daughters, much like wealthy families willed trust funds. At an early age, Erica decided she wouldn't continue the legacy, and her father's mother, Grandma Queeny, was the person who co-signed that determination.

Grandma Queeny could have easily turned her back on the girls when her son left. But she picked them up every weekend, making sure they had dance lessons, God, and home-cooked meals. Once a month, she took the girls to the Newark Museum for culture, and taught them how to make a way, "even when you feel like you're surrounded by dead end streets." She died when Erica was a senior in high school, bequeathing the girls her house and money for college. Erica was left in charge again.

"Peanuts or pretzels?" the airline attendant broke into Erica's thoughts. She was on her flight back from Los Angeles and accepted the pretzels, hoping that it was something she could keep in her stomach. Everything she tried to eat over the past five days just sat stubbornly on her belly, and she had run out of Rolaids. The trip to Los Angeles had been a disaster, certainly not worth the fiasco with Warren. His words, "I can't do this anymore" and "I hope you find what you're looking for," permeated her every turn.

Warren was what she needed, why couldn't he see that? She was so sorry. The last thing she wanted to do was hurt him. Things had gotten out of hand, and perhaps she had taken him for granted, but she never wanted this. Warren was her sun, soil, hydration and vegetation. Her body was retaliating by refusing to operate without him. Not being able to hold her food down was only half of it. She wasn't sleeping and the back of her neck was stiff. Five days was the longest they had ever spent without talking, and the mental distance was nauseating. She missed his voice, wanted him to comfort her and tell her things would be all right. While in Los Angeles she had worked up the nerve to call him from her hotel room, but when he didn't pick up she couldn't explain her hopelessness to his answering machine, and killed the line.

HARRIET LAKE HAD NEEDED constant hand-holding, making Erica feel more like a babysitter than a powerhouse publicist. To make matters worse, Harriet lost the Image Award when she was expected to be a shoe-in. After the defeat she reverted to Ms. Impossible Bitch, barking orders and nit-picking at everything: the towncar smelled smoky and she was allergic; room service didn't come when she called so Erica had to complain to the manager; her dress was too tight so Erica had to find a local seamstress. But the soot to fill her lungs was when Harriet demanded that she escort her to the Beverly Center to find a birthday present for her daughter. It was the last day of the trip and Erica's patience had puttered out, so she told Harriet, "Go ahead, I'll be waiting right here in the car."

Forty-five minutes later, Harriet called Claire hysterical, complaining that Erica had left.

Claire called Erica livid. "I told you to make her happy. Where is your focus?" and rattled off ways to rectify the situation but Erica was too pissed to take any of Claire's suggestions. Furious, she stormed into the mall, where she found Harriet having an ice cream.

"Oh, there you are, dear," Harriet said, and asked if she wanted a cone. It took all of Erica's strength not to smash the bowl in Harriet's face, and then dump the creamy mess in her blue-black hair.

Chapter Twenty-Seven
Stormy Me

Several weeks worth of clothes were piled in a heap on the bedroom floor. The kitchen sink overflowed with takeout containers and dirty coffee mugs. Loose papers were scattered about, and she must have tracked in something from outside because her bare feet kept sticking to the wood floor. But Erica had no intention of cleaning. Getting dressed for work took all the energy she could muster. That Monday morning, she slipped into the first thing she came across—black cargo pants and a faded v-neck. Not quite Monday morning work attire, but she dressed. Erica fixed her hair in a bun and stuffed a bottle of aspirin in her jacket pocket. On the five block walk to the train station, Erica gnawed at the skin on the inside of her jaw, begging for the physical pain to cancel out her internal suffering. She felt like a bicycle tire with a slow leak.

The train clanked into the subway station, and Erica battled for standing room. In the reflection of the train window, Erica recognized that she was the poster of misery. She hadn't slept more than two hours at a time for six days, and her skin had sprouted a blotchy pimple on her jaw bone just left of her chin. Even her dark sunglasses couldn't masquerade her gloom as she rocked with the train, staring at nothing. Every movement was robotic: get off train, cross the street, spin with the momentum of the office's revolving door, morph from weepy mess into a no nonsense publicist who ate difficult reviewers for dinner. But this time, she hadn't transformed once her feet stepped on the marbled lobby floor. It was a first.

"'Morning, Iris," she greeted the fourth floor receptionist, and shuffled down the hall. In the publicity department, Erica had to step over the large boxes of books lining both sides of the floor to get inside her office. She quietly cursed the assistants for not putting the books in the storage room. Gloom circled her movements, and by the time she got settled behind her desk, she wasn't surprised to see that depression had hitched a ride. She could feel it clinging to the gray walls, lounging on her bookshelves, swimming in the lake shown in the photograph, and attaching itself to the headlines in the *Daily News* that she had stretched across her desk. Erica could have been mistaken for a woman in an anti-depressant commercial. Perhaps that was what she needed: a little blue pill to make it all go away.

The telephone rang. It was the bail bondsman reminding her that her mother had court the next morning. Thanking him, Erica promised that she would have her mother there on time and jotted down the address. After hanging up, she swore again because now she had to take a personal day. Her mother couldn't be trusted to go to court alone, and Erica wasn't going to be stuck with the bill if she didn't show. While typing the e-mail request to Claire, her assistant, Prudence, knocked and entered.

"Sorry about the boxes, we're working on finding a place for them now." She looked Erica up and down. "You all right?"

"Yeah, why?" Erica wiped her hands on her pants.

"You look a little, I don't know, not like yourself," said Prudence. Erica assured her that she was fine.

"Well, here's the Jarvis update. Don't forget he's coming in to meet with you and Claire in an hour." Prudence gave her a thick file and took her leave.

Erica had forgotten about the meeting, but as she flipped through the pages, her fingertips started to lose their numbness, and a surge of energy slowly entered her body. Jarvis' story was one that had excited her when the sales teams presented the book at the spring conference. Most of the books Erica worked on were chosen for her because she could handle high-profile authors, or had key relationships with media outlets that wouldn't give ordinary books a play. Titles that she personally salivated over didn't cross her lap often, especially those authored by an African-American.

LaVal Jarvis grew up on the south side of Chicago. His mother was a heroin addict, and at the age of five he witnessed his father stab her seventeen times, killing her at a bus stop. His father was arrested for the murder, and LaVal became a ward of the court. He began selling drugs around age 10, and by fifteen he headed the largest fraction of the Billy Goat gang in Chicago. A jealous rival snitched, resulting in his arrest. In his memoir, *365 Degrees of Change: My Life on and After the Streets*, Jarvis explained how being mentored by strong men during that two-year sentence at a juvenile detention center saved his life. Once released, Jarvis abandoned his control of the streets and moved to Dayton, Ohio, with an older cousin. There he received his GED, went to college and graduate school, receiving his law degree earlier this year. Claire had kept her in the loop while the project was developing and now it was finally on her desk, providing a much-needed distraction.

"Erica, reception just called. LaVal Jarvis is in the lobby. Want me to get him?" Prudence offered.

"I'll walk over. Confirm that Claire is ready for the meeting."

Erica opened her top drawer but realized that she hadn't replaced her hand mirror. Instantly, she thought of Warren and abruptly jumped out of her chair before a new flood of emotions could catch her. While hurrying down the hall, she moved a few bobby pins around to tighten her makeshift bun.

In the reception area, LaVal was sitting with his legs crossed, flipping through the fall catalog. They had met last week at Hunter College, and just like then, he was suited up. LaVal was a good-looking man, muscular and tall, with skin the color of sand and penny-sized dimples. When he moved, it was with enough swagger to establish street creditability, peppered with just the right mix of charisma that put white folks at ease. But even under his expensive cologne, Erica could sense a grittiness about him that she wasn't sure she trusted.

"It's good to see you again." She extended her hand.

LaVal eyed her a second too long, and then replied, "Likewise."

WHILE WALKING DOWN THE hall, they made small talk about his flight and the weather in Chicago. Once they arrived in Claire's office, Claire hugged and gushed over LaVal like she was his professional mother. It was her way, and explained why everyone was comfortable in Claire's presence.

"It's so nice to finally meet you," she held him at arm's length. As usual she was impeccably dressed, wearing a bone suit and snakeskin pumps. Erica was pitifully underdressed, and quickly found her seat, hoping that the wrinkles in her shirt went unnoticed.

Claire gestured for LaVal to sit, and the show began. "We're all so excited to have the opportunity to work on a book with such emotional depth. Your story is phenomenal."

LaVal gave her a schoolboy's blush. "I just hope the public likes it."

"They'll love it," she continued, lathering him with charm. Karen entered holding a stack of papers and, on Claire's nod, handed a stapled pack to each of them.

"We've outlined your publicity campaign from start to finish. I wanted you to have every bit of your publicity tour in one place so that there are no surprises."

Erica took her copy already knowing the contents because she had written it.

"Eight cities in ten days?" LaVal looked up.

"It's important to keep you moving so that we can create buzz and momentum," Claire smiled, and then walked him through each page, illustrating how she hoped the campaign would play out. She was so awesome on her feet that Erica got lost watching her in action. That was how she aspired to be.

"Well, I really appreciate all of your hard work," said LaVal, and Claire stood clasping both of his hands with hers.

"Our best work is yet to come."

The two hugged again, and Erica offered to show LaVal out.

"So you're my publicist?" he asked, once they fell in step.

"Yes, I'll be managing your campaign."

"Well, I think we need to get to know each other a little better before I entrust my whole writing career to your hands. How's lunch?"

Erica wasn't in the mood. "I'm out of the office tomorrow," she pressed the button for the elevator while glancing down at her feet. How could she have come to work in her old ballerina flats?

"Then Wednesday," he said, sounding like a man who was used to women giving him what he wanted. Without waiting for a response he stepped into the elevator.

ERICA MOPED BACK THROUGH the halls, and just as she was about to turn into her office, Karen told her that Claire wanted her again. An instant nervousness flitted through her. The meeting was no doubt about Harriet. She could feel butterflies flapping their wings in her stomach. She should have stopped at the bathroom.

Claire was ending a call when she entered, and Erica sat waiting anxiously, like a child summoned to the principal's office after a schoolyard fight.

"You know about the call from Harriet." Claire rested her weight on her fingertips, letting her words take effect. "She said you were neglectful and difficult to work with in Los Angeles. She didn't call Genève so we got lucky, but what happened?"

"She was just impossible." Erica shifted under the microscope.

"But you knew that going in. What made this trip different?"

Erica was tempted to let loose her personal problems and sob on Claire's shoulders, but this wasn't the time. She also didn't want Claire to think that she was taking advantage because of the intimacy that they shared in Atlanta.

"My mother's been ill," the lie left her tongue before she could think it through, "and I've just been worried. I put in for a personal day tomorrow so that I can take her to an appointment. I hope that's okay." Erica raised her chin, to Claire's sympathetic eyes.

"Anything I can do?"

"No, tomorrow off is enough."

"Are you sure that's the only thing wrong?" Claire's eyes swept over her attire but Erica rolled back her shoulders and pretended not to notice. She wanted out of the hot seat and fast.

"That's it. It won't happen again. I'll send Harriet flowers and a little note before I leave today."

"Now you're thinking," Claire continued to study Erica, and then added, "Edie is out, and you're up to bat. We need your A game, kiddo."

Erica nodded her head, and assured Claire that she would have it, but on the inside she didn't feel so confident.

Work was suffering and she couldn't believe she had lied to Claire. But if she didn't take her mother to court then she wouldn't go. Being the responsible one was wearing Erica thin. Pamper the authors at work, manage up to Claire, manage down to Prudence, manage the expectations of the editors because their books were sure to flop, stay numb towards dad, send money to Jazmine, bail mom from the slammer. When did she get a break? For what felt like her entire life, she was jammed taking care of everybody. And now, in the midst of her heart vomiting all over her chest, she was still the go-to seamstress stitching up everyone's problems.

Erica returned to her office to grab her coat, and left for lunch with a cloudy head. Warren was the first man she had truly loved. Those puppy-eyed relationships in high school and college never panned out because Erica wouldn't allow them.

She had only one goal in mind—to be successful. There was no future in birthing babies by different daddies, and trumping up a fake disability so the government would take care of her with low income housing. The below poverty check each month was not good enough for Erica, and her focal point never wavered.

Warren was the first man who pried her open without permission, kissed away her shame, and dismissed that which she deemed ugly. The connection between them was fierce, and she felt revered by his attention and care. He was her best friend, that person she could call and tell that one quick thing. She missed him. A fresh batch of tears gathered as she tore through the revolving doors, and with each step she tried keeping her emotions behind her fogging sunglasses. But like everything else in her world, it proved impossible.

Chapter Twenty-Eight
On With It

A lump the size of a child's fist had been pressed against Warren's chest for the past three days, and he had done everything he could to distract himself from the breakup with Erica. He took on a difficult project at work, and went to Sweet Melodies on Tuesday. He went again on Wednesday and played even though it was amateur night. That morning he reorganized his record collection and cut back the leaves of his houseplants for a little natural therapy, but nothing worked. The mass stayed, and despite his best efforts, their break-up scene waltzed through his head more times than he wanted to admit.

When Erica proposed the Monday night getaway Warren had agreed, even though it meant missing yet another gig at Sweet Melodies, simply because she had asked him to. With everything going on, he never got to tell her about Shar's boys and what he had overheard at the church. Besides, he had missed her, and he would have gone if only for the pleasure of smelling her hair. Warren went with the hope of rekindling that spontaneous urgency that made being together necessary. Leaving Philadelphia was a knee-jerk reaction to her deception. Erica knew about the trip to Los Angeles and she should have told him right away, instead of hiding behind her creation of a romantic fantasy in which to deposit her bad news. What upset him more was her not being there for him. The red-eye to D.C. was bullshit. With Erica's track record something would have come up and she would've missed the plane, and even with that he still loved her.

The revelation made him pause, before slipping a 12-year-old bottle of Glenlivet from a brown paper bag. Ilsa, his cleaning lady, had come for her weekly visit and his apartment smelled like orange Pledge. He hoped that a spotless house and single malt scotch would make him forget his troubles. If only momentarily.

His keys dropped in the basket on the kitchen counter followed by his money clip, wallet and the ring with the two diamond stud that his father had given him for his twenty-first birthday. In the top right cabinet, he reached for the brandy snifter. It was next to Erica's favorite cobalt wine glass that they had picked up at a street fair. Originally they had bought two glasses, but once they got home Erica started dancing with a music video, accidentally knocking one to the floor. Warren pushed the remaining glass to the back of the cabinet until it was out of sight, cursing the memory.

When he was honest he had to admit that he had never devoted himself to a woman the way he had Erica. Not his high school crush or his college sweetheart. The wounded look she threw at him just before he closed the hotel's door was what seemed to torture him most, because he had seen the essence of it before. He called it her love burdened look, because in her eyes was a tender ache that magnified her raw feelings, stripping away all the shields that she usually placed to protect her soul. Hurting Erica was the last thing he wanted, but he was at his wits end from trying to make them work. His whole life seemed to be malfunctioning, and it was wearing him thin, like tattered soles on a pair of old shoes.

Cracking the bottle, he coated two ounces of the butterscotch colored mixture into his glass, nosed it with a swirl, and then sipped. In his kitchen, Warren longed for the old Erica whose appetite was greater than his, and who would go out on the weekends in a simple ponytail without make-up. He missed the girl who tried to outdrink him at the bar, and later let him love her in the backseat of his car.

With his glass in hand, he walked into the living room. He hadn't watched a single basketball game that week, and was not in the mood to play his trumpet, so he opted to listen to music instead. A female saxophone player named Tia Fuller sat in with his band last week, and she played with such depth that Warren bought her CD on the spot. He was rewinding the second cut of the album when his home line rang. The caller-ID read unavailable, but his instinct told him to answer.

"Salam."

"Hello?"

"Salam, brother."

"Billie?" Warren put his snifter down on the coaster.

"Oh, it's so good to hear your voice," she said.

"What's going on?" Warren pressed pause on the music. He couldn't remember the last time they had actually spoken. Billie had been on location for over a year working on a documentary about the dangers involved crossing the Sahara desert.

"Ready for Saturday? I'm so bummed I'm not going to be able to make it back because of our deadline to finish shooting. The producer has already threatened to pull the plug because we're behind three weeks. Dad understood but I still feel badly."

Warren wondered if she knew about the boys. He had so much to ask her, but she cut into his thoughts, "I have some big news. I was going to wait until I saw you but I don't know when that will be. I'm heading to Spain next Wednesday to start some editing."

"You don't let any grass grow under your feet," Warren said, borrowing one of their mother's favorite lines, and Billie laughed out loud.

"I'm engaged."

"You're kidding."

"It can't be that hard to believe with all of my fine qualities," she joked, but it was really only a modest tease. Billie was smart, good-looking and free-spirited. A killer combination that would make any man fall fast and hard. "His name is Enrique. He was the Boom Operator on the film."

"Well I hope he's a good man. You know mom always put me in charge of keeping you safe."

"Yes, and I'm so happy. I don't know when we'll marry but...we're expecting a baby in six months." Her voice rose with excitement.

"I'm going to be an uncle?"

"It'll slow me down a little. Okay, a lot. But I'm ready for the change."

"Are you coming home to have it? When will I see you?"

"We're thinking about coming back. I want the baby to have dual citizenship. Enrique is from Spain, so I think that's where we'll settle. He lives right along the coast."

The conversation continued quickly. Billie caught him up on all of the details of the film—the actors, the hassles with the crew. Billie was the same fast-talking girl, jumping from one idea to the next. Warren could barely keep up. Before he knew it, her calling card had run down to one minute. He hadn't gotten a word in edgewise and he wanted to tell her about Erica and ask her what she knew about Shar's sons.

"Give Erica my love. I'll call again soon. Take care of Dad," she said right before the line went dead.

He was going to be some little person's uncle, and with that he held up his glass, and toasted to their health. Finally there was something lovely to contemplate.

Chapter Twenty-Nine

There's No Place Like Home

It wasn't often that Erica returned to the house where she grew up, but every time she did, Monroe Street seemed smaller. Erica guessed it was her father who had kept up with the payments on the property. Otherwise, Erica was sure they would have been forced out a long time ago. The once desirable area had suffered when the middle class fled for the surrounding suburbs. The house located directly across the street had been abandoned because of fire. Planks of fat wood had nailed it shut. Ms. Frances, the neighborhood gossip who lived next door, had died a few years ago and left the house to her son Nelson, who was in and out of jail. The roof of her house sagged so far to one side, it looked as if the whole house was about to cave. Erica remembered the countless times Ms. Frances dished on her family, pegging Erica as the girl who would just end up pregnant. How ironic that now, Ms. Frances' house took first place in being the worst eyesore in the neighborhood.

The shrubs in front of her mother's house were overgrown, but the small patch of lawn looked good for this time of year. Erica slowly walked up the steps, instinctively avoiding the third one with the loose brick.

"Ma," she called through the mail slot, then banged on the door with her fist. The bell hadn't worked since she disconnected it when she was ten years old. She heard bedroom slippers scuffling toward the door. Two locks were released before her mother slid back the metal chain.

"Slim?" her mother mumbled, casting her eyes on the mosaic vestibule floor. Her ear-length hair that used to be full of luster and weight stood lifeless and transparent. A cigarette burned in one hand, while the other held up the stretched-out scrubs that served as pajama pants. The white T-shirt she wore hung past her waist, and her braless breasts shifted from one side to the other. Why wasn't she dressed and ready to go? Erica bit back her attitude as her mother moved to let her in.

Their living room always felt masculine, with wooden mini blinds and mahogany crown molding. Grammar-school pictures of Erica and her sister sat on the mantelpiece, and dusty sheet music was opened on the piano rack, though Erica knew no one had played since she had moved out. After tapping a few keys, she headed to the sofa. The only songs she could remember how to play were "Mary Had a Little Lamb" and a few bars from "Für Elise."

"Why aren't you dressed?" Erica reached for the table lamp with golden tassels hanging from the shade like fancy earrings. In the light she gasped; her mother's face was swollen and bruised as if someone had kicked her with steel toe shoes.

"What happened to you?"

The green plastic cup her mother now clutched found her lips. Erica watched as she gulped with thirst.

"I fell." Fuzz clung to her upper lip, which was bloated like mushrooms and caked with dried blood. Her left eye had a purplish ring around it and was slightly closed.

She was definitely lying. "Somebody hit you?"

"Can't go nowhere lookin' like this." Her mother tipped her cup to her mouth again.

"Well, I don't have ten thousand dollars to give the courts, so you're going," Erica snatched the cup of beer from her mother's hand and poured it down the kitchen sink, despite her mother's protests. Erica's heart thumped wildly against her blouse. Part of her wanted to know who, where, and what regarding the bruises, but most of her didn't. This wasn't the first time she saw her mother black-and-blue and Erica wouldn't be sucked into playing detective today. Her task was to get her mother to court. She couldn't shift her eye from the objective.

A roach scurrying across the kitchen counter made Erica jump. She wanted to smash the bug dead, but lost her chance as it ran for a crack in the wall. The yellow paint that had been so bright in her childhood had dulled and was covered with a slimy film of grime and dust. Erica was tempted to sneak up to her old bedroom and reminisce, but she had to get them moving.

Back in the living room, her mother sat on the arm of the peach floral sofa that needed to be reupholstered. A rust-colored stain had bled through two of the burgundy flowers, and the cushions were worn thin.

"What if they keep me?" Her voice was meek.

"Don't do this to me, Ma. The bondsman said you just had to show up and they would drop the charges." Erica crossed her arms, realizing that she hadn't even removed her coat.

"I can't stay here no more. I need a vacation." Her mother sounded exasperated.

Erica opened her mouth, tempted to counter with, "your whole life is a vacation, you don't work, what is it that you do all day exactly," but she stopped the sass from rolling off her tongue. This wasn't the time and they needed to go.

"Things bad 'round here now." Her mother's eye jumped, and tears dribbled. "Gunshots as common as flies on shit. Can't hardly walk to the store no more."

Erica helped her mother to her feet, trying not to look at her, but the desperation in her mother's eyes couldn't be missed. Then her tongue betrayed her as it always did when her mother's problems were shoved into her lap. She didn't know what possessed her to say it. Perhaps misery really did love company.

"Get dressed and pack a small bag, Ma. After court, you can stay a few days with me."

"Oh, Slim, thank you." She moved towards Erica for a hug, but Erica stopped her.

"The conditions are no drinking. This is a dry trip," she warned.

"Whatever you want," Gweny hopped up with new energy. "Whatever you want."

Chapter Thirty
Mommy Dearest

When the prosecutor dropped the charges, Erica's mother reacted as if she had just beaten a murder rap, throwing her hands in the air crying and thanking Jesus.

"I told you all you had to do was show up," Erica said, as she helped Gweny with her jacket and purse. After signing a few papers they were free to go, and headed out to the street. Bonnie hadn't shown, and Erica was happy when the judge issued a bench warrant for her arrest. Maybe if Bonnie was behind bars, her mother could get her act together. All she could do was hope.

Penn Station Newark was only a few blocks from the courthouse, but her mother insisted that she couldn't walk, so Erica hailed a taxicab.

"I sure appreciate it. My knees won't make it that far," she cranked the cab door closed behind her, and Erica wanted her mother to stop acting old and disabled. Something was always bothering her. If it weren't her knees it was arthritis, a bad shoulder or sore back. Was she ever just all right? Erica had to dig way back into her childhood just for a glimpse of her mother pain free.

When they reached the train station, Erica stopped at the deli kiosk and bought them both Pepsi-Colas. When she was younger, her mother would tell her that the soda was the next best thing to a beer, and as she watched her twist the cap and take a long slurp, Erica wondered if she remembered sending her on the countless trips for the replacement beverage.

"This feels like a real vacation." Sunglasses were perched on her nose, and covered the majority of her marks and welts. Her mother attempted to blend some lipstick on her twisted lip, but it did not mask the left leaning sag to her mouth when she spoke. Seeing it shot a pang through Erica. Turning away, she studied the pigeons snacking on crumbs. After standing on the platform for five minutes, a train slowed into the station. Passengers were scarce in the middle of the day, and they had no problem getting seats next to each other. Her mother spent the thirty-minute ride looking out the window.

In New York, they caught the subway to Harlem. Erica strained to lug her mother's postage stamp canvas bag.

"I haven't been up here in a long time," her mother said, stopping at the top landing of the subway stairs winded and breathing hard. She leaned against the rail for support, fumbling in her pocketbook for a cigarette.

"When're you going to quit?" Erica watched two teenaged girls passing in high-heeled boots swing their asses hard, searching for some attention from the three boys holding up the corner.

"One thing at a time, Slim." She cupped her palms and lit. After a few drags, they were on the move again. As they passed Sylvia's Soul Food restaurant, Erica offered to get her mother a plate but she declined.

"My arthritis is flaring up. I just wanna get to your house and get out of these clothes."

She was dressed neatly in a pair of wool straight-leg slacks and matching flats. Her leather coat had large silver buckles

"I'm glad you came."

"Thanks, Slim. That means a lot," her mother said, coming in for one of her bone crushing hugs. Erica surprised herself when she allowed it.

"There is nothing in the refrigerator but condiments, so I can order us something," Erica rummaged through her junk drawer for takeout menus.

"Whatever you want is fine." Her mother went into the bathroom, and when she came out she was wearing her panties and a stretched-out bra. Her breasts drooped to the rolls on her stomach. Spider veins crept around her jelly-like thighs and her belly hung over her waist in two chunky ripples. She had aged since the last time they had spent quality time together, but when was that? Erica couldn't remember because her weekends had been so consumed with Warren that she had little time for anything or anyone else.

Without overthinking it, she picked up the telephone and ordered burgers from Jimbo's, a diner-like restaurant a few blocks away whose number she had on speed dial. When she hung up, her mother walked over holding up a pair of nylon shorts that she found in the bedroom.

"Can I wear these?"

They were Warren's.

"No. Why are you going through my things?" Erica pried the shorts from her mother's hand and carried them back into her room.

"I was just tryin' to find something with some rubber in the waist," she defended herself, but Erica didn't hear her because she was searching the room for anything else that belonged to him. Just touching the shorts reopened the badly stitched wound, and when she looked around his imprints were everywhere. Had she not noticed it before? A dress sock was on the floor and the sheets hanging off her bed were the ones he'd slept on last. His copy of *Black Enterprise* was face down on top of the dresser, as was his favorite pen. Warren always left a pair of black slacks and a buttoned down shirt in her closet. In her top drawer were a pair of underwear and a bottle of cologne. Erica wanted all of him gone.

After yanking the sheets from the bed, she went around grabbing everything that said Warren and stuffed them in the sheets. The teddy bear that he had won for her at Six Flags, the watch he gave her for her birthday, the pink and red roses that she had dried marking their one year anniversary, their photo album—all of it she rolled into the sheets. Sweat dotted her forehead and her hair was sticking to her face.

"What's wrong with you?" her mother watched.

"You want to leave some damn body," Erica mumbled to herself, then started stomping the linen into a ball.

"Erica."

"Nothing, Ma." She kicked the bundle aside and pushed past her mother to the kitchen.

"I'm your mother, girl. Don't tell me nothing." She followed.

"Warren left me." She picked up the wineglass and started guzzling like her mother had. She didn't stop until she had licked down the last drop. A fiery sensation passed through her chest as she closed her eyes, hating that she was handling her crisis just as her mother would, throwing back drinks. She was supposed to be the strong one.

After a few moments, her mother placed her robust arms around Erica's body, and for the second time that day she didn't resist her mother's affection. Instead she collapsed, and rested her face in the sweet-smelling place between her mother's breasts.

"Life's filled with disappointments Slim, and I know I might be responsible for most of yours, but you going to be all right. I can promise you that," her mother said, rocking Erica in her arms after so many years of neglect.

Chapter Thirty-One

Friday Night Fever

Four days had passed since Warren left Erica. It was Friday night and in less than twelve hours his father would marry Shar, within a year of his mother's death. His sister Billie was engaged and pregnant, and wouldn't be coming home for the nuptials. James was hugged up with a lady friend. Spider, the band's pianist, wasn't answering his phone. Warren slogged through his condo feeling restless and agitated, searching for something mindless to do.

Growing up with a father who served in the military had made Warren orderly almost to compulsion, and when he pulled open the doors on his walk-in closet, it was as if he had stepped into a section of a men's department store. On the right, his suits were lined in a row with the sleeves folded forward. The dress shirts were color coordinated, shoes stacked with tree horns, and T-shirts and shorts folded with crisp edges. Warren's wardrobe was larger than most women's, and he rummaged through the neat racks with the intent to purge. He started with removing dressy pieces to donate to Career Gear, an organization that gave the suits to men in need. Warren had already pulled eight suits and heaped them into a pile when his fingers closed in on the sleeve of a navy Brooks Brothers suit.

It was arguably his best suit. The one he wore to job interviews, important dinners and his cousin Grace's wedding. It was also the suit he wore when he laid his mother to rest. He remembered selecting the suit because she always said that it was bad luck to buy new clothes for a funeral. Warren ran his fingers over the lapel, recalling the Sunday morning last spring when his father summoned him abruptly to the family house in northwest D.C.

His mother hadn't been feeling well. She'd been nursing a persistent cough for weeks. Warren had noticed the rattle and rasp during their biweekly phone calls. Erica was at his place, and convinced him to stop for cornbread and a hot bowl of chicken noodle soup from Devon and Blakely.

"Let's get those purple tulips too," she said when they passed a small Mexican woman selling flowers out of a white plastic bucket.

His mother was in bed when they arrived. The room smelled like bacon. On the nightstand was a pitcher of water, an empty plate, a roll of Ritz crackers with a jar of peanut butter, and a half emptied coffee mug. On the floor was an extra blanket, a jar of Vick's Vapor Rub and a stack of newspapers. From the looks of things it seemed that she was spending a lot of time in bed, and Warren grew concerned that she wasn't moving around enough. After kisses and hugs, Erica jumped in, telling his mother about a book that she was planning to send her. The ladies kept up a constant chatter while Erica fluffed her pillows and straightened the blankets and sheets.

"I can't wait to read it," his mother smiled broadly, which made Warren grin because he loved that his mother loved Erica.

"You bring your horn, baby?" his mother asked as Erica carried the flowers to the window seat overlooking Colorado Avenue.

"Play 'Favorite Things' for me, that song always..." she started hacking and her eyes popped like they were trying to escape from the sockets. Erica rushed over and poured her a fresh glass of ice cold water.

"Ma, you sure you okay?" Concern was etched into his forehead, but his mother took a few sips and then waved him on.

"Your father took me to see Betty Carter at the Village Vanguard in New York and, man, she tore that song to pieces. Play it for me, sweetie, so I can reminisce." She nestled her head into the pillow with her eyes closed. Warren unfastened his horn, pressed it to his lips and settled into the longer version of the song, the rendition that John Coltrane played in 1965 at the Newport Jazz Festival with McCoy Tyner, Jimmy Garrison and Elvin Jones. Three minutes into the piece Warren was lost beneath the cadence and cords, and changed keys to give the tempo a chilling effect. Traditionally, the piece is played slowly, but Warren pushed it, making the beat lively and danceable. When he finished he was out of breath and his T-shirt was soaked through.

His mother clapped with glee. "Music just makes me feel better. I don't care what anybody says. Don't you ever stop playing, you hear me? Never," she leaned forward, and in the next moment she started choking.

"Mama, I think you better go to the doctor."

"Your father took me yesterday and everything was fine. Stop worrying, son," she took a deep breath and then settled back on the pillows. "Erica, take Warren downstairs and feed him some of that soup. I'm not going to be able to eat it all. You two go on now. Let me rest," she smiled.

Warren kissed her cheek and followed Erica out of the bedroom and down the back steps to the kitchen. As always, the room smelled like warmed cinnamon and he couldn't figure out how that could be since his mother surely hadn't cooked anything all week. The 13-inch television that was sandwiched between the cherry cabinet and formica countertop was tuned into Bob Schiffer's show *Face the Nation*. Warren recognized the theme music as he handed Erica the remote and a spoon for her lunch.

"I'm going to talk to my dad real quick. Make yourself comfortable," he rubbed the back of her neck and then headed to his father's study, on the other side of the house.

Out of habit, Warren ran his fingers across his mother's piano before turning the corner and tapping on his father's door. "Sir."

"Son." His father looked up from the *National Geographic* magazine he was reading. His pipe and a tin of tobacco sat on the desk amid a stack of loose papers. A framed family photo, taken when Warren was twelve, sat appropriately in the right corner. The study had been the setting for several serious conversations with his father growing up; "the talk" about sex and girls, warnings on drugs and alcohol, why certain friends weren't welcome in their home, Warren's college choices, and the list went on. There was always a pipe, a brush brass zippo lighter with a soaring eagle, and a tin of tobacco. But Warren had never been offered a smoke. That day was no exception.

"Your mother has lung cancer," his father said without fanfare. He was not one to beat around, preferring to head right for the heart.

By accident, Warren bit his tongue and a small trickle of blood salted his mouth. "What does that mean?"

"Well," his father said, dabbing at the sweat forming on his forehead with a handkerchief. "They've given her a few weeks to live. Actually, they've suggested hospice."

"Hospice? What about treatment?"

"The cancer has already metastasized into her brain. Chemo and radiation might give her a few more months."

"So let's fight."

His father dropped his head in his hands and pushed his tight curls back over his head. "She refused to go to the doctors for so long. You know your mother, insisting that it was nothing and she could cure herself with oils and herbs. Now it's too late. It's just too late," he answered, and when Warren looked up at his father it appeared that he was aging right before his eyes.

Erica took the next day off from work and stayed with Warren when he couldn't get out of bed. Nine days later his mother had passed on.

WHILE PICTURES WERE PULLED, programs stapled, flowers selected, and food ordered for the repast, Warren concentrated on the song he would play to honor his mother. The choir wanted him to play "Eye on the Sparrow," but Warren decided on "Precious Lord Take My Hand" and asked Miss Rita, the church pianist, to accompany him on organ. "Precious Lord" had been his mother's favorite church hymn, and Warren watched videos of Mahalia Jackson and Aretha Franklin singing the song so that he could get it just right. There had been nothing pleasant about the funeral. Not one memorable thing about Pastor Davis' sermon. He disliked walking in the processional with piteous glances being cast on his family. Didn't like the laying on hands that people felt compelled to do as they passed his pew. The smell of so many flowers made his stomach churn and the Extra Strength Tylenol did nothing to relieve the ache in his head. Warren felt wretched down to his bones.

But at the very moment that Warren thought he couldn't take one more second of funk, Pastor Davis called him to the pulpit for his musical intersession. And Warren didn't just play "Precious Lord," he made his trumpet sing "Precious Lord." Shoulders started swaying and the congregation was moved to Amen, Hallelujah and Thank you, Jesus. By the second verse, Sister Clementine caught the Holy Spirit and had to be hugged and held by her teenage son. Warren played, feeling ordained, and understood for the first time what John Coltrane meant when he declared that, through his music, he had heard the voice of God.

When he finished, Warren didn't bow or even acknowledge the applause and calls on the Lord as he walked down the three steps from the pulpit. All he saw was Erica, sitting in the front pew. Falling into the seat next to her, she clutched his hand so tightly that it felt as if she was trying to extract all of his pain, like a presser would fruit for its juices. She squashed and squeezed, transferring his feelings into her body so that just for a time he could feel free. That's how Erica was or who she used to be, and it was going to be pure punishment for him to get used to his life without her.

Damn her.

Chapter Thirty-Two

Jumping the Broom

Tardiness was never an issue for Warren. He learned from his father the habit of arriving early: fifteen minutes prior to an event, twenty for work, and one hour if he were going to perform. For the wedding he arrived at Tabernacle Baptist church with thirty minutes to spare, but spent ten of those behind the wheel of his car scratching his foot. On the drive over his left toes started itching, all of them. As soon as he pulled into the parking lot, he removed his sock and raked his fingernails over the skin. Warren had had athlete's foot before, and hoped he hadn't caught something from the rental shoes his father insisted he wear. He found an old tube of hand cream in his glove compartment and slathered what he could squeeze across his toes. His skin still stung with irritation, but it would have to do.

Warren put his shoe back on and got out of the car. His truck had been washed and waxed two days ago, and before trudging across the lot he checked his reflection in the shiny paint. As if the itching wasn't enough, the black and white shoes were cutting into the sides of his ankles, and the heel rubbed with each step. The day was going to be a long one.

Two women walking in front of Warren commented on the loveliness of the church. He had to agree. Tabernacle's church was a building of beauty, with early century stone walls, ten-foot stained glass windows, a bell tower that still rang on the hour, enclosed in a steeple that could be seen for at least a mile in all four directions. Today, satiny calla lilies chased roses along the metal railings, which fanned to either side of the wide stairs. Oversized wreaths filled with blood orchids hung from each of the double doors, and something smelled plumy.

Warren's father, Maynard, greeted guests at the top landing. The two men were identically dressed in black, three-button notch-lapel tuxedos, with white shirts and trimmings.

"Son," his father embraced him while patting him on the back, and Warren caught a whiff of his spiced cologne. A smile as thick as a stack of pancakes played on his father's face as he looked Warren in the eyes.

"Thanks for standing with me today. It means the world to me," and then his father did something he had never done before. He kissed Warren's cheek and whispered, "I know how you felt about your mother, and I loved her too. But I can't stop living, I have to move on." He patted Warren's cheek, and turned his attention to three women dressed in wide-brimmed hats. Before Warren could recover from the comment, his father was gesturing for him to show the women to their pews.

Monkey-faced Sister Clara linked arms with Warren, and he cringed when she tried to explain.

"Warren, baby, I been meaning to call you. 'Bout the other day…" she started, but Warren cut her off.

"Enjoy the service." He left her standing at the last pew, despite the available seating up front.

As he walked to the back of the chapel, his seething subsided when he spied his great-Aunt Maggie, being pushed in her wheelchair by an aid from her nursing home. Warren kissed her forehead and offered to escort her down the aisle. The crowd then started pouring in, family members, distinguished members of the military, and friends of the family. After what felt like an hour of walking back and forth, his feet started itching again, and he was just about to duck away for a scratch when Blanche walked through the church doors. He had forgotten that his father invited her. She was wearing a turquoise scoop-neck dress that pressed her small breasts into buxomly cleavage. Her soft hair was gathered in a side bun, and a handbag with a chain-link strap hung from her arm.

"Hey, you." Warren took her hand.

Her face gushed pink. "I thought I was going to be late." She leaned in, kissing him on the chin.

The organist began a new selection while Warren escorted her to her seat.

"Where's Erica?" Blanche asked, sliding into the pew.

"I'll explain later."

"At the reception," Blanche assured him. Warren nodded, walking towards the vestibule, where his father was waiting.

"It's showtime, Son," he said, pinning a maroon gardenia to Warren's lapel.

They walked up the side aisle to the front of the church, past the stained glass windows depicting the birth of Christ. Once they were standing in front of the pulpit, his father nodded to the organist and the processional music began. Shar's younger sister, Bethany, who was both hippy and busty, made her way down the aisle dressed in a wine colored dress that bunched at the waist. Bernard, the older son, carried the broom, followed by Jared, clumping along with the ring pillow. Both boys were dressed in white, and looked uncomfortable in such fancy clothing.

Once the bridal party took their places around the pulpit, two ushers rolled out the white carpet and the wedding march began. The flower girl was so shy that she didn't drop a single petal. The organist pounded a heavy introduction and everyone rose to their feet.

Shar and her father stood in the entranceway and Warren had to admit that she was a beautiful woman, though very different than his mother. Shar's skin was the color of cumin and her small eyes had a distinguished slant. Her champagne slip dress fell delicately over her full breasts and exaggerated hips, and when she marched, the shiny material trailed behind her. As she descended the aisle, cameras flashed in every direction. But she kept her eyes fixed on her husband-to-be. The energy flowing between them was obvious. Shar's teeth stacked into a smile when Maynard left Warren's side and took his place next to her. Watching them both, Warren wondered about the development of their relationship over the years. How much time had they spent? How many memories shared?

Pastor Davis asked the church to be seated and the wedding rituals began. Rings were slipped on, vows exchanged, candles lit, songs sang, and then the pastor stopped for a dramatic pause. In his deep preacher's voice, he boomed, "Maynard Prince, please give the people what they want. Kiss your lovely bride."

The invited guests applauded.

THE WEDDING RECEPTION WAS held at the Museum of African-American Culture on Fort Place in Southeast D.C. A horse-drawn carriage sat out front with a sign on the rear of the buggy that read, "Just Married." Inside, the gallery walls were covered with African, Caribbean, and African-American art dating back to the early 1800s. An ice sculpture of two swans greeted the guests at the entrance to the hall. When Warren first walked in, there was something about the way the female swan curved her neck towards the male that made him think of Erica. She liked being kissed on the neck, and that was where Warren snuggled his face when they slept.

"Want some company?"

Warren was sitting at a table facing the dance floor, drinking his third glass of champagne. He had just sat back down after giving the wedding toast to his father and Shar and he was replaying his speech in his head, hoping he had done an alright job. Blanche dropped her shawl over the seat next to him without waiting for his response. His father and Shar were leading the room in a fast swing to "Blue Suede Shoes." Watching the couple encircled in each other's arms brought images of Warren's mother to his head. She loved to dance. On Friday nights, his mother was known to fry up a big batch of shad or porgies and potatoes, and push the carpet back so that Billie could teach her and Warren the latest steps. But he couldn't recall his parents ever dancing together.

"What's going on?" Blanche sipped from her glass.

"Not much," he was still watching the floor. The couple took a bow as the people standing around the edge clapped their hands. Maynard was a natural ham, and Warren could tell by the never-ending grin on his face that he was juiced from the attention. The waiter passed with the champagne tray and Warren grabbed another.

Maynard reached the bandstand and unclipped the microphone. "I'd like to thank you all for coming out to celebrate this day with me and my new lovely wife. We're off to honeymoon on a private beach in the Cayman's." Someone whistled.

"So in the words of the great Russell Simmons, who I think is a cool cat," Maynard raised his hand in the air, egging the crowd on. "Thanks so much for coming out. God bless and good night." He gave one last salute and then exited the stage. Back on the dance floor, he swept Shar up in his arms, spun her and then they dipped. The couple waved and made their way out of the reception hall. Guests followed them with cameras trying to get their last shots.

"Aren't you going to take pictures?" Blanche moistened her glittery lips.

"I'll get some from the photographer." Warren was enjoying the way the bubbly made him feel. Invincible like nothing really mattered. He could no longer feel his toes itching. The six-piece band was playing a Stevie Wonder hit, and a few die-hards danced across the floor. But most were heading to the coat check.

"I'm going to give you a lift home." Blanche touched his knee.

"Cool," he said, standing and stumbling a little. Warren knew he was a few steps from being wasted but grabbed another glass on his way out.

BLANCHE UNLOCKED THE DOORS from her keypad as they rounded her candy white sports car. The night air was unseasonably warm, and her wrap was loose around her pale shoulders. After opening Blanche's door, Warren slid into the cushy, leather passenger seat.

"Nice ride," he tipped his flute to his lips. The interior smelled like granny smith apples, and the radio station was playing a rock song. Warren nodded his head to the hard, heavy sounds of electric guitar, bass, and drums. The combination of instruments was the perfect compliment to his mood. Music was the seat of his being, and just as he started to disappear into its clutches, Blanche asked.

"So where is Miss Erica? I can't believe she missed the wedding?"

"We broke up," was all he offered, because he wanted to stay inside the bass line of the music. To his surprise she changed the subject, offering to buy him a drink.

"There's this place right down the street from my house. The waitresses are dressed like skimpy flight attendants, and treat you like you're seated in first class," her dress had slid away from her knee and exposed her milky thigh. Warren tried not to notice as he looked for someplace to put the empty glass.

"Give it here," Blanche tilted the flute to her lips for the last little drop. Smiling, she tossed the glass into the backseat and revved her engine.

Her townhouse was located just a half block from thriving Wisconsin Avenue in Georgetown, where the streets tipped over with hot bars, mediocre jazz clubs, and trendy restaurants. Her plan was to park the car in her driveway and walk over.

"How far is the lounge? I need to use the bathroom," said Warren, helping Blanche from the car. The split in her dress had slipped up further and he saw that she wasn't wearing pantyhose. Warren tucked in his shirttail.

"Come in." Blanche flashed her teeth. "I need to grab something anyway."

Warren followed her as she switched her narrow hips up the brick walkway to her home. The front door was red with gold trimming, and Blanche fumbled with the key. Leaning against the door frame, Warren wondered if it were a good idea for him to be there. It was late, and Blanche was his co-worker. What were they doing? What was he doing?

The lights were dim and Blanche grabbed his hand on the way up the three short stairs, which opened into the living room.

Her hands were cold but the house was much too warm. While she turned up the table lamp, Warren loosened his bow tie. The living room walls were beige, and the suede sectional was just a hue darker. Hanging above the stone fireplace was an oversized framed photo of Blanche, with a red silk sheet sliding from her right breast. Her hair puffed around her, and her eyes looked like the photographer had told her to make love to the camera.

"Nice photo."

"Thanks. The bathroom is down the hall," she pointed.

Warren wasn't surprised to find it small and dainty like everything else in her townhouse. He took his time washing his hands, but couldn't look at himself in the mirror. Maybe he should just leave. He thought of Erica, and all of the accusations she made about Blanche. Perhaps he should sober up on the cab ride back to the church to pick up his car. When he returned to the living room, the fireplace had been lit and Warren found himself mesmerized by the flames. Sitting on the mantel was a collection of sculptured angels, and he turned one over in his hand.

Blanche walked into the living room, approaching him from behind. The heat from her body reached him long before her words, and when he turned to face her she was holding two wine glasses. "They come from Brazil," she said, thickening her accent, saying Brasil instead of Brazil.

"They're nice." He took a glass. "Who's from Brazil?"

"My mother is from Bahia, but she lives in New York now. I never knew my father." Taking a step back, Warren bumped into the fireplace, and Blanche leaned her body into his to steady him.

"Do you go to Brazil often?"

Blanche unclipped her hair and tossed it around her shoulders, "Not really. I'm a love child. My mother is the daughter of a wealthy Salvadorian, and my father was of African descent. He worked in my grandfather's tobacco fields. My mother was disowned after I was born." Her eyes darkened.

The temperature by the fireplace was making Warren's armpits sweat, so he walked over to the sofa and dropped against the pillows. Blanche followed, raising her glass for a toast. She was leaning in so close that Warren could smell her. He knew what she wanted. Perhaps he had always known but could never admit it. Her fingers touched his wrist, and then she kissed him. Her lips were sticky, and tasted like raspberries.

Warren was the first to pull away. "What was that?" he asked, though it was obvious. Blanche kissed him again, with her tiny hands moving along the base of his neck. I should leave, he thought again to himself. It had reached that hour in the evening where only one thing happened when a man and woman were tipsy, by the heat of the fire, and for Warren, on the rebound with a cracked heart.

"Do you really want me to stop?" her voice was dim against the thick of his bottom lip. And as she sucked and pulled, all of his earlier hesitation withered away. Blanche pushed him further back onto the sofa, hiked her dress up and straddled his lap while her fingers worked his zipper. Slipping down her own dress, her breasts fell loose like lemons. Warren took one in each hand and was disappointed to realize that they weren't soft to the touch. Could they have been implants? But then it didn't matter because desire took over, and by the time the condom appeared from the side of Blanche's panties, Warren's sensibilities and thoughts had abandoned him. Blanche pushed him from the couch to the floor, and he navigated inside of her with a recklessness that surprised him.

Chapter Thirty-Three

Eat On

Erica was nervous, but wasn't sure why. Perhaps it was because the Wednesday lunch with LaVal turned into a Friday-night dinner. Blizzard-like conditions in the Midwest had delayed flights in and out of Chicago for two days. LaVal stayed in New York conducting business and had postponed their meeting until then. Under normal circumstances Erica would have never agreed to a Friday-night work dinner, but tonight she was relieved to have something to do. Staying busy was the key. Mind-numbing thoughts of Warren couldn't catch her if she was busy.

Her mother was still "vacationing" at her apartment and Erica was surprised at the easy rhythm that they had fallen into. Twice that week, they had stayed up half the night talking and giggling like school friends. Her mother had scrubbed the apartment until all Erica could smell was pine and Clorox. And she prepared home-cooked meals every day: crispy fried chicken, smothered skirt steak, stewed red snapper, yellow-corn casserole, collard greens, baked macaroni and cheese, sweet potato pone with walnuts and marshmallows, and her famous 1,2,3,4 cake that she frosted with homemade cream-cheese icing. But tonight was Friday, Erica's second weekend without Warren, and she needed something stronger than her mother's food and good company to chase away the bleeding-heart blues. As pathetic as it seemed, a work dinner with LaVal proved to be her best option.

Traffic was heavier than she had anticipated when she stepped out of the nail salon, and although she knew the subway was the best option, she flagged down a taxicab. In the backseat, she checked her work voicemail for messages, jotted down questions for LaVal, and before exiting the cab glossed over her lips. Rain was in the forecast and out on the street, she shuddered against the chilly wind. Her winter-white skirt swung just below her knees, and the leather knee-high boots she wore gave off the right amount of spunk without being suggestive. It was something that she took into account for appointments with male clients. Never overdo it.

They were meeting at Union Square Café on 16th Street and 5th Avenue. Erica was surprised when LaVal suggested that restaurant because it wasn't on the tourist map. The Café served American cuisine with an Italian soul, and was known for having an extensive wine selection that she couldn't wait to try. The dinner rush had already begun, and when she walked in she had to elbow between chatty couples to get to the host stand. The place was packed with folks who seemed high off the start of the weekend.

"Erica Shaw meeting LaVal Jarvis." She clutched her purse. The tight-lipped hostess scanned her book and then motioned for Erica to follow. They walked past the bar with the dinner specials scribbled on a chalkboard and into the main dining area. LaVal was seated at a table towards the back, looking triumphant as if he had just purchased a blue-chip stock. A bottle of white wine was sweating and breathing in the ice bucket, and he stood when she approached. The gesture made her stomach stiffen. Warren would have done the same thing.

"Sorry to keep you waiting," she said as LaVal pulled out her chair. He then caught her off guard by pecking her cheek.

Erica pushed her bag under the table, hoping that her face hadn't turned flush.

"I took the liberty of ordering a chardonnay and a plate of salt and pepper calamari." He only half smiled, but his dimples still weren't hard to find.

As usual, LaVal was dressed with guiltless style, and Erica complimented him on his chocolate suit and blond-striped tie. She asked him about his week in New York City.

While the waiter poured her wine, LaVal mentioned that he was vying to be the keynote speaker at the Black Lawyers of America conference next month.

"The original speaker canceled, so they're scrambling for a replacement."

"It would be a great way to kick off the book," she said, watching him dish a few pieces of calamari on her plate, before taking some for himself. The wine was tasty. "What is this?"

"It's Vernaccia di San Gimignano, a dry white wine from Tuscany. It's one of my favorites." LaVal pronounced the Italian label with no accent.

"What are you? A connoisseur?"

"Nah. Just know a little sumptin' sumptin' about entertaining." His eyes held her gaze a second too long.

"Do you speak Italian?"

"Piccolo. A little."

The waiter returned with mixed olives, warm bread and a dish of olive oil. They placed their orders and the menus were removed.

LaVal stretched back in his chair. "So, tell me about yourself."

"What do you want to know?"

"Are you originally from New York?"

"Newark." Erica took a sip of water. She wanted to be sure to stay hydrated and sober. She felt shy under his spotlight and changed the subject. "Why don't you tell me about you, since you're the subject that I have to sell."

"You're selling me," he chuckled. "I love it, but I'm sure there isn't too much that I can tell you that you don't already know."

"Tell me something that's not in the book," she leaned in, but it didn't take much to egg him on. In the time that it took for the first course to be cleared, it became obvious LaVal liked being on stage. His face was animated as his history unraveled, and Erica could easily picture him as a television personality, and told him so. LaVal laughed. "I've heard that once or twice before."

The waiter lowered his tray onto the wooden stand, and Erica's nose seemed to open up wide from the aroma of cheese, sherry and butter. Food had become her new lover and she couldn't wait for her fix. LaVal had the grilled lamp chops, Erica the creamy seared scallops. Forks and knives clanked and cut, while they chatted and chewed.

"Enough about me. You're the one I'm entrusting my entire writing career to. Who is Miss Erica Shaw? Is it Miss or Mrs?" Faint freckles dotted the bridge of his nose, and his sand dune eyes were intense but kind.

"It's Miss." She dragged her sliced scallop through the sauce.

"How long have you been with B&B?"

"Just over four years."

"Like it?"

She nodded.

"How much longer do you plan to be there?"

"Excuse me?" Erica put down her fork, and LaVal's face widened to a flirt.

"I was just testing your loyalty."

"You don't have to. I'm fabulous at what I do."

"So then I should be a *New York Times* bestseller this time next year?"

"Slow down, trumpet…I mean…cowboy." Erica looked into her plate, pinching her thigh under the table.

"You play the trumpet?"

"No." She sipped the last drop of her wine, and was grateful when LaVal poured her another without asking.

"So how did you make it out?" she turned it to him.

He shrugged. "There was always something in me that radiated greatness, even when I was on the streets dodging foster care."

"What was your breaking point?"

"You ever been to a group home?" he asked, and then continued without waiting for her response. "We used to put our names on our socks so that they couldn't be stolen, because you don't want to be caught without socks in a Chicago winter. That life wasn't for me," he shook his head, and as he talked about the past, his speech pattern changed. Erica could see darkness etch around his brows and in the slits of his eyes. His transformation made her feel cottony towards him. Women loved a reformed man with a glint of the streets. Once she got a picture of him in the local papers with a nice write-up, the women should flock to the book signings like cattle in a herd.

"When I met my mentor, it was a no-brainer. He set me up, and I changed from working the hood to getting my education. It wasn't hard. I was a smart dude. Every now and again I'd dip back for a little cash, but once I was focused that was it."

The waiter topped off their wineglasses and they both declined dessert. A WASPy couple entered the restaurant and took a seat at the next table. The woman's rosy perfume went straight to Erica's head.

"When're you headed back?"

"Tomorrow. So will you show me New York?"

"I need to get home." She straightened up in her chair.

"It's Friday."

"My mother's visiting."

The waiter placed the check on the table and LaVal grabbed it before Erica could.

"I'll pay." She summoned the bill with her pointer finger, but he refused to hand it over.

"I can't have a woman pay for my dinner."

"That's my job."

"Then I'll let you buy me a drink." He pulled a platinum card from his wallet. "Come on, just a quick one at the bar."

Erica knew she should stand her ground and bid LaVal good night. He was her author, and she was already two and a half glasses into the night, on the rebound and incredibly lonely. But going home was so unappealing that she agreed. When LaVal walked over to help her with her chair, she wasn't sure if it was the influence of the wine, but he smelled wonderful.

ON THE RIDE HOME, Erica wrote down everything that she could remember from their conversation. This was the part of her job that she loved: getting at the core of a writers' work so that she could twirl her pitch to the media just right. Erica anticipated reporters salivating over LaVal's book as if it were caramel-crusted pie.

Her mother was up watching a movie when she walked in. A 22-ounce can of Colt 45 was cracked open on the table.

"Where did you get that?" Erica pointed.

"Chile, you got some stairs. I walked down to the corner for some air. It's Friday, Slim, let me live."

Erica didn't feel like fighting. "Any calls?"

"Phone ain't ring all day. You eat?"

Erica dropped her things in her bedroom. It was the one room that her mother hadn't sparkled, probably because she couldn't figure out what was dirty or clean. Erica slipped into her yoga pants and got out of her bra. In the living room, the television was turned up too loud and her mother was fooling with her hair.

"You just washed it?"

"Yeah, and the back gets so tangled. Can you grease my scalp for me?"

"Now?"

"Before it dries up."

Erica sighed and tossed two pillows in front of the futon on the floor.

"You 'spect me to get down there, with these knees and my arthritis?"

Right, nothing on her mother's body worked. Erica went for the folding chair that she kept stored in her bedroom closet. Bringing it into the living room, she opened it up and her mother eased her plump bottom into the metal seat. She wore a faded, snap-front house coat, and cellulite dimpled her flabby arms.

"Thanks, Slim."

The weather report had been forecasting rain all day, and finally out of nowhere came the sound of the clouds opening and water pouring from the sky. It was that hard-hitting type of storm, with drops that were fast, furious, and fleeting, and would pass in five minutes. Someone out on the street gave a screech, and Erica could hear the slapping of feet against the soaked concrete. The apartment was warm and the pitter-patter of raindrops so soothing that Erica found herself humming while she parted her mother's hair and slathered the scalp with oil. She had a finer texture of hair than Erica's, but it wasn't as healthy. Whole sections were broken off and it was uneven with split ends.

"You want me to clip your ends? Make it even?" Erica knew her mother was too cheap to go to the hair salon. That wasn't the type of thing she spent her money on.

"You know what you're doing?"

"I trim Tess' ends all the time."

"Guess it can't look no worse."

"Thanks for the vote of confidence." She went into the kitchen drawer for the scissors. Her mother picked up the remote and flipped the channel to the basketball game. The Nets were playing the Wizards and Erica felt her insides curdle like spoiled milk. Covering the floor in three long strides, she grabbed the remote. "I can't watch this."

"Fine." Her mother put her hands in the air. She must have gotten used to Erica's temper swings.

Leaning against the arm of the futon, Erica clicked a few channels before settling on the Food Network. Emeril was cooking New Orleans style gumbo, and listening to the ingredients distracted her bluesy emotions enough to return to her mother's head.

As a girl Erica loved playing with dolls, brushing and braiding their plastic strands. There was something therapeutic about doing another person's hair. Untangling and greasing was like massaging and releasing. It was an intimate gesture that reminded Erica of when her mother would sit on the front steps and cornrow her hair. Her mother made sure to fasten colorful beads on the ends of Erica's hair, so when she jumped double-dutch, her beads would soar in every direction making music in the air. It gave her the sensation of flying.

On those days, when her mother said she was going to the store, she came right back with her Pepsi-Cola, and sometimes brought ten cent popsicles for all the kids playing outside. Erica enjoyed the attention she received when giving out the treats. Bonnie wasn't around and her mother was mostly sober. This would last for about a week, and it didn't take much for Erica to start thinking that her mother would get a job, stop drinking for good, show up for parent/teacher conferences, and pay back the candy drive money she had stolen from Erica's hiding place under her panties in her top drawer. But as soon as these thoughts started looking like clear pictures, the dreaded white Trans Am would appear in their driveway. Erica's bedroom was in the front of the house and she could hear the engine roar into the spot before anyone else. Bonnie would lift the mail slot and shout Gweny's name until someone opened the door. The bottle would be hidden in a brown paper bag for the neighbor's sake, but once Bonnie crossed the threshold, the bottle was cracked open. Each time, Erica felt like she could vomit.

"Finished," she took her mother by the arm and helped her from the folding chair.

"Ooh, ouch. You hear those bones crack? Where the mirror at?"

Erica pointed towards the bathroom, and then followed the few steps.

Her mother held onto the pedestal sink, turning her head from side to side. "Oh, my. Slim, who knew you could do hair? I look wonderful."

"New hair, new attitude," Erica found herself hoping aloud. The haircut was fitting. Shorter in the back, layered in the front with feathered curls falling against her forehead. The bruises on her mother's face were clearing up, but her lip still sagged.

"Next time, I'ma bring some color so you can dye all of this gray."

"Ma, you have like ten strands. That's good for your age."

"If you ain't have so many steps I would say we should go out, but I ain't going down. That rain got me aching already."

"You're not that old."

"Chile, you don't even understand." Her mother walked back to the chair and lifted her beer. "You got cards?"

In the kitchen, Erica found a deck in the same drawer as the scissors. A pen and pad was already on the coffee table. She and her mother had been playing Rummy 500 since Erica was old enough to count, back when they watched soap operas together.

"Ma, you still look at *Guiding Light?*"

"Every day."

Cross-legged on the futon, Erica shuffled the first hand. "Cutting?"

"Now you know I ain't choppin' up my aces." Erica forgot her mother's card superstitions. Most people cut for the winning cards but she just patted the top for luck, and the game began.

While they played, her mother caught her up on family gossip; which cousin was pregnant, on drugs, in jail, moved out West and started a new business. The conversation was easy, and it was good-natured moments like these, when iced tea was merely made from leaves, sugar and water, with no hidden baggage floating to the top, that got Erica to dreaming. Erica knew it was a dangerous feeling considering the disappointments of their past, but she just couldn't help it.

Chapter Thirty-Four
Girls Night

The next evening, Erica attended a book signing at the Barnes & Noble in Union Square. That location was reserved for only the most premiere authors, and Ms Elizabeth Mavis Samuels fit the bill. She was one of the ground-breakers and grandmothers of African-American literature. Her first manuscript was lost when she left it on a city bus. It had been typed on a typewriter, so she had to start the book again from scratch. Once she had finally finished, her manuscript was rejected thirty-seven times before being offered a meager deal for publication. She had since become a *New York Times* bestseller and her ten novels had been printed in fifty-two languages worldwide. Elizabeth had been Edie's author and Erica was happy to inherit such a legend. A beautiful woman, Elizabeth had long salt-and-pepper locks that hung past her back, some with cowry shells clipped to the ends. When she looked you in the eye, it seemed as if she were reading you. Erica had arrived earlier than necessary to make sure Elizabeth was comfortable. They hit it off right away.

"You remind me of my granddaughter." Elizabeth turned her soulful eyes on Erica, "Smart and savvy. But, dear, why are you so sad?"

Damn. "I'm fine, ma'am, really. Please let me know if you need anything."

"I've been a one-woman show forever. But it is always good to know that help is available." She squeezed Erica's hand, and then hugged her to her breast. The scent of lemongrass wafted from her shoulders and once she let go, Erica felt lighter, like she was fully in the room. Elizabeth patted her cheek and walked with the grace of a queen to the front of the room. Without waiting for a proper introduction she took the stage. Every chair in the room was filled, and additional fans filed around the edges of the stage and in the aisles. Elizabeth was long past coaching, so Erica had the privilege of just listening and absorbing.

After a brief question and answer period, Elizabeth moved to the desk and began signing books, shaking hands and posing for photographs. Erica's cell phone vibrated inside of her bag, and when she saw Tess' number on the caller-ID she moved behind a shelf of books to answer.

"What's up, Sugar?" chirped Tess.

"At a signing. What are you so happy about?"

"Got the night off. Where's Warren?"

Erica hadn't told her about the break-up, and simply replied that he was in D.C.

"Great. Let's meet for a drink?"

"Sure," she had nothing else to do tonight. "I'm in Union Square."

"Perfect. Madame X on Houston, I'll be waiting at the bar."

IT HAD BEEN RAINING off and on for the past twenty-four hours and a light sprinkle drizzled from the clouds as Erica stepped from the taxicab. Flipping the collar of her raincoat, she trotted down the few steps to the basement bar. Tess was seated on the suede bar stool. Her afro was picked out to its fullest and she was wearing a green halter dress that clung to her curves. Her ample cleavage, brushed with glitter, was at the center of attention.

"Hey, Sugar," she popped her gum and then kissed Erica on the cheek. She smelled like a cinnamon stick.

"Where're your clothes? It's not summertime," Erica dropped her tote over her chair.

"This is Ken, our hunk of a bartender," Tess smiled up at the thick armed blond. "Make her the same drink, sweetie."

"What am I having?"

"It's called a sexy motherfucker," Tess did a shoulder slide. "Can you believe they named a drink after us?"

Erica gave a weak smile and then looked around the dim room. The bar was outfitted in red velvet chairs from the seventies. Nothing matched exactly but it worked, lending the room a dark, vamp feel.

"I'm glad I picked this place, there's a live band at nine," Tess said, sipping. "Maybe I'll get up and sing."

It was just like Tess to walk on stage uninvited and outsing the performers paid for the gig.

"How was your day?" Erica stirred her drink.

"I just had a date with Hercules." All of Tess' men had secret nicknames. "Girl, brother man is so sexy the whole dinner felt like foreplay."

"So what happened?"

Tess batted her eyes. "I gave it to him in the bathroom of this snobby Upper Eastside restaurant *Unfaithful* style."

"*Unfaithful*?"

"Didn't you see the movie with Diane Lane and Richard Gere?"

Erica's face went blank.

"You don't watch enough television for me. Well, it was insatiable. I'm surprised my afro is still intact." She patted her 'do. Erica could feel Tess studying her and knew what was coming next.

"Whatcha looking so down about?"

"I'm not down." Was it that obvious? She had done her make-up, combed her hair and was wearing a stylish black ruffled top with fitted trousers.

"You can't outdress your problems," said Tess, reading her thoughts.

Erica didn't want to break down at the bar. Tess sensed it was something big and ordered a second round. The lounge area was half empty, but every seat at the bar was full and the talk boisterous. After another gulp of her drink, Erica told Tess about Warren. Every detail tumbled out, from their last weekend in D.C., the strong fights, Blanche, his father getting married suddenly, to him calling it quits in Philadelphia. By the time she finished, she had to pinch her thigh to keep the tears from welling up.

Tess moved to hug her, but Erica pushed her away. "Don't make me cry. This is so fucking unfair."

"So why are you taking it?"

Erica looked at Tess.

"Honey, I would have been on the train to D.C. by now. Warren is a good man. Go kiss and make up."

The thought had crossed her mind, but Erica couldn't take any more rejections. "I called twice, and he hasn't returned either call."

Tess told Ken to keep an eye on their drinks, pulling Erica outside for a cigarette. Huddled against the brick wall, they smoked while watching the cars and cabs zoom by. The drizzle was frizzing up both of their hairs but neither seemed to care.

"Want my advice?" she turned, but didn't wait for Erica to respond. "Relationships go through things. Just because he got mad doesn't make it a deal breaker. Warren is hurting too. If he doesn't answer your calls, then go after him."

Smoke curled from Erica's lips, and the nicotine rush was instant. She took a moment to enjoy the fuzziness it caused in her head. Tess was probably right, but just going to D.C. took guts that Erica wasn't sure she had. She felt wimpy and weak, and if he rejected her again, she didn't know what she would do. She stubbed out the cigarette and led Tess back to the bar.

Ken had poured them each a Kamikaze shot, and the three cheered, then threw the drinks back. Erica was becoming her mother. She couldn't remember the last night she had gone to bed sober.

The musicians were setting up their instruments on stage, and the drummer sprung into action, lightly tapping his drum sticks.

"What's up with your promotion?" Tess asked and Erica could tell that she was changing the subject to keep her mind occupied. The two had been sisters-friends-neighbors for the past three years and there wasn't another woman alive that understood Erica the way that Tess did.

"Just waiting to be acknowledged."

"Honey, you work for corporate America. Ain't nobody giving you shit you don't ask for."

"Edie is out. What should I do?"

Tess looked at Erica like she had just failed an elementary spelling quiz. "Request a meeting with your boss and tell her what you want," Tess touched her chin, "then go to D.C. and tell Warren what you need."

The music started, and a sun-kissed sister wearing a floor-length, red dress started singing her rendition of "That's the Way Love Goes," by Janet Jackson.

Erica wondered if it was a sign.

Chapter Thirty-Five

Purpose

It was dawn when Warren finally made it home. He kicked off his shoes before shouldering his front door closed with a thud. The blisters on his feet caused by the rental shoes had ruptured, and he could feel the pus oozing into his silk socks. He plopped down in his love seat, and peeled them off and massaged his swollen toes. What had he been thinking? Sex with Blanche? She wasn't his type, and had only served as a temporary fix to put some distance between him and Erica. Now, he dreaded the aftermath this would cause at work. What was worse, Warren fell asleep after sex, and when he woke up he thought it was Erica next to him. For three beautiful seconds his heart skipped happily and he actually thought that Philadelphia was nothing more than a bad dream. But then he heard a sleeping sigh and realized it wasn't her, and his entire evening rushed back: the wedding, seduction by Blanche and the sheer absence of Erica.

It was on his drive home that missing Erica had started like the onset of a toothache. It was a slow nag that worked its way to a pinching pain. By the time he was slumped against the sofa the ache had permeated his nervous system and reached a place where "Ouch" couldn't begin to describe his torment. All he could think about was Erica—her lithe touch, spirited voice, the way she stood war posing when she was upset, and the image of her bottom lip trembling with sexy rage when her mother called.

Sleeping with Blanche had given his body some relief, but it was his soul that needed soothing. Warren was restless and uneasy, but he didn't want to medicate with alcohol, or smoke marijuana until he was in a purple haze. What he needed was a friend, and from across the room his silver brass mate beckoned him. Warren took three steps to retrieve his horn and when he unclasped the metal case, his trumpet begged to be cradled and kissed.

Warren wasn't sure what it was, but something made him carry his horn down the hall until he was standing in front of his spare bedroom. The room was box-sized and had been closed off from the rest of his apartment since the day he had salvaged his mother's music collection. After her death, his father thought nothing of leaving her items curbside for the sanitation department. But Warren had rescued her piano stool that had been in her family for over a century, crates of vintage albums, and her favorite sheet music before the garbage trucks arrived. He had planned to make the spare bedroom a music sanctuary, but had never gotten around to it.

Blues, classical and jazz albums by Nina Simone, Dinah Washington, Muddy Waters, Mozart, Bach and Ray Charles were stacked against the eggshell walls, with countless others. Her wooden record player sat in the corner, with a thick film of dust covering the oak frame. When Warren lifted the top and dropped the needle, out belted Billie Holiday. Her sad, sultry voice was as much a part of his childhood as his favorite Spider-Man pajamas.

Some day he'll come along, the man I love.

Warren hadn't heard his mother's favorite song in ages. The emotions behind everything that he carried over the last month welled up inside of him until it was difficult to stand. So he sat on the stool. His mother had loved Erica for him as much as he did, and the tears flowed with a furiousness that forced Warren to shove the collar of his dress shirt into his mouth. The grief hit him like a whirlwind. Warren had spent so much energy burying his true self beneath objects that were supposed to make him feel good: his shiny SUV, the eighth-floor condominium, his high-salaried job, all of the things that made him look established on paper. But the death of his mother followed by losing Erica made him feel hollow inside, like a forgotten conch shell. Once he allowed himself to be honest, pent up misery began unraveling and he couldn't stop throwing it up. It left his body in spouts of babbling cries, coughing and clutching, kicking and screaming. This felt as though it went on forever, until Warren was weakened and wet, and his body just stopped and stooped over in silence. Then he heard the most familiar voice whispering in his ear, "Play son, play."

Warren was still sitting on the stool that his ancestors had shared, and as he placed his mouthpiece against his lips, he felt their kindred spirits traveling through his body. His mother's lilac scent filled the small room.

Now she was seated on the piano stool, her long fingers in position, nodding that it was time. A duet between Billie Holiday and Louis Armstrong was next, and Warren and his mother joined them. As his notes pierced the air, his mother's were soft, as if she were bathing him like she did when he was her baby. Warren replaced Billie with Bird, and as his mother's petite foot worked the pedals, her entire body danced up and down the keys. When he played Coltrane's "Favorite Things," his mother played faster, bringing Warren to his feet. Once he was up, her fingers swept across the keys as if she were sprinkling his body with her special oils, while whispering, "This is your Purpose. You are a King."

Warren mashed his valves in acceptance of her gift, knowing at that moment that if he lifted his arm, he would fly.

Once the records stopped, Warren's body was spread across the floor like he had just finished making angels in the snow, and he stared without seeing the ceiling. His lips were dry and chapped, and he had lost all sense of time. Instead of playing the music, he cradled his horn in his arms and whistled the melodies, mimicking the notes with his fingertips. A telephone rang in the distance, but Warren's ears only heard music.

A few days later, he was still there.

Chapter Thirty-Six
Second Skin

It was late Sunday afternoon when Warren heard an insistent knocking on his front door. He hadn't left the apartment since rediscovering his music room, and was enjoying being zoned out and disconnected from the outside world. The banging increased with a steadiness that was both annoying and hard to ignore. Rolling onto his side, he stumbled to stand on bare feet. His knees wobbled and head spun from the sudden movement. On the walk down the hall he leaned against the wall for balance.

"Who is it?"

"It's me," her voice was small.

Warren turned the knob and unlocked the door. The lights from the hall were bright and his gaze felt disoriented, but after squinting and stepping back he was able to focus.

Blanche Laurent stood there removing her sunglasses. "What happened to you? You look like shit," she touched his face with her hand. His bottom lip was bruised, and his chocolate skin ashen and dry. He was still wearing his tuxedo shirt and trousers from the night of the wedding, though damp and wrinkled. He smelled like sweat and spoiled salami.

"What're you doing here?" Warren backed away and shuffled across the room to the sofa, collapsing against the pillows.

"Why is the music so loud?" Blanche scanned the apartment. Warren could hear her heels clicking around. The living room felt stuffy, and the leaves on his favorite fern drooped like dog's ears. Warren felt weak and was slouched over when Blanche thrust a glass of water in his face.

"Drink this."

Warren obeyed, and finished half the glass before setting it down on the table. His stomach ached. When was the last time he had a meal?

"Bret was ranting about firing you on Friday..."

"Friday?"

"You know they don't play the no call, no show. How could you stay out a whole week? Are you insane?"

Warren scratched his head. He hadn't realized so much time had passed.

Blanche stood and paced through his living room. She wore a trench coat tied tightly at her waist and very high aqua and black printed heels. "In your defense I told him you called me sick. At first he didn't believe me but, you know I can be very persuasive," she looked down at him and smiled. Her lips were painted blood red and the sight of them made him nauseous.

"How'd you find me?"

"I know people in high places," she purred. Blanche stopped in front of him and held his gaze. Even in his current state, Warren recognized that unmistakable look of desire in her eyes, and when she propped herself in the seat next to him he knew she had come to bone.

Warren's head felt groggy. He needed time to think. "I'll be right back."

"Where are you going?" The front of her trench split and Blanche slid closer, showing off a pair of creamy thighs.

"I'ma take a shower."

Blanche scooted forward as if to follow him, but he touched her shoulder and said, "Alone."

TWENTY MINUTES LATER, WARREN walked slowly down the hall wearing his shawl-collared robe, drying his hair with a hand towel.

"I ordered Chinese," Blanche leaned against the kitchen counter. The buckle on her trench was loose, revealing a diamond-studded bra. But before Warren could comment, the telephone rang. Happy for a distraction, he picked up the cordless on the second ring.

"Hello. Hey, what's up?" he signaled to Blanche that he would be right back, and carried the phone down the hall and into his bedroom, where he closed the door.

"SEE YOU IN HALF an hour," he said into the receiver before ending the call. Ten minutes later he walked back into the living room, smelling like frankincense and dressed in black from head to toe. Blanche's eyes twinkled as she put her hands on her hips and said, "I hope you like lo mein."

Warren didn't want to hurt her feelings, so he kept his voice light as he confessed that he had to go.

"But I've ordered food, and I was hoping…"

"You can wait until the food arrives and then take it home with you," he had his money clip in his hand and dropped a few bills on the countertop. The music had started up in his head, and when he reached for his trumpet case he couldn't wait to shed.

"Just let yourself out," he replied, but when he glanced at Blanche the trench coat came down over her shoulders. Her panties were lace with the same diamond studs as her bra.

"If there is no time for dinner, surely we can skip right to dessert," she winked, cat-walking the few steps towards Warren. But when she leaned in to kiss him he pushed against her waist to hold her at a distance.

"Perhaps some other time," he tapped her wrist, and then eased out the door, shutting it behind him.

Chapter Thirty-Seven
Believe Me When I Say

"Like a moth to the flame burned by the fire." Erica hummed and rocked in her seat. "My love is blind can't you see my desire?"

Janet Jackson's "That's the Way Love Goes" became Erica's theme song. It was upbeat and lively and Erica needed upbeat. Upbeat gave her courage. So much courage that she was on the Accela express with a manuscript in her lap heading to D.C. After her night out with Tess she decided that if her relationship with Warren could be salvaged, then she had to cast pride aside and make the effort. Being put first was Warren's biggest gripe, and she was determined to show him how vital he was to her. Erica couldn't go on without him and she was prepared to beg, grovel and plead. She would even stand on her head while singing "I Apologize" by Anita Baker if that's what it took to convince him. They belonged together, and she wasn't leaving D.C. until he understood.

The train sped into the station and Erica was one of the fastest passengers to disembark. Taking long strides, she made her way out to the taxi stand on Massachusetts Avenue. The line wasn't long, and when she slid into the backseat of the cab she felt so optimistic that after rattling off the address to the driver she whispered to herself, "Please, get me to my man."

Her heart was beating like a conga drum when she reached his front lobby. She had no baggage, just her purse with an extra pair of panties in case he had gotten rid of her things. The doorman recognized her face and waved her through. On the elevator ride to his 8th floor condo her hands started to shake, and she reapplied her lip gloss and checked her nose through the reflection of the door for something to steady her. By the time the elevator arrived on his floor, her confidence had begun to waver. But Erica willed herself to continue down the hall by putting one foot in front of the other.

The original plan was to knock, but at the last minute she decided that she hadn't come all this way for him not to let her in. She decided she would use her key, and felt relieved when it turned in the hole with little effort.

"Sweetie. You're back. I knew you would change your mind." Stiletto heels clicked from down the hall towards Erica, but she was so shocked to hear a woman's voice that she couldn't locate her tongue.

"Honey, I…" Blanche turned the corner, but stopped moving when she saw Erica.

In all of the scenarios that ran through Erica's head, this one hadn't made the cut. The longer she stood there the harder it was for her brain to process what was happening right in front of her: Blanche, in the middle of Warren's apartment wearing a sleazy trench coat, under-damn-wear and some fuck me pumps. Erica could feel her eyes bulging from her head like she had thyroid disease.

Even though there was about fifteen feet between them, she could smell the woman's peachy perfume, and it added to the sickness rising in her stomach. Her nerves were sloshing around like runny eggs in a frying pan, but she had to make herself speak.

"Where's Warren?"

"Not home."

"What're you doing here?"

"I was invited. Can't say the same about you," Blanche stood her ground with composure, and watching her with that smug I-got-your-man-look made Erica want to fly across the room and fight her. Last-day-of-school-style, when it didn't matter how hard you beat a bitch's ass because you couldn't get suspended. Erica could already feel the thinness of the whore's hair in her hands as she flung her around the room, knocking down furniture. She could hear the glass splattering and smell the blood, but shook the vision.

Blanche tilted her head sideways, but she didn't move to close her coat. Like Erica wanted to see her bony ass.

"Look at you, standing there looking like a trailer whore. So tacky."

"That's not what Warren said."

"So how come he's not here?"

"That's none of your concern. Not anymore right? Don't hate, girlfriend."

Did she just say girlfriend? "Makes sense. Hoes are excellent on the rebound."

"I'm not going to take too many more of your hoes," Blanche's tongue slapped against the roof of her mouth, and Erica detected a little lower east side New York in her, but she wasn't scared. After all she had been through, Blanche could pull a gun on Erica and she wouldn't even flinch.

Erica took three long strides and shortened the space between them. "Where is he?" she demanded.

"Why? He's so done with you."

"Really? Is that why you're standing there looking like a video vixen trying to seduce him?" The walkway wasn't that long, and she had gotten close enough to see the nervousness cross Blanche's hazel eyes. "I know Warren's scent, and I don't smell sex in the air." Erica rolled her neck. "Looks a lot like rejection to me."

"Is there a message?" Blanche fumbled with her belt, as if she had just remembered her nakedness.

"Yeah. Fuck you," Erica shouted in Blanche's face, and then turned on her kitten heels and walked out of the apartment.

Erica's tough girl act was stripping down fast, and she knew she couldn't hold it together while waiting on the only elevator in the building, so she dipped into the stairway. On the sixth floor landing she started feeling winded, like a hammer was pounding against her chest. By the fifth floor, the tears were streaming, and at the top of the fourth she had to hold onto the banister for support. After three more steps, vomit shot from her mouth with such force she had to hold on for dear life. Her head was hot but her brows cold, and she was sweating like she had a fever. How could she have been so blind? Warren was messing with Blanche the whole time. Why else would she be sitting in his apartment half dressed? And buzzing around the office bringing him black coffee? The excuse Warren had given about them just sitting together at his father's dinner was bullshit. He had invited Blanche when Erica couldn't come. Probably screwed her in his car on the way home, that's how the condom slipped.

Erica's bag fell from her hand and she dropped on the step right next to it. The smell of her regurgitated tuna sandwich was noxious, but she couldn't go on. Her body had become like cement, too heavy for her to even curl into a ball and hide. It was really over. Dead and gone over. There was no way they could bounce back from this and no turning back after what she had witnessed.

Hot damn.

Chapter Thirty-Eight
Black Man Free

Warren had spent twenty-four hours locked in the room with his mother's spirit. As she was his first teacher, he trusted her and spent much of his life loving her more than anyone else. His pain had anchored him to the floor, so she knelt before Warren and brought him to his feet. Her vine-like hands held the rhythm of the beat, while she chanted in a language that he had never heard. Calling the confusion from his head and replacing it with pure beauty. As she pressed her fingertips to his ego, the power it held over him thinned and was replaced with the divine Light of his Spirit. Warren wept openly with his mother, until every ounce of moisture was drained from his body. Then she kissed strength into his third eye, throat, palms and soles of his feet while whispering, "My son, get up. God lives inside of you." She said it three times, and as he rose to thank her, she curled through the room like a puff of smoke and vanished. Once she did, Warren became conscious of the outside world again, and the person trying to break his door down.

It was James who called after Blanche arrived, inviting him to play a gig at "The Spot" in Arlington. Before he left home, Warren had anointed himself in frankincense, and the aromatic powers of the oil had him floating through the dark Virginia dive bar, like he was a weightless leaf. The college club was outfitted with wooden tables and a mixture of ladder-back chairs. A pool table sat in the corner on the right, with the platform stage taking up most of the space adjacent to the bar. The crowd was a blend of students seeking inexpensive beer and mature regulars who came to hear the music. James was always the first to arrive at a gig, and was on stage tightening his drums.

"Black man," he stood, wiping his hands on the front of his jeans, pulling Warren into a half handshake, half hug. "Fuck happened to your lip?"

Warren touched the open wound, having forgotten that it was there. "Shedding," he replied.

"Well I hope you can still play, because I have the mother of all gigs lined up."

Warren pulled up the piano stool. James was essentially the band's manager.

"I got a call from this promoter I know in New York. There's a major showcase going down. A&Rs, record producers, anyone who's anyone is going to be there," James paused. "And I got us on the list to play."

"Say word," Warren scratched his overgrown goatee.

"We get to play one song, five minutes, original tune. Talk to me, brotha. You're the best writer in the band. Tell me you've got something new."

Warren unfastened his trumpet case. Shoved in with his horn were sheets and sheets of new music. The songs had come to him so fast, that he had to scribble to keep up.

"We might need to work on some of the arrangements," Warren said, sorting the pages. Then he pointed to the notes while humming the highs and lows of the beat.

James' fingers started waving the way they did when he got excited, and when Warren sang out the finale, James slapped him five. "That's it."

IT WAS LATE WHEN Warren walked through his front door, and he was relieved that there was no sign of Blanche or her lo mein. He had been thinking about Erica on the drive home, and now that he was standing in his doorway it was like he could smell her. Being locked away for so long with himself had made him sensitive. He knew it was weird, but Erica's presence was suddenly so strong that he almost called her name. Once he flipped on the light the sensation passed, but he still missed her. A yearning had opened up and he had no idea how to quench it. Could their relationship be fixed? Warren wanted to see her, and the gig in New York proved to be his best opportunity.

Still antsy from the drive, he knew he wouldn't be able to sleep, so he pulled his laptop from his briefcase. His lip had started to throb and his fingertips were sore, but the music was still on in his head. The song they were going to play at the showcase was called "Love Burdened Eyes," and he had written it while thinking of Erica, and those wounded eyes she often turned on him at the end of their weekends. The song summed up the tug-of-war in their relationship and the constant battling that he felt, and he couldn't wait to hear it full out with all the instruments doing their part.

Ten new emails sat in his inbox. James must have gotten home fast because the first one was from him. It was the guidelines for their upcoming gig, and Warren almost dropped the computer when he read that it was being held at the Iridium Jazz club. Talk about serendipity.

The Iridium was where he met Erica on a humid summer night. Warren had been on stage at the jazz club jamming with a young quintet. They were rendering a song from Miles Davis' album *Sketches of Spain*, and Warren knew he was failing in comparison to Davis on the tune. When he looked out into the audience to see if anyone noticed, he saw Erica.

She was sitting alone, sipping a drink with her pink nails pressed against a red straw. Her reddish-brown hair hung loose on her shoulders, and the vanilla halter she wore reflected the tan on her summered skin. Warren was immediately attracted to her, so when he closed his eyes and blew, he envisioned himself asking her out. From that moment he didn't miss another note.

After the performance, he lingered on stage with the other musicians as they packed up their instruments, but his eyes never lost Erica. When she glided toward the exit, he excused himself from the guys and fell in step beside her. She thanked him as he pushed open the door for her, and it was then that he noticed miniature freckles on her cheeks. They were like cinnamon drops sprinkled on a slice of French toast, and when she smiled, Warren's heart really did stop.

"What would make a woman come to a jazz club alone?" They were on the corner of 51st and Broadway.

"My girlfriend was supposed to meet me but she flaked," Erica looked into traffic.

"Can I hail you a cab?"

She laughed. "We both know a black man can't get a cab to Harlem," she stepped into the street waving her wrist back and forth, making her gold bangles clank. When the taxi stopped, Warren opened the door for her, and then slipped into the seat beside her.

"Then I guess we'll have to share," he smiled. It was a bold move, but there was something in the way she flicked her hair that told him it was okay, even though they spent the first five blocks in frozen silence.

"Do you play trumpet full time?" she chipped at the ice.

He tucked his trumpet case under his feet and explained that he was interning at the United Nations by day, playing his horn at night. When he asked her the same, she told him that she had attended NYU and was now climbing the ladder in publishing. Their conversation flowed, and as the driver rounded the corner of 125th Street, Warren invited her for a nightcap, which she accepted.

The Lenox Lounge had been a landmark in Harlem since the late 1930s, serving as a popular backdrop for many jazz legends, and a place for Harlem Renaissance writers to congregate. The Art Deco club lured a spunky mix of local hipsters, students, and tourists, and as Erica and Warren shared a round of drinks in the semicircular booth, the top layer of their lives unfolded. When the house lights signaled closing time, Warren insisted on walking Erica to her apartment. And as they passed through her front gate, he remembered her apologizing for her landlady's idea of garden art.

"The house has been under construction since I moved here," she said referring to the wooden porch, which drunkenly staggered toward the left.

"When can I see you again?" Warren dabbed at the sweat forming on his brows.

Unlocking her front door, she stepped into the vestibule, quietly analyzing him for so long it made him wonder if she had heard the question.

"Tomorrow, I'll be at the diner on the corner of 135th and Lenox, ten o'clock," she whispered, and then closed the door behind her. Warren watched her through the glass pane as she walked the stairs, taking in the best pair of legs that he had ever laid eyes on.

The memory had come to him without effort, and all he wanted was to go back.

For the office on Monday Warren was careful in overdressing the part, selecting a brown suit with a paisley tie, wingtip shoes and silk socks. It had been over a week since he trimmed his facial hair. The rough look suited his mood, and he didn't care what the handbook said. As he walked through the door that led to his department, he collided with Blanche. He caught her by the arm to keep her from stumbling. She moved her bangs from her hazel eyes, studying him, like she was expecting something. When he didn't respond, she slipped him a piece of paper.

"It's a doctor's note explaining your absence," she whispered. "Your lip looks better," she squeezed his bicep on her way down the hall.

In his cubicle, Warren felt out of place. Brett, his manager, buzzed him before his computer had finished booting, and Warren could tell by the way he ordered him to his office that he wasn't happy. Still, Warren took his time walking over.

"You wanted to see me," he stood in Brett's office doorway. On the mantel sat an exorbitantly large portrait of Brett's perfect family: prom queen wife, blonde daughter, blue-eyed boy and a dog named Prissy.

Brett had been reading the newspaper and took his time folding the section back and making a neat pile before acknowledging Warren. "Nice of you to grace us with your presence," his tone wore spiked heels.

"I have a doctor's note," Warren stretched the slip toward him, but Brett batted at it like it was an annoying flea.

"What do you think you're pulling, missing work without calling, and then strolling in here with some bogus note? You're taking advantage."

"Of what?"

"No one else on the team would ever pull a stunt like this. If it weren't for your father…"

"What does he have to do with this?" Warren replied hotly.

"You might not be standing here."

"Is that a threat?"

"Call it what you like it. I'm just telling you to watch what you do, Buddy. Big brother's eyes are all over you." Brett turned back to his paper, "And Daddy can't help all the time." His last remark was a whisper.

Warren knew his worth, and at this point it had nothing to do with his father knowing Stan. Brett had a lot of nerve threatening him. Warren was the one busting his ass while Brett shuffled papers and called meetings every ten minutes masquerading as the expert. Jackass.

If they fired Warren it would be a relief.

Chapter Thirty-Nine
Unwanted Guest

Erica didn't know how long she sat in the stairwell in Warren's building with the lyrics of "Fool of Me" by Me'Shell Ndegecello playing in her head. Erica felt dumb. Stupid. Blind as a one-winged bat. What kind of idiot was she? How long? That's what she wanted to know, and as she found herself sinking into the seat cushions of the train back to New York, she felt like the playlist of every broken-hearted love song. This pain hurt worse than brand new shoes, Ms. Sade. It was the type of suffering that offered no cure, no amount of prescription drugs could help her now. All she could do was ache.

When she emerged from the subway back in Harlem, she tried walking away her misery on the five block stretch to her house so that her mother wouldn't ask questions. The woman was like a bloodhound when it came to detecting Erica's mood and she couldn't go through it with her, not tonight. Her excuse for leaving had been a book signing in Baltimore, and her mother wasn't expecting her until the morning. Hopefully she'd be asleep, and Erica wouldn't have to explain coming home in the middle of the night.

As she got closer to her brownstone, Erica spotted Tess sitting on their saggy front porch, wearing a ratty French beret and an oversized army coat buttoned to her neck. No wig, no lashes, and lips covered with a thin layer of Vaseline. Something was wrong, she didn't look herself.

"What're you doing out here in the cold?" Erica pulled her hat low so that Tess couldn't see her face.

"You look like shit," Tess flicked an ash. "Where're you coming from?"

Erica couldn't discuss it now, and stuck with the work story. Tess must have been too preoccupied with her own problems to detect the lie, because she just pulled over a vinyl kitchen chair and patted the seat for Erica to sit. The sparse furniture on the porch could easily be mistaken as trash, but anything nicer had the potential of being lifted. Even with the gentrification taking place in Harlem, where developers were constructing hundreds of million-dollar condos on every other corner, there was still a certain street element that couldn't be ignored. Tess lit a second cigarette and passed it. Erica dragged hard.

"Mercury must be in retrograde, 'cause now Hercules and I are on the outs. Why can't I find a guy who sexes well and just wants to have a good time? I'm not trying to get married, don't want no babies. Just a good damn time," Tess pulled a crumpled brown paper bag from a side pocket in her army coat and passed it. Erica sipped from the pint and coughed, then wiped her mouth with the back of her gloved hand.

"What was that?"

"Bourbon."

"You drink like an old woman."

Tess shrugged and puffed on her cigarette. A crackhead wobbled down the street lugging two shovels, and both girls watched him, knowing that the tools were stolen. Erica was glad for the moments of silence. There was no way she could tell Tess what happened in D.C. without falling apart. She was exhausted physically and mentally.

Tess flicked her cigarette into the garden of dead art, and Erica watched the last bit of the flame die in the air before it hit the porcelain sink. Her butt was frozen and her toes freezer burned.

"Come on, it's getting cold," Tess stood and unlocked the door. Erica followed her inside, happy for the warmth. Tess made it to the second floor before stopping and leaning her thick frame against the banister. She coughed hoarsely. "Before I forget, I have a big gig coming up."

"I'm there." Erica replied, pleased to have something to look forward too. Tess sung like an angel and Erica was one of her biggest fans.

When they reached their floor, the smell of cigarette smoke was as strong as air freshener in the hallway between their two apartments, and noisy, raspy voices were coming from Erica's end.

"Why does she have the TV on so loud?"

The door was unlocked and when Erica pushed through to her living room, she was face to face with yet another person she didn't want to see. It was becoming obvious that Erica had fallen out of favor with Lady Luck the instant she broke the handmirror at work, because since then her life had steadily headed downhill without a set of sturdy brakes.

Bonnie, the devil herself, was sitting in Erica's living room with her feet propped up on the coffee table like it was the most natural thing in the world, and it was almost funny.

"My bad, E. Long time no see," Bonnie waved her hand in the air and then reached for the remote control.

Erica nodded her hello. It had been years since she saw Bonnie, but she hadn't changed. She wore stark-white glasses that were too large for her mousey face. Her cocoa-colored skin was still pocked by black pimples, and her short hair was snatched together with a pink glittery clip. Erica knew without looking that the pink glitter was repeated in her nail polish, socks and perhaps even her shoes. For as long as Erica had known Bonnie, she had been flashy to a fault. Wearing bright-yellow running suits with matching sneakers in January, floor-length fur coats and earmuffs in April, bodysuits and cutoff jeans worn with fishnets in November. The kicker was when she showed up to Grandma Queeny's funeral wearing blood red in the dead of July.

Bonnie Thomasetta Clark, the woman who took her mother away, caused her parents to split, and changed Erica's life forever. Just being in the same room with her brought up the agonizing times Erica went to bed hungry and scared, ran "code badman" to protect her and Jazmine when the doorbell rang, couldn't call her friends at school because they didn't have a telephone, ate spoiled food because the electricity had been shut off, all because her mother had been more concerned with Bonnie.

"Heey, Slim," her mother slurred, waving like they were meeting someplace other than Erica's own living room. "Don't be upset, we'll clean this mess up." The alcohol had her eyes protruding like oversized marbles, and her head was rolling around her neck like a newborn's.

A near-empty liter of Bacardi, two red plastic cups, and an ashtray of butts overflowed on the table where they had been playing cards. The smell of lemons and pines had been replaced with the stinking scent of betrayal.

"You said you weren't comin' back til tomorrow. Bonnie came to keep me cump-nee." Her mother was attempting to stand, but the futon was dipped so low, she kept sliding backward. The more she concentrated on getting up, the further back she fell.

It was a dilapidating picture and Erica felt traumatized. "You need to go," her voice was deliberate.

"See, I knew I shouldn't have come," said Bonnie. "I told you."

"No. Her house is my house, you welcome anytime." Her mother touched Bonnie's hand. "I'm still the mother round here," she mumbled under her breath for Bonnie's benefit, but Erica had dog ears.

"Are you?" Erica clinched her fist. "Were you?" she shouted. "When? Please tell me when. Because that's not the way I remember it." The wrath pushed hard against the fibers of her face, rearranging her loveliness into pure pit-bull rage. Tess piped up, "Ms. Gweny, why don't ya'll come over to my apartment and give Erica a chance to get settled." Bonnie grabbed her purse and switched her narrow hips over to where Tess stood in the doorway, but Erica's mother didn't move.

"I ain't raise you to be disrespectful."

"You didn't raise me at all. You were out running the streets with her," she pointed to Bonnie, "and you left me to fend for myself."

"I did the best I could."

"No. You didn't." Erica moved closer. "You were never around and when you were, you were drunk or in the bed. I'm sick and tired of you acting like I owe you something, calling me for money every other day. I'm not responsible for you. It was supposed to be the other way around. And you never got it right." Erica's mouth scrunched as she sliced her hands through the air. "I'm done. I'm so F-ing done."

She tried to take a deep breath, but the words continued to fight for freedom. "How could you treat us like that, like you didn't give a damn? What was more important than taking care of your children? I really need to know. Where were you all those nights? How could you leave us unprotected? What kinda mother would do that to her babies?" The tears welled and Erica brought her hand to her lips. She had finally said what she had been thinking for so many years, and it felt like the guck in her chest had loosened.

Her mother's hands shook as she reached across the table for her cigarettes, squeezing one from the package. "This ain't the time," her voice sounded almost sober. The lighter flickered but wouldn't catch. "What is it that you want from me?"

The guck had started to separate, and the untreated wounds that Erica had buried whole with her fancy degrees, company cars and job titles emerged without permission. When she parted her lips the little girl who had long since died inside of her was resurrected.

"I wanted you to stop drinking and love me. Get a job and pay the bills. I needed you to show up at my school sober and not embarrass me. Put gifts under the Christmas tree and pretend that Santa had come. I wanted you to take me shopping at the mall, read stories, tuck me in at night..." Tears spilled down the little girl's cheeks and her voice was soft and trembling. "I…I wanted a mother who would take me to ballet lessons and be waiting for me in the lobby when I came out of class, not outside on the pay phone. I wanted you to be my goddamn mother. And for my entire life I could never figure out why that was so damn hard for you to do."

Erica's mother had started rocking in her seat and her arms were shaking so badly that her cigarette dropped. She had finally figured out how to maneuver her ass to the edge of the futon. When she leaned her hearty body forward for the cigarette, her fingertip grazed the filter. But she bent too much, and before she could catch herself she missed her footing and slipped to the floor.

"Damn it, that's my bad hip." She rolled on her side.

"That wouldn't have happened if you weren't so drunk," Erica's voice came out like a mad whisper.

"It's the weekend Slim, cut me a break."

"Every day it's something, and all I've done is cut you breaks."

"Well, could somebody help me up?" Her mother looked like Humpty Dumpty who fell off the wall, with a cigarette clasped between her fingers.

"I'm tired of helping you, Ma." Erica stepped around her, pushed past Tess and Bonnie, who stood suspended in place by the tension.

"Please don't be here when I get back," Erica said. And when she walked out of her apartment, she left the old Erica behind.

Chapter Forty

Nothing Left to Lose

Warren was fucking Blanche.

Her mother had once again chosen Bonnie.

Now the only thing Erica had left was her job. Deciding that it was time to cast her personal life aside, she focused on her promotion. With Edie home on maternity leave, Erica had to make her move. She shoved her feeling inside of her gray tailored pant suit, hid what didn't fit in her French twist, and covered what was left beneath with shimmered eye shadow and a fresh coat of clear gloss.

In the office, she headed over to Karen and requested a meeting with Claire.

"There's a ten o'clock departmental scheduled today. She has a small window directly following," Karen replied, and Erica thanked her.

Inside her office, Erica sipped her coffee and rehearsed what she wanted to say. This was the most important conversation of her adult life, and she only had one shot at getting it right. Erica wanted the Director's position now more than she ever had before.

At ten o'clock sharp, the publicity department filed into Claire's office and took their appropriate seats. Assistants on the floor, publicist and above on the sofa, but no one sat in Edie's chair. Claire stood glowing in a heap of jewels behind her desk, making her petite frame seem taller. She asked about their weekend, and once everyone finished bantering, she cleared her throat to begin.

"I have some good and bad news," she pressed her fingertips together. "The good is that you have all done a phenomenal job in Edie's absence. Erica, Reverend Black is still singing your praises."

It was always an honor to have your name recognized in the meeting, and Erica smiled her thank you.

"The bad news is that Edie will not be returning," Claire paused to let her words sink in, and Erica knew her face was caught between a grimace and smile. She wasn't sure where the conversation was headed and she prayed she wasn't too late. Claire went on to say that Edie had decided to stay home full-time with the baby, and the disappointment of losing her business partner was obvious in her eyes.

"But I've found someone to replace her."

Erica's stomach turned. Would Claire announce her promotion without consulting her first? Wouldn't they need to discuss the details like salary, office with a view, and the other perks that come with moving up?

"His name is Athan McKinley," Claire said, and on cue Karen passed around his bio to all fifteen people in the room. Erica was struck silly. Claire had gone outside of the company to hire someone without even considering her. How could she do that?

"I'm sure you'll all love him. He comes from Miramax films. He was their head of publicity for seven years and has been a good friend of mine for ten. I've often bounced ideas off him in the past, and I think he will fill Edie's irreplaceable shoes just fine," Claire smiled.

Erica had grown tired of feeling like the wind had been knocked out of her. Work had been the one safe haven, until now.

"I went ahead and pulled someone from the outside because I wanted fresh, innovative ideas; someone who could come in and shake things up a bit. He starts a week from Monday, and I hope you will all do your best to make him feel welcome. Any questions?" she asked.

None.

"Great. The announcement will be made companywide this afternoon."

The meeting adjourned, and the department filed out of the office in the same schoolyard manner in which they had entered. Karen motioned for Erica to stay, but she really just wanted to go.

"What do you think of my news?" Claire gave her that motherly smile that usually put Erica at ease, but it didn't help. "I know you're going to love Athan. He's so smart, and I'm really looking forward to him showing us new ways of doing business."

"How come you didn't consider me for the position?" Erica stared straight into Claire's eyes. "From day one I've handled the top-notch campaigns, worked with the most difficult authors, all with stellar results. Why not me?" she knew the anger was oozing out, but she decided that it was now or never.

Claire reached for her bottled water and took a long sip before returning Erica's steadfast gaze. "You are doing a wonderful job, and it's true that you are my go-to-girl. Experience is what Athan has that you're lacking, and I think he will be instrumental in teaching you how to hone those skills needed."

"How much longer?"

"It's hard to say. Why don't we see how the spring plays out and revisit this conversation?" Claire extended her hand, which meant it was time for Erica to go. "I'm really counting on you to help Athan get settled."

Of course she was; wasn't that always the case? The black woman gets passed over by some white man, when in fact she has to teach him the job for which she had long since been qualified. Returning to her office, Erica called over her shoulder that she was going for coffee. Outside, the air wasn't fresh enough. She bypassed the truck on the corner with the stale bagels and headed to the new gourmet shop three blocks away. She needed to put some distance between her and Claire's news. Light jazz was playing when she walked into the coffee shop, and the small wood-burning fireplace was lit. Indian throw rugs and overstuffed cushiony chairs lent the room comfort but did little to lighten Erica's mood. Sweets would do that, and she ordered a fatty latte and a thick slice of marble cake and wolfed it all down.

SHE TOOK THE LONG way back to the office, and no sooner had she removed her coat, Prudence bounced, in swinging her brown hair, with two message slips. The girl was so cheerful that it was sickening.

"Warren called and so did LaVal Jarvis," Prudence handed Erica the slips.

Warren called? Her insides fluttered and she couldn't concentrate on the next five things that Prudence said.

"Goldie was emphatic about needing it by the end of the day. Erica?"

She was pulled from her thoughts. "Yes. Sure. Fine. Thanks."

Prudence backed out of the office. What did Warren want? Had Blanche told Warren about her showing up at his apartment? Erica picked up the telephone, hesitated, and dialed LaVal.

"Jarvis."

"LaVal, Erica Shaw from B&B returning your call."

"How are you?" his voice was husky, and he made small talk before getting down to the nature of his call.

"I'm in New York at the end of the week, and there's something that I'd like to discuss with you. Can we meet?"

"Of course," Erica replied, and scribbled down the appointment.

Warren's message stared at her from the desk, and although she was itching to call him, she balled it up and tossed it in the trashcan. Being hurt twice was not an option.

WARREN BROUGHT HOME SOME files from work, along with an 18-year-old single malt Scotch. The Knicks were playing, but it was no fun watching the game without Erica. Even when it was a weekday game, they would watch over the phone. Why hadn't she returned his calls? Warren had left a message with her assistant, and tried her cell phone so many times that he felt as though he was becoming a stalker. He was ready to talk and clear the air. Could she have moved on?

His bottom lip was still slightly swollen, and it had curbed his thirst to shed. The love affair he had with his trumpet was like being in a marriage—some days his lust was so strong that he couldn't keep his hands off of her, while on others he didn't want to be touched. Right now it was the latter, and he was glad that his band didn't have rehearsal until Wednesday night.

Blanche had offered to buy him a drink as he was leaving the office but he declined, deciding that it was best to put some space between them. He really hoped that she would get the hint. Alan seemed to be watching them, and the last thing Warren needed at work was Alan scheming behind his back, especially with Brett's chest puffed out over Warren's unannounced absence.

Warren was used to getting looks from women, but lately they had become bolder. Monday night, a short-haired girl with a nice smile was practically throwing the booty at him when he got off stage. Warren was flattered, but he only wanted Erica. Once he made up his mind on something there was no turning back.

ATHAN MCKINLEY, THE NEW Director of Publicity, had reported to the office, and Erica spent her days explaining campaigns and operations, while Claire carted him around to meetings showing him off like a brand new kitten. After a few days with him, it was clear to Erica that while Athan may have come with more publicity experience, she knew publishing. And the two professions were as different as swimming in a four-foot lake and deep-sea scuba diving. The fact that he had stolen her job and was benefiting from her knowledge was like a noose around her neck. Her only act of refuge had been leaving the office each day at five. No more working ten- to twelve-hour days. If Claire noticed the change, Erica didn't care.

She had read once that in a single day, 75 percent of an average person's thoughts were negative, and as Erica moved through her day, her negativity went from thoughts to actions. She snapped at her assistant for forgetting to give her a message, cursed out the guy at the mail desk because two boxes of books that she needed were missing, accused the clerk at the deli of giving her the wrong change, pushed her way onto the subway, knocking a too-skinny woman out of the way so that she could squeeze into the last seat. Her day had been out of sorts, and to remedy what was left of it, she stopped at the fish shop on the corner of 125th and Fifth Avenue and waited in line behind ten people for a large order of fried porgies, hush puppies, collard greens and potato salad. Nothing was more comforting than salty soul food, and she practically ran up the four flights of stairs to her apartment with her tongue dragging over the wet paper bag.

Since she sent her mother back to Newark, and was passed up for the Director's position, Erica couldn't stand to be in her apartment alone, spending most of her time over at Tess'. Hercules had turned out to be another dud, and the girls distracted themselves from their man troubles by eating, listening to old music, and watching every Diana Ross movie that Tess could get her hands on. They drank woo woos by the pitcher, a drink made with peach schnapps, vodka, and cranberry juice. Tess swore the drink had healing powers and Erica didn't complain because it helped her sleep through the night. But after so many consecutive nights of boozing, she couldn't help wondering if her mother's addictions had begun this way, couch-potatoing with a girlfriend while pity-partying over some man. She still hadn't returned Warren's calls, and once Tess heard the full story of Blanche, she called Erica a ditz.

"I woulda slapped that bitch upside her head and kicked her out of the apartment. Sugar, I don't know why you didn't wait for Warren to come back. I'm sure there was a logical explanation," Tess said every time the subject came up. But Erica had stopped listening. Tess was such a hopeless romantic that Erica had to take her advice in small doses. Erica was sick to pieces of feeling like a wheelbarrow on wobbly wheels, and although she missed Warren like an amputated limb, she was done. It was time for her to develop the thick skin of a rhinoceros and move on. She would only do what was necessary to survive, and once Erica had set her mind to something she could be as stubborn as the Arizona sun.

Chapter Forty-One

Love-Burdened Eyes

Friday came like it did every week, and Erica was determined to have a good weekend from the minute she hit the lobby of her office building. She hopped the 1 train, which rattled uptown to 28th Street. She was meeting LaVal at the Plush Bar and Grill, a lounge with thatched ceilings and a bamboo-inspired theme restaurant that as of recently was getting a lot of play. The 28th Street station deposited her across the street from the restaurant, and when she swept through the doors, she made a mental note of how long she could stay. Erica needed LaVal to get to his point quickly. After their drink she had to hurry to midtown for Tess' performance. She was the opening act, so Erica couldn't afford to be late.

He waved her over to a corner booth and jumped up to help her with her coat when she rounded the table. Erica felt his eyes on her back and tried not to quiver. It was the most male attention she had received in what felt like a long time.

"Is this spot okay?" he asked, smoothing out his pecan-colored tie against another stylish suit. She could smell aloe vera on his hands when he slipped next to her in the wrap-around seat.

Erica had a hard time that morning finding the right look, but had settled on a clingy wool dress with a floppy turtleneck and gold-beaded jewelry. It was still early, so the after-work crowd was sparse around the bar, with only two other couples sitting in the lounge area. Popular shoulder-moving music played at a volume that was good for conversation.

"Mind if I order a few appetizers?" he asked when the waiter approached. Erica did mind, but nodded politely. What did he want? She tried not to look at her watch as he ordered a Pu Pu platter and two glasses of pinot noir.

"I'm just getting in from Scottsdale. I had a lecture at the university and then squeezed in a few rounds of golf."

"You play?" she chuckled.

"Don't look so surprised."

From the drug corners of Chicago to the exclusive golf courses in Scottsdale, LaVal Jarvis is sure to open the country's eyes to a new breed of black men with his memoir, *365 Degrees of Change*. Interesting, Erica thought.

"What are you thinking?" he grinned, making those dimples pop, but she didn't have the heart to utter such a rough pitch.

"What did you want to discuss?"

"My lectures. I've been receiving quite a few requests, and it's getting harder for me to get back to everyone," he paused. "I was wondering if you'd be interested in working for me part-time," he placed his glass on the table.

Erica studied him, wondering if this was some sort of trap. "I have a job."

"Just a side venture, I'd pay you a percentage of course."

"Why not hire a lecture agency?"

The waitress brought the platter, and LaVal helped himself to a little of everything.

"Because I don't trust them, and they charge huge fees when I'm doing all the work."

"So you're looking for cheap labor?" Erica reached for a spring roll. The aroma had made her hungry. Fried food was her new weakness.

"Concentrated labor," LaVal flashed his teeth. "You're an enterprising woman, so I know you realize by now that a nine-to-five isn't going to keep you satisfied."

Did he sense what she was dealing with at the office? It was a risky move. She was his publicist via B&B, and she was sure that there was something in the handbook that would say no to doing outside business with clients. Nonetheless, the opportunity intrigued her.

"I need to think about it," she placed her fork on her plate.

"It's a big decision, I know," he wiped his mouth.

Erica told him that she'd get back to him in a week or so and began gathering her things.

LaVal dropped his napkin on his plate. "What are you doing later?"

"A friend of mine is singing tonight."

"Can I tag along?" His eyes held hers.

Erica hesitated. She didn't want to say yes, but how could she say no? He had just offered her a job. Maybe Tess would find him interesting. She was on the rebound from her fling with Hercules and LaVal was fine.

"Okay," she reached for her coat, "but we have to hurry."

Erica had printed Tess' email with the show's information before leaving work, and was in such a rush that she stuffed it in her bag without reading it. LaVal was rambling on about his lecture in Scottsdale when she read out the address and realized that she was heading to the Iridium, the club where she met Warren. Why was this happening when she was on the verge of growing her rhinoceros skin?

On the drive up the Avenue of the Americas, LaVal kept up the chatter, and although Erica nodded and laughed, she had let her mind wander to the details of that first time she and Warren came together. When the taxi pulled up to the curb, LaVal insisted on paying the fare and Erica didn't have the time to fight him. Tess was going on in five, and the Iridium always began on time.

Jazz clubs in New York City were notorious for cramming in more tables than was comfortable, and the Iridium was no exception. Erica followed the hostess to their table with her handbag pinned to her chest, saying excuse me and trying in vain not to bump her hip against people's shoulders and heads. Tess had made the reservation, and since she was on the program, Erica's table was front and center. The odd-shaped furniture, quirky gold-trimmed mirrors, and hanging light fixtures were what Erica remembered most from her many nights there with Warren. Nothing had changed.

Three tables to the left was where she sat on the night she watched him struggle through one of the longer cuts of Miles Davis' *Sketches of Spain*. One table back and two tables to the right was where they had celebrated their one-year anniversary, and every table in between was where she had watched him jam session after session. The Iridium had been their place, and even though LaVal was just her client, it felt weird to be sitting there with him. Erica kicked herself for not reading the location on the flyer before allowing him to come.

LaVal must have sensed something because he touched her elbow and then ordered them both dirty martinis. Alcohol was just what she needed, and as soon as the waitress returned with their drinks, the lights went down and on glided Tess. She had changed her hair to a jet-black straight 'do, which was tucked behind her ears, pinned with a lavender gardenia. Her mint dress criss-crossed at the breast, showing off mounds of cleavage dusted in glitter. The gardenia was her tribute to Billie Holiday, but when she parted her mouth, it was the whispery sound of Diana Ross that held the audience still.

"That's my friend," Erica whispered.

"She's good," he mumbled, but Tess was better than good. Her voice was surreal, like the first cry of a newborn, seconds after being pushed from the womb. Angelic. The room seemed almost afraid to breath for fear of missing a note.

Shimming her hips halfway to the floor, Tess threw up her arms, and then belted out the last note, holding it longer than humanly natural. The audience was awestruck. Erica was the first on her feet, clapping until her palms stung.

Tess' signature was to bow three times before blowing two kisses and sashaying off the stage. No sooner than she did, the lights changed from bright yellow to the color of dust, and a horn started wailing in the wings. The sound was as pure as hungry chicks chirping, announcing the onset of spring. Suddenly, like warm sun pushing through thick clouds on a rainy day, the music opened into a soulful Sunday-morning swing. The lighting moved from dust to bright orange and Warren strolled onto the stage, with that cocky walk that was either to be admired or despised. He wore black from head to toe, and his almond skin glistened from the sheer joy of sharing his gift.

Erica was iced to her seat. It was like seeing and hearing him play for the first time. Goose bumps prickled her arms, and she reached for her martini in an attempt to cool herself. Damn he looked good. Her insides did a push-and-pull. She loved him, no she hated him.

Always a master at his craft, Warren took his time playing and riffing his notes with an intensity that seduced Erica beyond her will. The rhythm synced with her breathing and within seconds she was inside of the melody. Even though she tried fighting the feeling, Warren's horn knew her well and pulled on her vulnerabilities, smothering her between its clutches. It seemed like the two of them were in the room alone, and each chord he crooned reached the shadows of her pain. The sound of his healing made Erica feel like she could stay in that space forever, and she closed her eyes and allowed the power of his music to possess her.

Moments later James interrupted her drift by ramming his sticks into his drum and picking up the pace. He played on top of the beat while the bass took a walk and kept time. The melody ran across the range of instruments, giving the tone a light and happy feel. Each musician had a chance to strut his stuff and solo before the quintet rejoined in a faded tune that was as soft as bare feet, tiptoeing across a bed of tulips. Warren blew into his horn even slower, and it felt like Erica could feel his mouth on her chin. The other musicians made their instruments whisper, as the song ended almost like it began, in a series of cries, each one more piercing than the previous.

The crowd went berserk. Warren waited a beat and then brought the microphone to his thick lips. The trumpet dangled from his left hand and he looked so happy.

"Love Burdened Eyes," he announced, and the magnitude of the words hit Erica as their eyes met and embraced.

It has been said that body language is subject to interpretation. But, if someone had asked Erica what happened in that moment that passed between them when the rest of the room seemed to disappear, she would have said that Warren reached for her face and kissed her full on the mouth, resting his tongue against hers, breathing into her body with urgent regrets.

WARREN COULDN'T BELIEVE ERICA was in the audience. But who was the dude sitting next to her?

A CLASSIC JAZZ STANDARD played in the background, and the audience moved around for smoke breaks, bathroom visits, and phone calls, while the waitresses brought drinks before the next set.

"Who's that?" Tess snuck up beside her, and Erica mumbled out of the crook of her mouth that he was the author she had been telling her about. She wanted to scream at Tess for not telling her that Warren would be there, but Tess was already extending her hand flirtatiously to LaVal. They exchanged pleasantries before Tess was pulled by an admirer in the opposite direction.

"This place is hot," LaVal tapped the table with his fingertips, and Erica wondered if it was the club or Tess that he was talking about. It didn't matter because she needed to leave. She couldn't bear sharing the room with Warren, and just as she turned to tell LaVal, a tickling sensation breezed through her reddish hair. Erica felt Warren before his fingers touched the exposed skin above her shoulder. All of her anger was lost in the shuffling of her feet as she turned his way. Warren's beard had grown thick like vines, and he seemed taller, or lighter, definitely different, and when he opened his arms smiling his crooked grin her feet carried her right in. She was such a nut, she thought to herself.

Warren's shirt was damp and smelled of frankincense.

"Great title," she raised her eyes.

"Yeah, you were awesome," LaVal interrupted the union by holding out his hand to Warren. The two shook hands and Erica could feel the men sizing each other up like boxers in a ring. She started to clarify, but enjoyed the wonder in Warren's eyes.

"Erica, can I talk to you for a minute?"

"I was just headed to the ladies room," she fumbled with her purse and excused herself in the opposite direction. The nerves in her body seemed to have congregated in her stomach, and she really wished they would move down to her feet.

Once she was in the sea of women fighting for mirror space, she spotted Tess, and turned an evil eye in her direction. "How come you didn't tell me Warren was going to be here?"

"Sugar, I didn't see him until I was halfway on stage."

"If I had known I wouldn't have…"

"Brought LaVal? I'm glad you did. Makes it look like you're not sitting around waiting on him. He broke up with you, remember?" She dropped her brush in her purse.

"The song was about me," Erica said and then explained.

"So you have a chance if you want one."

"What about Blanche?"

"For the umpteenth time, stop worrying about her." Tess started for the door. "You staying for the second set?"

Erica said no. She needed to get away from Warren. Being this close had hindered her ability to think. They agreed to meet outside in five and share a cab back to the house. LaVal was waiting for her at the table.

"I need to go," she leaned in over the music.

"You can't stay for the last set?"

Erica shook her head, and LaVal got to his feet, helping her into her coat. With his hand resting on the small of her back, they parted the crowd and headed for the front door. Erica searched the room for a glimpse of Warren and didn't see him.

But he saw her, leaving with the next motherfucker, and it took all his control not to stop them.

Chapter Forty-Two

A Can of Whoop-Ass

Erica had been tossing and turning since she crawled into bed, so when her buzzer rang she was only half asleep. She opened her eyes but didn't move, wanting to make sure she wasn't dreaming first. The buzzer rang again, longer this time. Annoyed, she slid from the warmth of her goose comforter and pillow-top bed and shuffled across the cold, hardwood floor. If it was someone looking for her neighbor Lula from the second floor, Erica was going to lose it. Lula's guests had a habit of touching the wrong bell.

"Who is it?" she barked into the intercom, but heard nothing. Just when she was about to give up, she heard him.

"It's me."

The sound of Warren's voice went straight into her chest, pumping her blood so fast she felt light-headed. What was he doing here? Her hands shook against her head scarf as she pulled it down and fingered out her hair. The apartment was a mess, but she knew he hadn't come for the décor. Just that thought alone dampened the seams of her shorts.

Warren waited in the hallway for Erica, asking himself again why he was there. He had gone back to the hotel with the other guys but couldn't sleep. He raided the wet bar and took a few shots, but even that didn't settle him. He couldn't stop picturing Erica with Dude, and needed to know the score.

"You do realize what time it is?" Erica wore only a camisole and a pair of satin sleep shorts that displayed her pretty legs. She was a timeless beauty, never needing hair, make-up or clothes. Beauty belonged to her in the raw sense. Her look was delicate and exotic, like a bird of paradise at the height of bloom. Her buttery skin looked supple, and her eyes were so tender that he wanted to lay down in them and rest his head.

This was Warren's favorite time to catch her, right after she had been sleeping, and he was tempted to kiss her, but not yet. He needed to know if she had moved on first. Just one sniff in her bedroom would let him know if they had boned, and although it would crush him, he had to know. Erica motioned him in. The living room was cluttered with used cartons of takeout, bottled drinks, papers and clothes. Erica was never as neat as he was but this was ridiculous. He stepped into the entranceway of her bedroom and stuck his head in.

"Excuse you," she stood behind him.

Three quick sniffs only revealed weeks of dirty laundry and salt-and-vinegar potato chips, her favorite.

"Just trying to see what you've done with the place."

"Can't you see it's a mess?" she said, and as he looked into her face, her cheeks reddened. Warren's eyes darted around searching for a sock,T-shirt, something to confirm his suspicions. He knew he had asked for space, but he just needed to sort some things out. They were sorted now and he hadn't expected Erica to be on to the next man so soon, it had only been a month.

"Can I use your bathroom?" He could feel the Scotch working through his bloodstream.

"You know where it is."

Warren strolled into the bathroom and closed the door. The metal hinges squeaked. The WD40 that he'd put on must have worn off. Dude wasn't even doing his job. What was she keeping him around for if he wasn't even useful? Warren flushed the toilet to mask the sound of him snooping in the cabinets and drawers. All of Erica's familiars greeted him like an old friend. Nothing. He opened the door and walked into the kitchen.

"Do you still have that WD40 that I bought you? Your bathroom door is squeaking," he said, leaning against the counter. He could smell rotten broccoli and something that smelled like old milk coming from the sink. Maybe they had done it in Dude's apartment, but tomorrow was Sunday and Erica would have wanted to spend the night and cuddle. Unless she was just fucking him with no strings attached. She had never been casual with him. But people change. She pointed to the cabinet under the sink. The kitchen was barely big enough for two people, and as she moved for the stove and Warren towards the sink, her breast grazed his wrist. She wasn't wearing a bra, and the thought of her nakedness went straight to his manhood.

"I'm making tea, you want?"

He nodded, and left to fix the door. She was sitting on the sofa when he finished, and he sat two seats away from her. Even with the distance between them, the heat from her body still reached him.

"Thanks for fixing the door," she folded her legs under her, pushing her hair from her face.

"Why did you bring that guy with you to the club?"

The teakettle whistled.

"Excuse me?"

"He had his hands all over you," came out sounding more envious than Warren intended, but it was the truth.

Erica stood and moved towards the kitchen. "You jealous?"

Warren followed. "I'm just saying."

They were only a few feet apart.

"We came to hear Tess. I didn't even know you were going to be there." She poured hot water into the mugs.

"You would if you had returned my calls. That's our club."

"You left me. Remember?" Anger flashed across her face. The kitchen was hot. "Why are you here?"

"Are you with him?" He ran his teeth over his bottom lip. "Just tell me. Were you sleeping with him all along?"

"Like you and Blanche," she said matter-of-factly.

"Huh?" Whoa. Where did that come from?

"I know all about it," she placed her hands on her hips, war posing. "Just get out?"

A wave of panic crossed through Warren. It was one thing to accuse her of messing around, another for her to accuse him. It had only been the one time with Blanche and Erica had no way of knowing. He decided to play the bluff.

"Why do you always bring her up? We work together."

"Just go, please."

"Why can't we talk about this?"

"Because you're a lying asshole." She moved in close, pressing her fingers into his chest until he was backing towards the front door. The anger had frenzied her in such a way that he could smell her. He touched her face and she batted his hand away.

"Fuck you, Warren," her mouth said, but he knew from past fights that her body didn't agree. Warren mashed his lips against hers, forcing her mouth open with his tongue. The kiss tasted like toffee, until Erica shoved back, panting hard.

"Did Blanche tell you that I stopped by?"

Warren's eyes blinked several times. "Wha…what're you talking about?"

"The day she came over in the trench and heels?" Erica closed her eyes, and it only took a few seconds for the memory of her showdown with Blanche to stretch across her face. "How long have you been fucking her?"

Warren watched the rage bubbling through Erica but stood there without answering. How could he? He was damned either way. Erica was shouting at him, and then out of nowhere came the sucker punch. It hit him smack on the jaw.

"Damn it," Warren said, caught off guard, but Erica wasn't finished.

"How-dare-you-cheat-on-me-when-I-was-nothing-but-good-to-you?" she said, accenting each word with landing fists. Upper cuts, jabs and then she came at him with the windmill.

"I should have known. I should have known, I should have known," she said over and over again, and now she was kicking him in the knee, the thigh, the foot. Warren was double Erica's size and could have stopped her if he wanted, but it was clear to him that she needed to get her feelings out, so he stood there like a punching bag, protecting only his face.

"I…trusted you," she was out of breath, and then for good measure sent one more blow to the chest. Exhausted, she stopped. Leaning her butt on the arm of the futon she told him again to get out. Warren came towards her.

Even though her mouth was telling him to go, she wanted him to stay, and these conflicting feelings were pissing her off. Warren had turned her from a woman of strength to a watery bowl of chicken noodle soup. Why was his hand on her, circling her wrist then moving up her arms? It was such a simple touch and her pressure seesawed.

"Stop," she batted him away. But by then his lips were on hers and they were kissing. A wet open-mouth kiss that never felt so honest, deliberate, vital in all of Erica's life. And she kissed back like the world was ending in thirty seconds and this was her last shot at passion. Warren folded her into his big arms and pressed his fingertips into the small of her back. Damn, she loved him. His hands were on her camisole. Don't let him, her mind whined, but Warren did, taking a breast in each hand, and doing that thing she liked with the tips of his fingers. The fever for him was overwhelming as he nibbled on her neck, ear, throat, and kissed both eyelids. The hardness had swollen against Warren's thigh and without thinking she was up on it. Her body was getting away from her, betraying her honest-to-God feelings.

"No," escaped from her lips. The fantasy of everything being well and right between them was so easy to get lost in, as his tongue touched that special spot on her collarbone that always sent her to the place of no return. But she couldn't.

"No, don't," she said again, shaking herself from the trance. Erica had never been a cheap screw, and she wouldn't be one now. Pulling away and breathing hard, she mumbled. "You really need to go."

Warren looked confused. "Serious?"

How could everything be so wrong but feel so necessary? Erica needed to think and moved out of his reach.

Warren had always been a gentleman and she knew he wouldn't ask again. Why was she doing this? What did Erica have to prove? Tess would have bedded this fine stallion with strong history an hour ago. But Erica was not one to blur the lines. He left her, probably for another woman. He should go. Not trusting her voice, she shook her head.

This time, she didn't run after him.

PART 3

We're living in an age where people need to talk.
They don't communicate.
Queen Latifah

Chapter Forty-Three
The Legacy

Most of the women in Erica's family had mastered the government's welfare system by the age of sixteen and were generally grandmothers before thirty-six. During tax season, these women wouldn't hesitate to let someone else claim their children, as long as the payoff was profitable. If they worked, it was at jobs that didn't require much education: managing fast food, filing charts in the doctor's office, and ringing up items at retail stores.

They only knew single-parent homes, and that's what they offered their offspring. Men came into their lives, but never stayed. Along the way, some of Erica's aunts and cousins fell victim to the streets, developing drug habits, an unhealthy taste for alcohol, and an affinity for prescription drugs. As the years passed, their overweight bodies wore down from disease: hypertension, diabetes, arthritis, anxiety, and always depression.

This was the legacy of poverty that was predetermined for Erica before she was born, bequeathed like a family's coveted christening dress, passed from one daughter to the next. But at an early age, Erica decided that she didn't want to be the next woman in line and turned her back against the looming family baton. These thoughts wandered through her mind as she walked to the diner two blocks from her job. Her mother had called that morning and asked if they could meet. They hadn't seen or talked to each other in two weeks, since the

Bonnie incident. Erica knew her mother had waited until it seemed that all had been forgotten. Such was her way.

The lunch crowd was heavy, and the waitresses slung heaping plates and icy drinks through the thick aroma of cheeseburgers and gravy. Erica glanced at the specials written on the glass board behind the counter while working her way to the table where her mother sat. Gweny was using the window as a mirror to apply a coat of worn-down burgundy lipstick.

"You got some on your teeth," Erica offered, removing her sunglasses.

Her mother swished her tongue around, and then opened her lips wide to confirm that the spot was gone. Erica nodded yes.

"How you been, Slim?"

Erica could tell that she had put effort into her appearance. The lipstick suited her, as did the navy wool sweater. Soft rolled curls hung damply against her forehead. It was a glimpse of the mommy she had loved without inhibition, and the thought burned her throat.

"I haven't had a drink in three days," her mother said, trying to catch her daughter's eye, but Erica kept her gaze on the checkerboard table and waited for their Pepsis. She was tired of throwing her pom poms in the air. They were mired in disappointment.

"What you thinking?" her mother asked after a long bout of silence, but Erica didn't speak.

Twirling her napkin between her shaking fingertips, her mother spoke in a voice much deeper than her own. "It's time I told you something," she said, "Should have a long time ago."

Love in a Carry-On Bag

Erica knew her mother, Gweny, had a troubled past, but didn't know the weight of the story until that afternoon at the diner. Gweny had been raised in a sanctified home, and her mother was more interested in praising the Lord than raising her only child. The slightest mishap—spilling milk, using too much syrup on her pancakes, answering the telephone before the mandatory four rings—could land Gweny a merciless whooping. Gweny had been a beautiful child, with corn-silk braids that reached the small of her back. All the kids in the neighborhood thought she had Indian in her family. When she wasn't getting the devil beaten out of her, she was paraded around the church like a porcelain doll. She was never hit where the marks could be visible.

Her mother was the choir director, and often had rehearsals at their tiny Irvington, New Jersey home. The men always came early and gathered in the basement until the women arrived. Gweny's mother would send her down with refreshments, telling her to keep them entertained while she finished dressing. Louis, the tenor, was usually the first one there. He was in his late twenties, a skinny man with bloodshot eyes, a pug nose, and lips as big as bubbles. He always had a fifth of brown liquor tucked in the inside pocket of his tweed sports jacket. The alcohol seeped through his pores and made him smell. His advances started with a hug when Gweny was nine. That lent itself to searching hands, which graduated to pulling Gweny on his lap with his sweaty fingers in her flowered panties. Eventually he took what wasn't his, and Gweny remembered asking herself, where is my mother, from against the cold basement wall.

"Had anything like that ever happened to you?" she asked.

"Uncle Bobby paid me a dollar once for a kiss on the lips, but that was it." Uncle Bobby was Gweny's sister's on-again off-again boyfriend.

Her mother sucked her teeth. "How old were you?"

"Like twelve."

"I knew something was up with that man," her mother shook her head in disgust. "How come you never told me?"

"It wasn't a big deal, and it only happened once."

Erica could see the thoughts speeding through her mother's head while she waited for her to continue. "Your father was the first man I trusted after that because he didn't believe in church," Gweny fumbled a cigarette between her knotty fingers, but remembering that she couldn't smoke, placed it on the table. "So I went straight from my mother's house of sin, to my husband's house. No healing in between. I wanted a family desperately to soothe my pain, but I wasn't whole. You were born and then Jazmine. I wanted y'all. But I couldn't cope with the demands. No one taught me how to mother, so I pretended. When the game got to be too much I checked out. I'm pitiful, and I don't blame you for how you feel 'bout me." Her sad eyes welled. "Lord knows I can hardly stand to look at myself in the mirror."

"But you didn't even try. You just gave up, long before Daddy left. Do you know what that felt like for me to have to just figure it all out? It was horrible. I'd never do that to my children." Erica nibbled the end of a French fry but couldn't taste it.

"That's because you are a much better person than me," her mother searched her face. "All I can do is ask for your forgiveness, Slim, and hope that we can move on."

Erica had read somewhere that forgiveness wasn't for the offender, it was for the offended, and refusing to forgive was like refusing to breathe to prove a point. On the one hand she wanted to get past the hurt that she lugged around like a hump on her back. It had become a part of her bone structure, but whenever she tried to get over it, her mother would do something to mess it all up and the cycle of regret and bitterness would start all over again. Erica needed help, perhaps therapy, and her mother must have wanted to stop the pendulum of their relationship too, because before Erica had a chance to reject her, her mother was on her side of the table, smashing her head into her boulder-sized bosom. She smelled like talcum powder, and Erica could feel the heavy baton pressed between them threatening to cut through her wind pipe.

"I'm so sorry that I hurt you and will do everything in my power to make sure it won't happen again."

A stubborn tear appeared in the corner of Erica's eye as she muttered. "It's cool." They squeezed a second more before Erica pulled away. She rolled her shoulders back and looked her mother dead in her eyes. "With that said, I can't keep taking on your problems. I'm done being responsible for you."

Her mother leaned back against the booth. "I'ma stop callin' on you. I know I'm too much. Just be patient with me," she said, and then kissed Erica's forehead like she did when they were simply mother and child.

Erica couldn't stop walking after she left her mother. New York City was inviting in that way. The distance between the streets was short, and before she knew it she smelled hot dogs drifting from Gray's Papaya, on the corner of Sixth Avenue and 8th Street. After crossing Broadway, and then Lafayette, she strolled down St. Mark's Place. At the corner of Second Avenue, she passed Dallas BBQ's, where as a budgeting college student she drank Texas-sized beers, and ordered oversized rotisserie chicken platters that she would stretch for three meals.

As a girl, when she sat between her mother's legs getting her hair combed, Gweny would wave the brush in the air declaring, "You don't know how good you got it."

Erica's mantra had been, "Don't end up like Mommy." She had worked hard to defy the cycle that fought to enclose her, thinking that graduating college and climbing the corporate ladder would make her better. But now, thinking back to her mother at the diner, she realized that they were the same. They had both gone through life motherless. They attempted to re-parent themselves, failed, and wallowed in the sacrificial pain. Erica was who she was because she stood on her mother's shoulders and glimpsed a better view. And it was time for her to stop condemning and start accepting her mother for who she was. In that moment Erica realized that she was the one who needed to change.

When she got back to the office, Prudence assured her that Claire and Athan had been in meetings and no one had noticed that she was gone. Since being passed over for the promotion, Erica hadn't been behaving like her powerhouse self, and needed something to reignite her.

There was a message slip on her desk saying that LaVal had called. She picked up her phone and dialed him back.

"It's Erica Shaw."

"Just the woman I needed to speak with. I have a lecture in D.C. the Friday after next and I'd love for you to come see me in action."

She thought about Warren. The last time they had walked U Street when he talked about losing his mother, his hand wrapped in hers.

"I'll see," she replied.

"It'll give you a better idea of what I do, especially if you decide to represent me."

Erica paused. "I'll have to see if B&B will cover the expenses."

"No need. The trip is paid for. All you have to do is show up."

LaVal was so aggressive that he made it hard for Erica to think logically, so she told him to give her a day or so to get back to him. D.C. represented Warren, and when she got home she couldn't stop thinking about how he had barged into her apartment thinking that he could make love to her and all would be solved. Most nights Erica couldn't stop picturing that she had.

Her apartment was beyond trifling, and if Grandma Queeny were alive, she would give Erica a good tongue-lashing. The rooms had degenerated so far that the clutter was suffocating. Erica hadn't intended to clean, but once she turned her radio to the Quiet Storm and unconsciously placed clothes in their designated drawers it just began to happen. The sour bed sheets were replaced with fresh linen, and once that was taken care of the rest of the room was a breeze. Laundry was separated, and she arranged her heels on the tiered shoe rack that Warren had made for her. It was one of his many attempts to organize her, but hadn't worked. When she pushed the shoes toward the back of her closet, she spotted the balled up sheet with all of Warren's things in the corner. Without thinking she brought them to her face. Warren's scent was strong, and she put her head on the pile and hugged them to her chest.

Vesta Williams came over the radio singing her hit song "Congratulations."

Erica thought about her encounter with Blanche as she removed the dirty dishes and food containers from the kitchen sink. The song kept playing and Erica could picture Vesta in the video standing outside the church as her man married another woman. Was that to be her fate? Alone, congratulating another woman for marrying the man that she had loved with fever?

'Cause as long I can breathe

You'll always be the one for me…

She had felt that Warren was her destiny. As a young child, she had always believed in the great tales of true love, and it was hard to accept that her one chance had passed. He was the perfect yin to her yang.

Warren had done things for her that no other man had done before. Last year, she was so drunk on her birthday that when they got back to his place she forgot she was on her period and passed out. Before putting her to bed, Warren changed her sanitary napkin, and the next morning when he told her what he had done, she was mortified.

"I'm so embarrassed," she remembered burying her head in his pillow, but he soothed her embarrassment with tenderness.

"Girl, I love all of you. Nothing's off limits."

A month after they had met, he drove to Atlantic City to get her mother out of the loony bin without hesitation. He missed his gig with Bobby Watson to bail her mother out of jail. He encouraged her career and listened to all her crap. So why weren't they together?

Erica ran the dishwater so hot it was scalding.

Chapter Forty-Four

Father, What's Real?

There was something about being turned down by a woman that could make a man wilt like a thirsty rosebush. Since Erica had thrown Warren from her apartment he felt like a drying grape, shriveled up and small. He had no appetite, didn't want to get dressed, play his horn or leave his home. But it was Friday night, his least favorite day of the week, and he had to go to his father's house. His dad and Shar were hosting a fund-raiser that evening for the D.C. public schools. So Warren had no choice but to shuffle down the hall, turn on the showerhead and slather his body with soap. Once wrapped in a plushy towel, he used his hand to wipe away the cloudiness from the bathroom mirror and studied himself. His facial hair had grown coarse and wild. Warren knew that it was in his best interest to shave before the event, but he just didn't have it in him. The overgrown beard gave him a sense of freedom and he wasn't willing to let it go, not even for his dad.

Blanche called an hour before saying that she had a ticket for tonight's fund-raiser but needed a ride. Warren had been short with her at the office, and had even worked from another cubicle so as not to have to deal with her. Tonight was the first time she had phoned since showing up at his place. He hadn't even gotten around to asking her about running into Erica, and at this point it didn't matter. He agreed to give her a ride, but for him it was with the intention of clearing the air and setting the record straight. Blanche was a resourceful girl, and he was sure that she would understand that he was in love with another woman.

The gold cuff links with his initials carved through in script slipped into the cuff of his buttercream shirt. The last thing Warren was in the mood for was a party crowded with phony people and corny small talk, but his dad would be disappointed if he didn't show. It was his and Shar's first party as a married couple and everyone who was anyone would be there, throwing money at the cause.

When Warren pulled up to Blanche's townhouse, she was standing in the doorway dressed in a flamenco-style dress with her hair pulled to the side. Warren got out of the car and opened the passenger door for her as she hurried down her walkway.

"Hi," she kissed his cheek.

The truck needed to be washed, Warren thought, observing the layer of dust sitting on top of its red paint. Warren had always been meticulous about his ride, and he couldn't believe he had let his car get this bad. Tomorrow he'd take it to his man in Southeast and have it detailed, the rims and all. If he got there by nine, he'd be out and at the gym by ten.

"Ha-llo," Blanche interrupted his thoughts. "How do I look?"

"Oh, nice." Warren steadied her elbow while she stepped up into the SUV. When he slid into the driver's seat, Blanche rested her hand on his thigh.

"Thanks for the ride," she squeezed.

Warren's stomach tightened and he moved his leg with a jerk, causing her hand to slip away. It was obvious what Blanche wanted, but he decided to save the "chat" for the ride back. They drove the next few blocks with a Wynton Marsalis cut covering the silence.

Warren's family's house was a four-bedroom Georgian that sat in the middle of the block. When he turned the corner he could see that there wouldn't be parking close to the house, so he parked at the neck of the street.

"Nice neighborhood." Blanche pulled her wrap tighter around her arms as they walked. "Is this where you grew up?"

"For the most part," he gave the short answer.

"Must have been nice coming up with D.C.'s finest."

"I don't know about that," Warren commented as they turned up the cobblestone pathway.

"Wow, look at this house. I'd give my left arm to live here." She was looking through the picture glass window.

The curtains on the house were thrust open, and party-goers in fancy evening attire could be seen from the street. The door was ajar and Warren removed Blanche's wrap and handed it to the butler who waited in the foyer.

"Thank you," said Blanche, looking around the room; her eyes shining with amazement. Warren could see why; the house was very impressive, boasting high cathedral ceilings and hardwood floors that gleamed like polished glass. There were two large buffet tables to the left and the staff busied around holding trays of hors d'oeuvres.

Warren's eyes naturally fell on his mother's grand piano. It was the only personal item of hers still in the room and he saw Shar's boys leaning against it. A flame flickered inside of him. How dare they? That was his mother's piano and he didn't want them touching it.

"Blanche, can I get you a drink?" His eyes stayed on the boys.

"Yes, please. Merlot," she said as she removed a buffalo Wellington from the waiter's tray. "This looks delicious."

Warren made his way through the crowd towards the piano but was slowed down by greeting a few familiar guests. His dad and Shar were at the opposite end of the room laughing with a local congressman and his wife, so Warren decided to save his hello for later. One thing he had learned at an early age was not to interrupt his father when he was engaged in business discussions.

By the time he reached the boys, they had moved to the rosewood bench that had replaced his mother's stool. Warren relaxed.

"Hey guys. You boys home from school?"

"We just got here today," replied Jared.

"Mom made us keep these dumb uniforms on," Bernard imitated his mother, "because she thinks we look so handsome in them."

With a pang in his ribs, Warren told the boys that his mother used to do the same thing. "Is Mr. Brown still the gym teacher?"

"Yeah, he coaches my basketball team," answered Bernard. "I'm the jump shot king." He raised his hands in a swish motion, and Warren glimpsed his father's smile in the young boy's eyes.

"There you are," Blanche reached for Warren's arm. "Who are these handsome creatures?"

The boys introduced themselves as Warren flagged down the nearest gloved waiter. "Sorry about that. I almost forgot your drink." He handed a glass of red wine to Blanche, and took a white for himself.

The room had swelled with D.C. politicians, dignitaries, CEOs, and renowned local artists. The fund-raiser would be good for the public schools, and Warren was glad to see so many people turn out.

His father waved to him, and Warren excused himself from Blanche and headed over to say hello.

"Sir."

"Son," his father embraced him. "What's going on with the beard? Didn't you have time to shave?"

"Just something new I'm trying."

"Well I'm sure I don't have to tell you that I don't like it." He narrowed his eyes.

Blanche swept over and grabbed his father's hand. "Nice to see you again, Mr. Prince," she said, reminding him that they had met at the Man of Honor dinner.

"Thanks for supporting such a worthy cause."

"Well, the children are our future," she said brightly.

The music began, and Shar waved his father over from across the room. Warren watched as the tension from his father's body lightened when he reached for her. They kissed with passion, and then he pulled Shar close to his heart as they led the party's first dance. The newlyweds were dressed in black—Shar in a sequined cocktail dress and his father in a traditional three-piece suit. Even when other couples joined them, Warren couldn't help notice how their bodies swayed into each other as naturally as if they had been dancing for years. What was it about this woman that had turned his father into twinkle toes?

Already Warren found his father more gentle and affectionate with Shar, and wondered if it was because of their history together or lack thereof. With his mother, his father had often been agitated and restless, barking orders and criticizing her, which only made his mother work harder at pleasing him.

In the beginning of his Army career, money was tight because Maynard wouldn't allow them to live on base. Warren's mother did her best to create a loving home. She clipped coupons and could stretch a roasted chicken to chicken noodle soup to chicken-salad sandwiches. She mended socks and underwear so that they'd last a little longer, and didn't complain when told to pack up the family with only a moment's notice because of military orders. It was her prodding that secured his father the coveted position of chief of staff, and now that he was a groomed man, Shar sat reaping the benefits.

"I'm telling Dad," Jared stood crying. Bernard quickly hushed his younger brother by offering his wristwatch.

Dad? The couple hadn't been married a few weeks, and "Dad" was already slipping from the young boy's tongue? The anxiety that had been building since Warren overheard the gossip at the church crashed through him like a wave hitting a breaking point.

From across the room Warren watched his father whisper something to Shar and then walk towards the back of the house. Warren knew he was heading to his study to steal a smoke. Bravery surged through him. It was such a ballsy feeling that he knew he had to strike before he lost his nerve. After giving his father a head start, Warren followed down the center hall adorned with original paintings by artists such as Leroy Campbell and Georgia O'Keeffe. The family portrait of Warren, his father, mother and sister was gone.

Turning the sharp corner that led to his father's private study, Warren pushed the heavy oak door open without knocking.

"Son, when did you start barging in?" his father demanded, startled.

"Were you ever planning to tell me?"

"Tell you what?"

"That Shar's sons are yours?" The words shot from Warren's mouth.

His father looked down at his pipe and took his time to pinch in a chunk of tobacco before bringing it to his lips. After the smoke cleared, he replied. "I had planned to tell you about the adoption as soon as it went through."

"I'm not talking about an adoption," Warren clenched his teeth. "It's all over the church. Apparently everyone knows but me."

"Watch it, son," his father set his pipe down and glared, fixing Warren with the same look he would use to intimidate him as a boy. "Have you lost your cotton-pickin' mind?" His father's polished speech dropped Southern. Clearly, he was upset.

"You owe me an explanation," Warren took a few steps forward, refusing to back down.

"How dare you come in here with this nonsense. In the middle of a party? I have guests roaming my house. You've got some nerve," he pointed his pipe.

"Just tell me the truth and I'll go."

"Boy, you better watch your tone, before something happens that we both regret," his father stared him down.

"Then you're a coward," Warren spat, unable to believe his own nerve. "After all of your rules about what a man is? Now you can't even look me in the eye and tell the truth?" He turned on his heels and left the door wide open. Another no-no.

BLANCHE WAS HOLDING COURT with the wife of a senator when Warren stormed through the party.

"I'm leaving," his face was misty with sweat.

Blanche excused herself, and hurriedly followed him across the living area to the front door. Outside she had to trot down the street to keep up with him. "What's wrong with you?"

"Why are you here?" Warren looked at her. The street was empty in both directions, but music could be heard coming from the house.

"I wanted to support a worthy cause."

"No. Why are you really here?" He ran his teeth over his bottom lip.

Blanche fidgeted with her clutch.

"What happened with you and Erica?"

She stared at him.

"What did you tell her that day I left you at my apartment?" Warren demanded.

"Nothing . . .that it was over between you. Isn't that right?"

Warren could hear the desperation in Blanche's voice and he didn't want to hurt her, but he had to come clean. "That night I was really drunk, Blanche."

She moved closer and reached for his cheek. "That wouldn't stop us now."

Warren swatted her hand. "We work together, Blanche. And I'm not over Erica. I'm sorry," he offered.

"You're sorry," she mustered, spit flying. "Fuckin' asshole. You want to have your cake and eat it too. First you wanted me, now it's Erica. What a jerk," she said flatly.

Just then two women stepped outside of his father's home for a smoke.

"Blanche, calm down."

"Don't fucking tell me to calm down. What about how I feel?" she retorted. "Ever consider that? Or is your world so small you can only think of yourself?"

Warren grabbed hold of her arm to try to control the scene but she pulled away.

"Don't touch me," she said, pointing her finger in his face. "What a wishy-washy pig." She moved away from him, back up the cobblestone path and into the house.

Warren started to follow, but he knew it would do more harm than good on all accounts.

Sitting behind the wheel of his Yukon Danali, Warren could only think of one thing. Erica. He removed his cell phone from his hip and called her. After four rings the machine picked up.

"Hey it's me. Warren. We need to talk, please call me back."

When he got home he tore out of his suit, paced his living room floor and tried her again. No answer, another message.

"I really need to talk to you. Call me when you get this."

An hour later, his heart felt as if he had been running a twenty-one-mile marathon with no water and Erica held the icy cup. He needed her. Damn it, he couldn't take any more. He tried her again.

"Leave a message." Beep.

This time, when she didn't answer, he started singing. It was the wimpiest thing he ever did, but he was beyond caring. Erica needed to know how he felt.

He sang the first three verses of "Wild as the Wind." It was the song that they listened to over and over again in the car on the way to the Pocono Mountains, and Warren wanted her to remember when things were good. Although he sounded nothing like Nina Simone, he had perfect pitch and could carry a tune. *With your kiss my life begins…*

Warren put the phone to his heart, hoping that she could hear the pattern of his thump, bringing it back to his ear. "I can't go on like this, baby. I'm like a leaf clinging to a tree. I can't breathe. I can't think. I'm drying up without you. You've got me begging…"

The message space was filled, and the line went dead. Warren clicked off his phone, suddenly feeling like he played himself. What kind of dude sings on a woman's answering machine? Stupid. That was so high school, but the sad part was that he meant every verse.

Chapter Forty-Five
Stepping on Faith

Erica caught the 5:00p.m. Amtrak from New York City to Washington, D.C. It was the train that she always caught on Friday night, the train that got her to Union Station at 7:47p.m. sharp. When she was goofy and in love she had timed how long it took her to walk from the platform, through the station, and outside to where Warren waited curbside, dripping with that crooked smile that she loved so much. Three minutes is what it took for her to sashay through the crowd with her skinny heels click-clacking against the shiny floors, and her carry-on bag trailing behind her. Erica remembered how those minutes might as well have been hours, as her ache for Warren would escalate with each switch of her hip, smile hello, and elbow to the person holding up the line in front of her. Her body would fever with anticipation as she predicted how Warren would look, feel against her breasts, smell when he pressed his lips to her earlobe, and taste when their tongues touched. These thoughts would bustle inside of her with each anxious step, threatening to set her on fire. On some trips she'd find her feet scampering when she rounded the automatic doors, but she would force herself to slow down, so as not to appear flustered.

Now Erica was making the trip to see another man, LaVal Jarvis. He had been aggressive about bringing her to D.C. to hear his lecture, and pursued her intently to manage his speaking engagements. It was only part-time, but the opportunity had forced Erica to really examine her work situation at B&B Publishing. Weeks had passed since Erica was stepped over for the Director's position by Athan McKinley, and he still had no clue how to help Claire run the department. Working with him had been draining, and Erica didn't see any signs of her much deserved promotion down the pike.

Moving on was a thought that had been constantly ticking at the back of her brain, and for some reason when she opened her eyes that morning, she knew it was time to consider leaving. The heart to heart that she had with her mother made her realize that she no longer needed the office with the view, the fancy title and write up in *Essence* magazine to exorcise the family's demons. She had already escaped them. Erica was exceptional right now. But she wasn't great because of what she had accomplished, she was great because of who she had always been, and this self-realization was what put her on the path to restarting her life.

Erica knew that if she wanted to she could jump ships and go to another publishing house, but why not take a leap of faith and venture out on her own? After all, entrepreneurship was in her blood. Her father had owned an auto repair shop in Elizabeth, New Jersey, until he sold it and moved to South Carolina. According to Jazmine, he had opened another shop five miles from his house in Charleston, but this one also had an auto detailing department with a small line of products that he manufactured himself. It was probably why he still paid her mother's mortgage after so many years apart. The act was chivalrous, and the only reason her mother hadn't been forced onto the streets. Erica had to admit that she was grateful to him for keeping up with the bill, because she could only imagine how much worse things could have been.

When the train pulled into Wilmington, Delaware, Erica wondered why she was thinking about her father when she spent most of her time pretending that he didn't exist. If Grandma Queeny were sitting next to her she would have pulled her shawl tighter around her shoulders and declared, "Chile, that's because it's time for you to till the soil and dig up that toxic stuff that's hindering your good crops from growing."

Erica stared out the window but looked at nothing in particular. She supposed that it was time for her to deal with her feelings towards her father. Ever since she saw her mother in the diner she couldn't stop thinking about how forgiveness was for the offended, not the offender. For almost two decades Erica had been lugging around bags teeming with bitterness against her dad, and like a corpse it had grown heavy with rot, and the noxious fumes were killing her. When her father left Erica swept her suffering under a sturdy mat, stepped over it and moved on. She ran, flipped, and tumbled, doing everything to outsprint the agony of her abandonment.

But in that moment as she sat alone listening to the chug of the train, she knew that she was tired of outracing her past. She needed to make amends with her father so that she could go forward and love a man with an open heart. Perhaps that had been the problem with Warren, and Erica pressed her jacket to her lips to keep herself from crying.

"But he abandoned us. How could he not know that he was leaving us with a mother who wasn't capable? He was married to her for Christ sake. We were supposed to be his main girl, two halves of the same whole and he left," screamed the little girl picking the scabs from inside of her. Erica felt the wounds split, and bit down harder on her collar until her teeth ached from the pressure. Then she wrapped her arms around her waist and squeezed as tightly as she could. It hurt to think of the father that she had loved with unabashed innocence. So much time had passed since she had even heard his voice. He must have grown sick of calling without her answering, but the fifty dollar bills came every month like clockwork. Perhaps that was his way of repenting.

Erica rocked herself. The tears kept betraying her as she realized that she didn't want to end up at his funeral listening to folks proclaim what a good man he had been, and her having missed out because she had spent her life holding a childish grudge. Everyone deserved to be forgiven, and it was time for her to put down the corpse, scrub herself clean, and get on with living.

THE TRAIN CRANKED INTO Union Station, and as Erica took the three-minute walk to the street, she averted her eyes from where Warren usually parked, making a mad dash for the taxicab stand on the corner of Massachusetts Avenue. The driver helped her with her bag and then zigzagged through a sea of cars. Traffic was light, and it only took a few minutes for him to pull in front of the Jefferson Hotel on the corner of 16th and M street.

"Thanks," Erica slipped the cabby a twenty and told him to keep the change. The doorman asked if she needed help with her luggage, but she declined.

The Jefferson was an intimate, residential-style hotel, boasting old world charm located four short blocks from the White House. LaVal had booked her a suite, and once she slid in her keycard and opened the door, she could see that it was much more space than she needed. The sitting room was beautifully situated with Victorian antique furniture and tapestry, while the master bedroom's focal point was a four-poster bed. Erica kicked out of her traveling shoes and parked her bag against the mahogany chest of drawers. She had always been a sucker for a view, and when she pulled back the drapes there was a narrow door that led to the balcony. Erica stood stocking foot on the stone walk, gazing at the Washington Monument, thinking about Warren's voice messages.

She must have played it over a dozen times. Her heart was telling her to believe every word, but she was paralyzed with fear. Even though she was now conscious of forgiving her parents, it was different when it came to a man/woman relationship. Hurt me once, shame on you, twice…well that was a risk she was having a hard time taking.

The evening was unseasonably warm, and Erica breathed in the fresh air, trying to let the coolness clear the clouds from her head. Then without a second thought, she pulled her cell phone from the side pocket of her dress and scrolled through her contacts. The phone rang three times, and she didn't realize that she was holding her breath until she heard his voice on the other end.

"Hello," it had turned slightly southern.

"Hi, Daddy…it's me."

"E-bird? Oh, wow! It's so nice to hear your voice. How're you doing sweetheart?"

She could hear the crank of a jack lifting a car, and could almost smell Valvoline. A giggle crept into Erica's voice and the nervousness slipped off the balcony and disappeared into thin air. "I'm fine. Everything is going well."

"Yeah, Jaz tells me that you are a big shot working in New York City."

"I wouldn't say all of that," she felt herself blush.

"Still modest, I always knew you'd do big things. The way you'd tackle that fast math that I taught you on Saturdays at the shop. You remember that?"

"Yeah, I do."

"You were always quick as lightning. Anything I taught you, you'd eat it right up. Man, it's good to hear your voice," he said again.

"Same here."

They fell into an easy rhythm of catch up, and before Erica knew it the sun had dipped, and she was running late for LaVal's lecture.

"I hate to go, but I've got to get to work," she said.

"Okay, I understand. But promise you'll call again soon. How's Sunday afternoon?"

"Um, that should be fine." Erica replied, and then allowed her father to pin her with a time.

As she bounced through her hotel room she felt lighter, like she had left ten pounds of baggage behind on the balcony. The guck from inside of her chest felt scraped and shoveled bare. It was almost as if she had swallowed a decongestant pill, opening her up and leaving her feeling unblocked and free.

In the bathroom, there was only enough time for a quick shower, and after oiling her skin, Erica slipped into a gray kimono-sleeved dress, and accentuated the look with round-toe heels and a three-string beaded necklace that she'd bought at the African market in Harlem. There was no real time for make-up, but she swiped the mascara brush over her lashes and packed a little shadow and gloss to apply on the drive.

LaVal had sent a towncar for her, and on the ride over she noticed that the center where he was scheduled to lecture was only five blocks from Warren's house. Through the tinted back window she watched as the corner coffee shop where she picked up their bagels drifted by. Two blocks over was their favorite flea market, and a block up was De Vinos, where they went for wine. She was so close to him, and everything felt familiar.

LAVAL WAS SPEAKING INSIDE a neighborhood recreation center on the edge of Northwest. It was a neighborhood that ten years ago was labeled dangerous, but gentrification had changed the tag to up-and-coming, and then to good. When Erica hustled through the door, a woman with bright tangerine braids handed her a yellow program.

"Thanks," Erica nodded, and then made her way down the center aisle, just as a scrawny teenage boy started with the introduction. Erica took a seat to the left and then glanced over her shoulder to take in the crowd. Every inch of the moderate-size hall was lined with rows of folding chairs, and although all the seats weren't filled, the audience was scattered enough to give the appearance of a full house. Erica pulled a notebook from her bag and held it in her lap. After a round of applause, LaVal strolled across the stage with one hand waving in the air.

"Thank you," he said, adjusting the mic. His quarter-sized dimples dented his cheeks. LaVal appeared as polished as always, in a fudge-striped suit and dotted tie. His hair was cut close and his sandy eyes were bright.

"You know, it wasn't too long ago that I was just like you," he said, directing his attention to the young African-American boys who slouched in the front row.

"I used to carry a gun, and I earned so much money selling drugs that it made people who worked look like field laborers. And they were, in a sense," he paused for effect. "Why do the hard work for pennies, when the easy money was like taking candy from a baby?"

The room was still, and within seconds LaVal had swept them all into the palms of his hands.

Although Erica had read his book, hearing him tell his story live and on stage was like thumbing through his life for the first time. The crowd was mostly Jewish women and young black men bused in from a Southeast community center. Both groups hung onto his every syllable. It was amazing how he could play to both crowds without seeming pretentious, and Erica knew that it was because of the chameleon skin of the black man.

As a young girl, she could remember being in her father's auto shop, watching him change colors depending on the needs and background of the customer. "Know how to talk to people on their level, and they'll keep coming back," he'd say, and as she watched her author speak, she saw that it was true.

Forty-five minutes later LaVal opened the floor to questions, and then concluded with a pitch for his new book that was so tight Erica scribbled it in the margin of her notebook. She would use his own words to get the major media to cover him. LaVal was a star, and she was happy to be on his team.

"THANKS FOR COMING," LAVAL said to Erica, as he shook his last hand goodbye. The auditorium was mostly empty, and Erica had waited for him in the last row.

"No problem. You were great."

His eyes traveled over her. "Are you hungry?"

"Not really. Is there someplace where we can talk business?" she reached for her work satchel.

"I thought we could try a restaurant down the street."

"It's late LaVal, I'd really rather…"

"Promise not to keep you out long," he held out his hand to help her from her seat, and then stepped aside so that she could pass through the door first. Erica decided to go with it.

Five minutes later, the hired car dropped them in front of a swanky Southwestern-style restaurant. Although the kitchen was about to close, LaVal did a bit of smooth talking with the hostess, and she ushered them to a quiet spot in the corner. Erica dropped her napkin in her lap and glanced over the menu. The waiter appeared, and LaVal took the liberty of ordering a bottle of Chilean wine for the table and a few lite fares.

"Thanks again for setting everything up for me," Erica looked up. "The hotel is lovely."

"My pleasure," he flashed his dimples. "So what did you think of the talk?"

"Like I said, you were great. Poised, charming… the book should do really well," she fingered her beads.

The waiter returned with the bottle and served LaVal a taste. Once he nodded his approval, wine was poured into Erica's glass. Their table was pressed against the window, and Erica gazed at the street lamp.

"You know, you really look beautiful tonight," LaVal said, interrupting her thoughts.

An uncomfortable feeling trickled down her spine. "Thanks."

"Are you seeing anyone?" he looked her dead in the eye.

"Excuse me?"

"I was just wondering."

Erica picked up her wineglass and took a sip. What the hell was he thinking? This was a business meeting, not a date, she thought.

"So?" he tilted his head, looking her over like a man who was accustomed to making women swoon.

"So, what?"

"Are you?"

Erica rolled back her shoulders. "I really don't think that's any of your business. I thought you brought me down here to discuss your lectures."

"I did," he hurried. "But I just had to put it out there."

"For what?" Her patience was waning.

"Because if you're not seeing anyone, I thought we could get to know each other a little better." He leaned in on his elbows and Erica was floored by his boldness. She couldn't believe he thought that putting her up in a fancy hotel entitled him a glimpse into her personal life, or worse, that they were going to sleep together. She had come to D.C. to discuss work and now felt like a trapped possum. Disgusted, she pushed back from the table.

"Where are you going?"

"Home," she glared.

"I'm sorry. I didn't mean to offend you. That night at the jazz club I thought we made a connection."

"This is work for me, LaVal," she was still standing.

"Please sit. I misunderstood. It won't happen again."

Erica looked around the restaurant, and could tell that she was causing a small scene. So she sat back down, but with her chair pushed slightly away from the table. LaVal drank his wine.

"I take my work very seriously, Mr. Jarvis," she chewed on his name and spat it from her lips, like a high school principal would a child about to be suspended. "So please don't waste my time. If you are interested in me being your lecture agent, then you'll have to remain professional at all times. I will not tolerate you crossing the line. Ever."

LaVal's sandy eyes flickered with surprise, and Erica knew he was caught off guard by her forthrightness. But she didn't care. Men in business were notorious for blurring the line, and Erica wouldn't stand for it. She had come to D.C. depending on closing the deal. It was her first step in getting out from under B&B, and she couldn't let him ruin it for her.

"Does this mean you've decided to represent me?" he asked.

"If we can agree to the same terms, which include the utmost level of discretion and respect, and my fee of 20 percent."

"I was thinking more like 15," LaVal tossed.

"Eighteen, with the possibility of renegotiating in a year's time."

LaVal put his hand out. "Deal."

"Great," she left him hanging. "I'll get a contract over to you as soon as I return to my office. Enjoy your dinner," she said, throwing her napkin in her plate, and then she moved towards the front of the restaurant before he could stop her.

Chapter Forty-Six

I Just Don't Know

Warren hadn't been able to get himself on track. He had drifted through his week on auto pilot, only doing what was necessary to survive: go to work, eat, shower and swallow as many cups of coffee as it took to accomplish the minimum on the job. Erica never returned his calls, and his heartache sat in his stomach curdling like expired sour cream, making him feel nauseous and nasty.

"You look like shit," Alan paused at the new cubicle that Warren had taken over since his encounter with Blanche.

"Whatever man," Warren fingered his beard.

"Things not working out with you and Blanchey?" Alan leaned in, and Warren felt his fists roll up into an involuntary clench. Punching Alan in the face, knocking him to the ground and stomping him until he vomited would make Warren feel so much better.

"Why don't you put your efforts into trying to get laid for the first time? What are you, like forty now?"

Alan turned pink in the face. "I'm not a virgin."

"Forty years. Damn, that's a long time."

"Shut up."

"Or what?" Warren stood up, pulling himself to his full height. He was about three inches taller and twenty pounds thicker than Alan. "What're you going to do?" Warren mocked, begging the geek to give him a reason to punch him out.

The two were staring each other down when Blanche breezed past wearing an extra short mini dress, carrying a stack of folders and ignoring them both. Alan took the opportunity to step away and slink back to his corner of the room. Warren unclenched his fists and opened his mouth so that his teeth would stop grinding against each other like a salivating dog.

A FEW HOURS LATER, he reached home. His place was much messier than usual. Empty soda cans, cheeseburger wrappings, banana peels and the crust of a two-day-old pizza littered the kitchen countertop and the glass coffee table. His plants needed to be watered, and his socks and shoes were left wherever Warren had taken them off. His life lacked order, and Warren couldn't see a sliver of relief in sight.

The only saving grace was his horn. The showcase at the Iridium had plenty of promoters calling, and James was negotiating with one of them to get their band on stage at Rhode Island's Newport Jazz Festival. The band would only perform the opening song, but the exposure would be tenfold. Every night that week, Warren had come home, slipped into the same funky sweatpants, and composed new music. It amazed him how much beauty could be sketched from shattered pieces.

He had tried not to think about his last conversation with his father; in fact, Warren had let that part of himself drop numb. So when the doorman buzzed from downstairs telling him his father had arrived, Warren was more than surprised, and dashed around his apartment tidying up while trying to make sense of the visit.

Five minutes passed, and then there were two swift knocks on the door. When Warren turned the latch and pulled it open, his father filled the hall with the presence of royalty. He stood erect with his shoulders back and his head held high, reminding Warren of James Earl Jones as the king in the movie *Coming to America*.

Warren stepped aside.

"Sorry for not calling first. I just happened to be in the neighborhood."

The only sound in the apartment was the hum from the refrigerator. His father removed his overcoat and pointed to the easy chair. "Do you mind if I sit?"

Warren gestured for him to take the seat.

"You left the party without saying goodbye."

Usually when Warren played, it took the music forever to halt in his head, but with his father sitting in his living room the sound had gone silent.

"What were you doing before I came?"

"Practicing for a gig in Newport."

"The Jazz Festival?"

"Yeah."

"That's a mighty big deal, Son. Your mother would have been proud."

"What about you?" Warren was done tiptoeing.

"What do you mean?"

"Are you proud?"

"Son, I couldn't be prouder if I gave birth to you myself. Brett tells me that you're irreplaceable at work."

"I'm a musician, Dad."

His father took a deep breath, and then replied, "I know, Son."

"So why haven't you supported me?"

"You had your mother for that stuff. You didn't need me tagging along."

"I can't remember one recital that you attended."

"Well, I was somewhere working. I didn't think it mattered."

"It mattered, Dad." Warren looked him straight in the eye. "Do you know what it's like as a kid to feel like your father doesn't accept you? You treated me like an outcast. It was like growing up living a double life."

"And it's served you well. You've got the high salaried job that I've always wanted for you, and you still have your music on the side. Seems like a perfect balance."

Warren shook his head. "You just don't get it."

"But Son, I do. You wanted me to make it easy for you. Tell you to go off and follow your dreams, but the world doesn't work that way. I've had to work hard for every damn cent that I have," he punctuated the words by slapping his thigh. "Nothing has been easy for me. Do you know that I grew up in a shack smaller than this room with four brothers and three sisters?"

Of course Warren knew, and nodded his head.

"Well my daddy was a flugelhorn-playing drunk. He didn't give a damn about us. He was too busy chasing music, pieces of tail, and corn whiskey in juke joints up and down the Mason-Dixon Line. Ain't no fun starving, I can tell you that," his father looked away. "My mama picked cotton and did days work for the little white family over the hill that wasn't much better off than us to put scraps of food on the table, but it was never enough. I was the eldest child, so I had to help. That's why I joined the army, for survival, not because it was my lifelong dream. That's how things were done in my day."

Warren threaded his fingers in his lap.

"Then I met your mother, and she got pregnant with Billie so we had a shotgun wedding in her mama's living room. Then you came and we tried to make it work, but we never really fit. As beautiful as your mother was, we were too different. She wanted one thing and I wanted another," he paused, and then finished softly. "She knew everything. We had an agreement, Son."

"Knew what?" Warren leaned forward in his chair.

"That I was in love with Shar," his face sunned into a smile. "I've been in love with that woman since she walked into my office over ten years ago. I remember it like it was yesterday," he said, almost getting lost in the memory. "Your mother knew, Son, so you don't have to hold this against me."

"Well why didn't you tell me? And what about Bernard and Jared?"

"Your mother was the one who didn't want you and Billie to know. She didn't want her church friends looking at her differently, so she just asked me to be discreet and I did, out of respect for her. But when she passed away I couldn't wait any longer. I needed Shar to be my wife. I needed to make her an honest woman. It was what she deserved, and what I wanted more than anything in life."

His father removed a handkerchief from his inside pocket and sopped up the wetness from his forehead.

"So the boys are your sons?"

"Yes."

"Why didn't you just say that in the study?"

"Because you barged in on me in the middle of a party, like you had no cotton-picking sense. That wasn't the time for this type of conversation."

Warren was up pacing the floor. His whole family life had been a farce. His mother knew? How could his parents keep this from him?

As if reading his mind, his father interrupted. "We were just trying to protect you. Your mother wanted you and Billie to have a two-parent household, that's why she didn't want to split. I realize this is a lot, and you may need some time to digest it all."

"That's an understatement," Warren said with more sarcasm than he intended.

"Well, I know Shar can't replace your mother, but I would like you to give her a chance, and your brothers."

"You dump all of this on me and I'm supposed to just what?" The vein in Warren's forehead protruded through his skin like a thick slab of bacon.

"Accept me. Accept us, for who we are right now. Even if all of my decisions up until this point haven't made sense to you. Believe me when I say life is short, Son." His father chuckled to himself and then said, "and I don't want to be on the Maury Povich show saying I haven't seen my son in ten years, can you help me find him?"

Warren didn't take to the joke.

"Does Billie know?"

"I need to tell her too."

Some fresh air was what Warren needed, and he walked over to the window and opened it a quarter of an inch.

His father stood and reached for his overcoat. "I'ma take leave. We're having dinner at the house after church on Sunday, and we'd love for you to be there."

Warren moved towards his father and picked up his cashmere scarf that had slipped to the floor.

"I understand, no pressure," his father draped the scarf around his neck, and then held out his hand to shake Warren's. The two men locked eyes, and then his father pulled him to his chest and hugged him. "No matter what you're still my son," his father said, pressing his palm into Warren's back before releasing him.

Warren followed his father into the hallway to see him to the elevator, and when he looked down the hall, there she was standing in front of the elevator, looking breathless.

Chapter Forty-Seven

Swallowed Pride

Erica took a step forward, leaned in, and gave Warren's dad a squeeze. He smelled comforting, like a pot of warm spices bubbling up on a cozy day. His fatherly embrace eased her shaking nerves.

"Mr. Prince, it's been too long."

"We've missed you, dear. Where have you been?" He held her at arm's length and Erica smiled sheepishly.

"I've been caught up with work and a few personal things."

"Well, I'm happy you're here now. You know Shar and I got married?" he chatted, as if they were two friends catching up over lunch.

"Yes, and I'm so sorry I missed the ceremony. I know it was a beautiful affair, and all of the who's who of D.C. showed up to pay homage."

"Well, I don't know about all of that," he chuckled.

"You don't have to play modest for me."

"It was a very nice affair," Warren cut in. "So, um, Sir? I'll call you and let you know about Sunday."

His father looked him over, surprised, and then replied. "Don't wait too long, Son. A wise woman once told me: life is short, live it. Love is rare, grab it. Anger is bad, dump it. Memories are sweet, cherish them."

With that he saluted his son and then took Erica by the hand. "Please drop by the house before you leave. Shar would love to fatten you up."

"Will do."

The mobile on his hip started chiming and the goofiest grin appeared on his face. "See what I mean," he said, stepping inside the elevator. "Hey baby, I'm on my way home."

THE ELEVATOR DOORS CLOSED and Erica and Warren were left in the hallway alone.

"I'm in town on business and thought I'd stop by. Hope I'm not intruding."

"Of course not. You are always welcome," Warren wiped his hands on the front of his sweatpants. "Come on in," he said, stepping aside so that she could walk down the hall and into the apartment first.

Erica had imagined what she would do if she ever saw him again, and now that she was here with Warren she felt as flimsy as a wet paper towel. Unconsciously, she wrung her hands to keep them from bursting into a cold sweat.

Warren dipped his head into the refrigerator and came back holding a can of ginger ale.

"You want?"

"When did you start drinking soda?" she dropped her bag on the kitchen bar stool.

He clicked the can open and slid it across the granite countertop towards her. "Comes free with Chinese food if you spend ten dollars or more," he mimicked a Chinese accent. Erica turned the corners of her mouth upward, hinting at a smile.

Warren couldn't help watching her, noting everything: the lovely fitted dress, pretty glass beads, pout of her lips with just a touch of gloss, reddish hair free and loose, eyes soft but confused. She looked like his girl standing in his kitchen on any ordinary weekend, and he wanted to grab and kiss her until his lips felt cracked and dry. But he played it cool.

Erica was here for one of two reasons—to clear the air and end things on a good note, or to give it one more try. Warren slipped his crossed fingers into his pockets and hoped for the latter. Awkwardness had entered the room, and he searched the kitchen cabinets for a conversation starter.

Erica beat him to the punch. "I got your messages. They were nice."

"I played myself. You can say it."

"Well, just a little bit," she teased. "But it was cute." She couldn't keep her eyes off of him. Warren's strapping frame leaned against the refrigerator with both hands plunged deep into his pockets. Erica couldn't remember the last time she thought sweatpants were sexy, but they were doing the job on Warren. Their eyes met and clung, like they did a few weeks ago at the Iridium jazz club.

"What do you want?" he asked.

"What do you want?"

"You."

"But you left me."

Warren pulled his hands from his pockets and sighed. "I felt like I was running into a brick wall. Every weekend there was something. I don't operate well in gray space."

"What was gray?"

"Your commitment. I was going through a lot and you had no idea."

Warren recapped what he had overheard about Bernard and Jared at the wedding rehearsal and how he just lost it.

"When I confronted my father, he practically kicked me out of the house in the middle of a party. That's why he was here," and he told her what his father had just revealed about his parent's marriage and their agreement.

"So all this time I'm all bent out of shape, and Shar really is the great love of my father's life."

"Wow, that's crazy."

"It feels crazy, like my family had been living this great lie just to keep up appearances."

Warren grabbed a bag of Utz party mix and started eating out of the bag. He offered some to Erica but she declined, and sipped her soda.

"I've been struggling with making peace with my parents too. You won't believe who I called today."

"Who?"

"My father," her eyes widened as she ran down their catch-up conversation. "It was much easier than I thought and I felt a lot better afterwards."

"I'm proud of you. That was a really big step." He folded over the bag of chips and fastened them with a clip.

"Yeah, it was." Erica looked down at her toes. "You still haven't answered my question. Why did you break up with me in Philly?"

"Because you checked out long before I said the final word."

SHE HAD PREPARED HERSELF for Warren's answer, but was still unsure how to respond. Erica wanted him to understand where she had come from, and when she opened her mouth, she told him things that she had never said to anyone.

Erica took him back to her earliest memory and walked him through her life. She told him about the legacy of the women in her family, her parent's fights, the overwhelming responsibility that she had at an early age raising Jazmine and herself, while the neighbors on Monroe Street whispered about her family, and pegged her as the girl to get pregnant and ruin her life.

"No one gave me anything. I had to make it up as I went along. And I'm talking about from the smallest detail, like being out at a business lunch and trying to figure out which fork to use, to the big stuff like negotiating my salary, and presenting myself like I came from the same stock they did," she paused. "Then you came along, giving me all the love and comfort that I hadn't experienced since my father left. It was almost too much. I felt myself needing you, and I'm not the needing someone type of chick." Erica stood up.

"Not being able to support myself was never an option for me, that's why I worked so hard, because I thought the higher I climbed, the less likely I'd fall. It was never enough for me. As soon as I reached a goal, I wanted more, the next position, the next salary, the bigger office with the view. It was almost like an obsession," she took a band from her pocket and pulled her hair into a ponytail. "I was running, scared shitless that my upbringing would catch up with me and rip the new Erica down that I had worked so hard to construct."

Warren leaned across the counter that separated them with the urge to grab her hand, but resisted.

"You were worrying about not needing me, but I was the one who needed you."

"And so you turned to Blanche," Erica flung her words, and the fury of catching that heifer in Warren's apartment crashed through the room like a hurricane.

"I never cheated on you." Warren walked to the edge of the counter and stood in front of her. "I swear on my mother's grave." His fingers were on her chin, and he lifted her face so that their eyes met.

Erica hated when he did this because it was hard for her to hide when Warren looked so deeply into her soul. But the trench, the heels, what was she doing in his apartment?

Warren talked fast. He told her that those first few days after they broke up were like being swallowed by hell. "I know I said the words, but losing you was like a death. I couldn't sleep, wasn't performing at work..."

"What does that have to do with Blanche?"

Warren explained how he went into his music room, connected with his mother's spirit and played for so many days straight that he had lost all concept of time.

"Blanche came over that day because I hadn't been to work in a week. I don't even know how she got my address," he slapped his palms against his thighs. "You were right about her, she did come after me, but nothing happened. I left her here to go play in Arlington with James. She was waiting on takeout."

Erica sat quietly.

"You've got to believe me, baby."

Warren had a way of calling her baby that made her feel like the most precious thing in the world. Like she was really his baby, his charge to care for, nurture and protect. When she looked up he was standing against the wall with his shoulders sagged, eyes heavy, lips hung, and the need to touch him overwhelmed her. But it also frightened her.

He reached for her but she moved him aside. "Let's go into the living room," she offered.

The neighborhood seemed quiet for a Friday night, except for someone leaning on a car horn outside his window. Erica chose the easy chair, and when she sank into the cushions she put both hands on her head to think, but Warren pulled them away and forced her to look at him.

He was on his knees in front of her. "Do you think I could ever not want you, Erica?"

"I don't know."

Her answer seemed to take him aback. She could see the weary lines etched into Warren's face and wondered if he was growing sick of trying. Her back ached. It was past late. Going to bed was the sane thing to do.

"I'm going to head back to my hotel."

"Stay here. You can have my bed."

Her brows crinkled.

"I'll sleep on the couch."

Erica realized that she was too tired to argue. "Can I borrow some shorts?"

"You know where they are," Warren walked over to the sofa and dropped a few pillows in the groove for his head.

ERICA WAS SO EXHAUSTED that she couldn't sleep. She laid there for what felt like forever with her mind moving a mile a minute. When she did doze, it was into an uncomfortable fit of dreams; tossing, turning, running, stumbling. Then she thought she heard Grandma Queeny's deep voice, "Chile, stop moving ever witcha way. It's time to plant your feet in the soil and sprout up new trees." That was what made Erica sit up and wipe the perspiration that had gathered on her temples and moistened her chest.

She clicked on the table lamp and let her eyes adjust to the colors of the room. There was a framed photograph of Warren as a teenager playing his horn in what looked like his daddy's suit because of the way it hung off him. Erica picked up the picture from the nightstand and held it to her face.

Slowly, she pushed the patterned duvet aside and slipped barefooted into the hall. On the balls of her feet, she tiptoed into the living room, where Warren was nestled into the sofa and dead to the world. His chest rose and fell, and a light snore drifted from his nostrils. Warren could sleep through anything. Watching him, she could picture what their son would look like curled up taking a nap. Erica pulled a throw over herself and waited for him to stir.

Two hours later, the sun's rays bled through the mini blinds. Warren opened his eyes with a jump and seemed startled that she was sitting there. Then his body relaxed as the memory of the night before entered.

He stretched and yawned. "How'd you sleep?"

"Eh."

"What're you doing?"

"Waiting."

"For what?"

"To tell you that I'm sorry," she moved to where he had slept. The cushions adjusted under her and her bare knee grazed against his.

"Warren, I need you too. I've been suffocating without you. You are my perfect complement," her fingers found his face. "But I'm scared."

Warren looked at her, but no sound came from his lips. It was his eyes that cleared away her confusion. Then they were kissing, morning breath and all. Slobbering like two teenagers in the back of a parent's car.

"You are my number one draft choice." His mouth was on her chin.

"I'm so sorry." Her hand stroked his neck.

"I've been sick without you." His shirt came off and was flung to the floor. Her shorts slid down around her ankles, then disappeared. A quick shuffle dance and Erica was on her back. His chest rested against her breast, pelvis swelled between her thighs, fingertips gripped her wrist, while his lips slow dragged with hers. The intense weight of Warren's body made Erica teary. Dear God she had missed him.

Their bodies synced. Hugged and held. Sweated and panted. But then Erica's body got away from her. A fiery sensation blazed in her groin with an intensity that pushed her to a place she had never gone. She moaned deeper than the walls could absorb. Warren tongued her ear, egging her further. The room felt fuzzy. Her midsection burned. Nothing else mattered. Just them, their rhythm, and all Erica wanted was to swallow him whole.

But Warren pulled back and fanned her face with his hand to cool her down. Bars of a Keith Sweat song popped into Erica's head as Warren whispered. "You're so beautiful. My pretty girl. I would do whatever for you. Walk in the rain. Sing you every song," he held her hands while moving his body in that marching band tempo that always sent her over. Erica could hardly breathe as she tightened her legs around him, thrusting her hips like she was tapping a drum. Ta, ta, ta, ta, ta, ta, ta, ta. Neither could hold on, a burst of wetness soaked the crevasses between them, healing their grievances and christening the start of another weekend, together.

Chapter Forty-Eight

Chocolate Covered Every Day

The next morning, Warren drove her back to the Jefferson hotel for her things. In the elevator, his hands found her waist and she rested her head against him. Erica's room was three doors down on the right, and as soon as she slipped the keycard into the lock, Warren's fingers worked the back zipper of her dress.

"You want me to order some room service?" she asked. The heavy sheets gathered around her bare waist. Her reddish hair was tossed and tangled, but she had never felt more beautiful and alive.

"I'll do it," Warren walked across the room, opened the curtains and stared out at the Washington Monument. He whistled at the view.

Erica let the sheet fall to the floor and came up behind him. "You never asked what I came to D.C. for?"

"You said work, right?"

She turned him around so that they were facing each other. "My author brought me here to make me his speaking agent. We agreed on eighteen percent."

Warren looked as if he didn't understand.

"I'm starting a business."

"What about B&B?"

"They don't know yet," Erica tightened her arms around his waist. "I'm considering leaving the company."

"Whatever," he chuckled.

"Seriously. I've decided that I can do better than killing myself trying to climb somebody's corporate damn ladder. Entrepreneurship is in my blood. I get it from my daddy," she said, tipping her chin. "I'm thinking about trying to start something full time. On my own."

Warren ran his hands up and down her shoulders. "Baby, that's wonderful. Where? When?"

"Well, I haven't decided on all of that, trumpet boy. But maybe I could spend more time in D.C."

"You'll move?"

She grinned. "Doesn't seem like such a far-fetched idea. I don't want to spend another Monday without you."

Warren picked her up off of her feet, and kissed her like she was the last woman left in the world.

"Or Tuesday, or Wednesday."